I would like to dedicate this book to the memory of Jonesy.

First published in 2017 by Barrallier Books Pty Ltd,
trading as Echo Books

Registered Office: 35-37 Gordon Avenue, West Geelong, Victoria 3220, Australia.

www.echobooks.com.au

National Library of Australia Cataloguing-in-Publication entry.

Creator: Armstrong, Ron, author.

Title: Tiger tears / Ron Armstrong.

ISBN: 9780648074502 (paperback)

Subjects: Adventure stories. Friendship--Fiction. Mateship (Australia)--Fiction.

Book layout and design by Peter Gamble, Canberra.
Set in Garamond Premier Pro Display, 12/17 and Downcombe Regular.

www.echobooks.com.au

www.ronarmstrongauthor.com

TIGER TEARS

RON ARMSTRONG

ECHO BOOKS

CONTENTS

FOREWORD

So you are sick and tired of watching reality TV and thought you would give reading a go. Well if that's the case good on you. Why don't you buy my book so I can give half the money to the government and buy a beer with the other half. Come to think of it that's giving even more tax to the government. Fair enough I suppose since they do such a cracking job.

This book is about a group of colourful adventurers that manage to get themselves into more strife than a first homebuyer in Sydney. Still reading about them stumbling through life should provide you with hours of amusement and take your mind off burning issues like Jonny Depp is getting divorced again, a speeding fine has just arrived in the mail, whales are still being killed for scientific research, the polar caps are melting, your health insurance is going up and a politician has just spent your tax dollars on some dubious activity like travelling to Norway to study traffic flow.

Anyway, that's enough from me. You get reading and have a laugh. Me I will get cracking on the second book of the series, as once you fall in love with Ant and his depraved Global Angel crew, you will no doubt want to know what they will get up to next. You can check out my progress at www.ronarmstrongauthor.com

Antonio

HIS EYES STRUGGLED TO FOCUS in the dim light as the smell of bleach attacked his nostrils. A faint light partially illuminated the tiny room revealing a large porcelain low-set sink in front of him. His mind started to comprehend the situation but to do so it had to struggle through an alcohol-induced haze.

'What the...?', the man protested as he realized he was urinating in the sink. 'Oh bloody hell!'. In his surprise, he stepped backwards into bucket and then stumbled into the door that had been left ajar. The collision knocked the door open further and this time it cast enough light for him to realize he was in a cleaning closet.

He peeked through the doorway to see 365 etched on the wall in the hotel corridor. 'Bugger!', the man thought to himself, 'I must have been looking for the bathroom in my inebriated state and instead walked out of my room and pissed in this broom closet. Oh well not to worry, I will just go downstairs and get them to let me in'.

He took a step into the corridor and heard an immediate gasp. He spun around to see two Japanese ladies. It was at that moment he realized he was completely naked. His hands in a reflex movement sprung to cover his bowl of fruit.

Unfortunately for the two ladies the naked man in front of them was not known for being a small man in this department, hence his nickname Ant.

Ant's failed attempt to cover himself left one of the two ladies in hysterics whilst the other elven-looking lady in her early 30s just eyed him up and down with a smirk on her face.

Ant sprung back behind the door. God, not again he thought to himself. Why do I always end up nude in public? 'Umm, excuse me ladies, I was wondering if you could do me a favor? You see I'm locked out of my room and can't get back in. Is there any chance you could send someone up from reception with a room key for 365?'

The shorter of the two ladies continued to giggle into her hands, but the tall elven-looking women with a face that would have had Angelina Jolie off to the plastic surgeon to try to replicate, simply continued to stare. 'Please ladies, I'm in a bit of a bind here!'

The tall women glanced up and down like she could see through the door he was cowering behind and replied 'You sort it out big boy'. With that the two women disappeared down the hallway.

'Right', Ant thought, 'I need to work something out here'. He searched the closet and found a garbage bag. He tore two leg holes and attempted to fashion it into a plastic pair of shorts. Ant hung his head. With his solid physique and the garbage bag fashioned around his waist in the form of a plastic nappy he figured he looked like a half-naked, furry man-child.

He shuffled over towards the stairwell and descended to the ground floor, ready to undertake his humiliating walk to Reception across the entrance foyer of the plush hotel. The two young Thai reception staff looked up as the red-cheeked man-child lumbered towards them.

'Umm, excuse me ladies, I seem to have accidentally locked myself out of my room'.

One of the women just smirked and motioned towards the bellboy. Ant's Thai wasn't very good but he got the distinct impression he was being ridiculed as the two ladies behind the resort's front desk chatted enthusiastically whilst pointing at him.

'Great!', he thought 'No doubt my predicament will be brought up at the next hotel staff meeting and will be a source of great amusement for them all'. He could see it now, 30 Thais ranging from 16 to 60-years-old pissing themselves as they scoffed down fish cakes and satay skewers.

After a short trip in the lift back to the fourth floor he was let back into his room. He tipped the bellboy and bid him farewell. He then decided to clean up.

After a nice hot bath, a Berocca and headache tablets, he cleaned his teeth, combed his bushy moustache, and examined himself in the mirror. He wasn't the best-looking man in the world. He was 5ft 9in tall, solid and hairy. He had broad shoulders, a thick chest with strong powerful forearms and hands and a somewhat non-existent neck. His physique had landed him in the front row as a hooker in every rugby team he had ever been in. He was a strong man, although, now aged in his mid-thirties, he had allowed a little bit of flab to cover the once rippling muscle.

Despite all this he had a friendly demeanor and a rugged, manly face. Despite his kind nature people who crossed him, when fixed with his stare, would sense the darkness lurking beneath. He was after all a killer, albeit a reluctant one.

The man that Ant was today had been largely forged from eighteen-years' service in the Australian Army. In the early nineties, the then seventeen-year-old went to the Parramatta recruitment center with the ambition of becoming a soldier and donning the glamorous slouch hat with dreams of adventure and travelling the world being his goal. He had walked straight into the office where he stood in front of a square-jawed, wiry man covered in tattoos.

They weren't the fashionable designer tattoos you see the youth of today wearing as they attempt to imitate their Hollywood heroes. These were poorly-drawn tattoos that had been collected during service in the far-flung corners of the globe.

Skulls and daggers underpinned by slogans such as 'Brothers in Arms' and 'RIP Thomo KIA Vietnam'.

The sergeant's hair looked like grey steel wool. The man gave the sense that he could kill you with his stare. 'How can I help you, young fella?' the sergeant said, eyeing the young Ant.

'I want to go to join the Army and fire a machine gun', said Ant.

The sergeant snatched the file from the young man's hand and examined his higher school certificate marks.

'Sooo, you want to be a private in my beloved infantry yet your marks are high enough to get into university and study medicine. Are you sure you have thought this through mate?'

Ant stared the sergeant in the eyes trying to look tough and determined. In a firm committed voice he stated, 'I want a life less ordinary'.

The sergeant paused reading for a moment and looked at Ant with his intense stare. He had seen a lot in his time, most of the planet, beautiful landscapes in places that civilians will never reach. In his 28-year career in the military he had witnessed acts of bravery, compassion, and sacrifice in circumstances so intense that they brought out the best and worst in humanity.

He had also witnessed death and unspeakable violence, the likes of which had no place in the civilized society in which he now lived.

He was due to retire soon from the Army which filled him both with relief and regret. Standing in front of him was a fresh-faced symbol of the next generation ready to take up the fight.

God knows what this young man's fate will be. Will he survive the future conflicts that he will fight in? Will he keep his limbs? Will he keep his sanity or will he disappear into a bottle? Only time will tell. What could be guaranteed is that the military would test him both emotionally and physically. There will be mateship, travel, adventure, terror, and boredom in this man's future.

'A life less ordinary eh? Well, be careful young fella cause on the path you are about to tread you just might get it', said the sergeant as he moved towards a filing cabinet to fetch some enlistment papers.

Four-months later Ant got his wish. He spent two-years in the infantry carrying the machine gun in Australia's parachute battalion.

One afternoon he was summoned to the battalion headquarters to see the Commanding Officer. This was rarely ever a good thing for a private soldier. Maybe the Boss had found out about Ant and his mates getting drunk last night. The evening concluded in the defiant act of Ant doing a nude midnight run around the base. Surely not, he had taken precautions. He had even had the forethought to wear a balaclava so the duty officer wouldn't know it was him. Nonetheless here he was standing in front of the Commanding Officer.

'Come in Private Lucciano.'

Ant marched into the Colonel's office as smartly as he could manage and halted in front of his desk looking straight ahead.

'Ant relax take a seat', the CO said, motioning him towards a comfortable-looking leather seat.

Ant allowed himself to make eye contact with the man of authority. This man had the power to send a private to military prison or staff his discharge from the Army. He could promote him or demote him. Ant felt as though this man held more power over him than his parents or even the police. This was an extremely busy person running a battalion of some seven-hundred personnel. Yet here he was taking the time to invite him to take a seat, why? He wouldn't be invited to take a seat if the old man knew that he had been running around his unit nude last night. No, he would have him at attention screaming at him that he was about to take disciplinary action.

'I would like to talk to you about your future.'

'You're not what I would call in-flow with your career.'

The Colonel paused so Ant could digest what he had said.

'You see, Ant, you are a very good Infantry soldier. In fact, maybe too good. You are popular, a great shot, tough and above all a fantastic rugby hooker for the Battalion. But you see Ant, you have been cursed with a rather high IQ. Your platoon commander and myself started discussing your future after the last unit exercise.'

Ant and his unit had just returned from a military exercise where Ant, despite his inexperience, had stepped up to second-in-charge of an eight-man squad. On the exercise an Eastern Brown snake bit the Corporal in charge.

It was Ant who sprang into action. Tasking his fellow privates to establish radio communications and call in their position, deep in the NSW border ranges.

He grabbed his map and searched for a place with minimal vegetation where a helicopter could land and dispatched two of his mates to take off ahead of them to clear and establish a landing zone or an LZ, as they were called, for a helicopter. The remaining four men were tasked with constructing a stretcher so they could carry the stricken man to keep his heart rate low during his evacuation.

Those who have been in the border ranges know how physically taxing negotiating the steep slopes and thick vegetation can be. He treated the man just like he had been taught.

He didn't suck the venom out of the wound like you might see in a poorly-scripted Hollywood movie. Instead he tightly bandaged the wound away from the trunk of his body towards the extremity of the limb, so as to delay the movement of the venom through the lymphatic system.

He then organized the back-breaking rotation to carry the stretcher through the mountainous and heavily-vegetated terrain to the LZ. It was a complete success; his actions resulted in the quick extraction of the bitten man from the very remote location where the incident occurred.

The patient made it to the hospital within 70 minutes of the bite; enough time to have been fatal had the man panicked or had to walk to the extraction site. But the corporal made a full recovery, thanks to Ant's quick thinking and leadership.

Now Ant sat in front of his CO discussing his future. 'But Sir, I am happy in my job and with my mates,' said Ant.

The Colonel looked at Ant and with a dismissive gesture of his hand continued in his preplanned speech, 'Your platoon commander and I believe you could best serve the Army as an officer. You see, as an officer your mind would be more challenged and you would get more of an opportunity to utilize that effective leadership style that we saw on exercise. I am prepared to recommend you personally Ant. This is a wonderful opportunity for you.'

Ant got the impression he was to be recommended for commissioning whether he wanted it or not. As he sat there considering his situation he realized he was actually feeling chuffed. A chance to train as an officer and swan around with the private school kids in the Officers' Mess. Extra pay and as far as he could see less work. His heavy machine gun would be replaced with a lighter officer's weapon.

Sir that would be great, thank you very much for your support,' said Ant.

'No problems, I will make the arrangements for you to attend selection for officer training at the Royal Military College Duntroon. You're dismissed, keep up the good work.'

Ant stood to attention, saluted, and started heading for the door. 'Oh, and one more thing.' Ant stopped and turned to face the Commanding Officer. 'Keep your bloody pants on when you are running around my unit or I will cancel all your time off until you're ready to collect your pension.' Ant blushed, saluted again, and exited the office.

Some 16-years later Ant was standing in front of the mirror in the hotel after being let into his room by the bellboy. He had just left the Army three weeks ago, after countless adventures, travelling most of the globe and serving in two wars.

He remembered some of the great mates he had served with as he examined some of the badly-drawn tattoos he had collected with them over the years and laughed.

The feeling of euphoria was washed away as he looked down at the fresh tattoo on his forearm 'Ando KIA Afghanistan lest we forget'.

A feeling of immense sadness washed over him as he fought off the memories. 'Fuck it', he sniffed, 'It's a beautiful day, I'm going to the beach'.

He put his rugby shorts on, slung one of the hotel towels over his shoulder and jogged down to the beach. It was a humid sticky day in Phuket. Despite that, Karin Beach was occupied by what appeared to be only a dozen or so hotel guests.

He threw his towel on a sunbed with his wallet and keys and slipped a few baht to the waiter, 'Beer thanks mate and keep the change old china'. Ant ambled down to the water and flopped backwards into the surf. He could feel his hangover drifting away in the cool water.

'This is the life', he thought to himself, 'Beats the shit out of that hot dusty forward operating base where I just spent nine months of my life in Afghanistan'.

After 15 minutes frolicking in the surf he spied the waiter return with a frosty cold beer. Beauty, time to kill what's left of this hangover.

As he walked back to his day bed he noticed that a woman wearing a large floppy sun-hat, with a great set of legs, had occupied the sunbed next to him to take advantage of a nearby palm tree's partial shade. It wasn't till he sat down that the women elegantly lifted the brim of her designer sun hat to reveal a familiar, beautiful elfin-shaped face.

'You again', Ant spat with a false air of contempt. 'You didn't have to abandon me in the hotel. I had to do the walk of shame down to the lobby with nothing but a garbage bag wrapped around my waist.'

The Japanese woman looked at Ant with her unusual blue-hazel eyes and replied with a cheeky smile, 'Abandon you? I was running away! You looked like a drunk furry ape with an anaconda hanging between your legs'.

Ant sniffed with an indignant tone, 'Yeah, well I s'pose I should be grateful you and your girlfriend didn't act like most Jap tourists and start clicking off photos to load on your bullshit Facebook accounts'.

The woman glared at Ant, 'Yes OK, let's continue with your racial stereo types. Why would I bother photographing such a common occurrence as a drunken Aussie bogan running nude around a hotel?' With that the woman smiled and went back to reading her book, once again ignoring Ant's very existence.

'I don't blame her', Ant thought, 'She's quick-witted, beautiful and well out of my league'. He put his sunglasses on, flopped on his sun lounge and studied her with his peripheral vision. She was undoubtedly an elegant creature. She looked very athletic, yet feminine. Moreover, she oozed class and good breeding, amplified by a non-to-subtle air of arrogance and contempt for the proletarian masses of which she clearly considered Ant to be a card-carrying member.

'Reminds me of someone else I know', Ant thought to himself. It wasn't a woman Ant was thinking of that possessed these personality traits. No, it was a long-term friend, a man named Lachlan, that he had met in officer training some twelve-years ago.

Lachlan was a very different person to Ant. Whereas Ant was gruff-looking, stocky, genuine, intelligent, caring, and playful, Lachie was tall, lean, handsome, charming, self-centered, disingenuous and conniving. Unlike Ant, Lachie was born into money; old money from England.

The two had become friends at the RMC Duntroon completely by chance. They had been allocated rooms next to each other and Ant had been assisting Lachie and others with getting their gear sorted as the others, unlike him, weren't familiar with the basics of preparing military equipment.

Their friendship was sealed 3-months into their time at Duntroon when they were granted their first leave. Ant was at this stage the ripe old age of 21, whereas most of the other cadets were aged 18 to 19 years of age.

It was only around 2200 hours on their first night's leave and most of the cadets were drunk, en masse, and pumped with new-found strength from the fifteen weeks of intensive physical training. Lachie was no exception; he felt like a superman. That coupled with his long-standing superiority complex made it very likely that before too long he was going to attract trouble in the rough Canberra pub called Mooseheads Pub & Nightclub.

It was a favorite watering hole for the military cadets looking for the three F's on a night out. Well you might not have been able to get the feed but you could certainly get into a fight and occasionally a fuck.

Mooseheads was the veritable 'Star Wars bar'. In addition to the cadets, it was full of Rugby and Aussie Rules football teams. Joining them were the Canberra hard men, all looking to test their mettle and hoping to pick up one of the pretty girls.

The Canberra girls went there to hang with the cashed-up cadets. Some of them were looking to settle down with a cadet at the end of his training and possibly earn themselves a ticket out of Canberra. The girls were, however, hugely outnumbered by the men. Add in some hard-drinking in a packed environment and it was a powder keg.

Lachie was holding court running a drinking game and causing a stir. He was keen to establish himself in the pack of cadets as a leader and the life of the party. He was also trying to attract the attention of three beautiful young ladies off to the side of a large group of rowdy junior cadets.

Lachie stood on the bar, 'Okay men, the last three to finish sculling their beer gets the next round'. The call went up. Ant who had reluctantly been dragged into the game finished his beer first. The Infantry had prepared him well for this game. Surprisingly, pretty boy Lachie finished fourth and safe from the shout.

Of course, what Ant and the others didn't know was that Lachie had been buying himself mid-strength beers and strategically spilling several mouthsfull of his beer on the floor before the start of the races—just enough of an edge to guarantee not losing the race and not enough to be caught cheating. The light beer gave him a glow but ensured that his wit was remaining disproportionately high to that of his peers, which would no doubt help him manipulate the group and chat up the pretty blond that had been eyeing him off. Yes, he was better-looking and much less drunk than his mates–he would be in for sure.

Before long Ant moved away from the group. He was bored with the young drunk man bullshit. He started talking to one of his female Army mates who was an athletic and intelligent Canberra girl. She was attractive but somewhat of a Tom Boy. It was not uncommon for her to burp and fart in front of her male counterparts. As a result, her classmates changed her name from Barbara to Barry or Baz for short.

Baz and Ant positioned themselves on the other side of the room away from the blaring music so they could have a semi-civil conversation. Ant was fond of Baz as she was performing well in the Army and had quickly risen to the rank of corporal in what was at the time a male-dominated macho environment.

She was physically and mentally robust. She was funny and likeable and shared a common interest with Ant in Rugby Union about which they were now deep in conversation.

Ant looked across the room to see that the drinking games had finished and Lachie was now dirty dancing with a beautiful girl in front of the whooping and hollering cadets. 'Yep', Ant thought, 'That friggin show off is fast establishing himself as the alpha male'.

Baz leant across to Ant and said, 'See that girl your mate Lachie is dancing with? Well her name is Alison and her boyfriend is bad news. He won't be happy when he sees Lachie grinding against his woman'.

'Yeah well', Ant replied, 'She's not acting like a girl with a boyfriend, maybe they broke up'.

'I guess we'll find out soon because the boyfriend just walked in', said Baz.

Ant spun round to see five men standing at the door. The big one standing in the front of the group looked like he was fit to commit murder.

Apart from Ant, the five men were a couple of years older and more solid than the other cadets. They also looked well-organised as they split up. Two hung at the door and the other three approached Lachie who was by now sucking face with Alison oblivious of the danger approaching.

'Shit!', thought Ant, 'this ain't going to be good'.

The big man slapped Lachie hard in the back of the head and hissed, 'That's my fucking girlfriend arsehole'.

Lachie stood straight-backed and looked the man squarely in the eye and said, 'Well it appears she is looking to trade up sport'.

'Fuck you mate', the man spat and, with that, drove his fist into Lachie's solar plexus. Lachie fell to the ground where the assailant and one of his mates commenced giving him the Balmain tap dance on his head.

Ant thought to himself, Lachie may have deserved a punch in the stomach but the gutless act of more than one bloke kicking into his head for no good reason was too much to allow.

With that, Ant swung into action. He jumped in between Lachie and the two men kicking into him and shouted, 'He's had enough, back off'.

'Yeah, what's it to you Super Mario? Fuck off or the same is going to happen to you!', the man hissed into Ant's Face.

The man was a big lad standing 6ft 4in with a solid physique and big hooked nose that made him look even more menacing. His mate, who had originally hit Lachie, had a shaved head and was around 6ft–still big enough to be a problem. The other two men in the group were now starting to close in. One was tall and skinny and the other was rolling the sleeves up on his red striped shirt.

Ant looked into Hooknose's eyes that were now just inches from his, glaring at him as though he was ready to rip Ant's head off. 'Well there is no talking my way out of this one', Ant thought.

The five men had sized him up and figured although he was solid, he wasn't a tall man and it was five versus one, so soon he would join his mate on the floor and the patrons of Mooseheads would again be reminded of what bad asses they were.

What they couldn't have known was that Ant was a pretty proficient fighter and as tough as hell. He had represented NSW twice in Judo and boxed regularly at the Parramatta Police Boys Club with the street kids. That, plus two years serving in the Parachute Battalion, had resulted in Ant becoming one hard bastard.

It was time for these guys to find out how tough Ant was. He prioritized his targets. Hooknose, due to his size and proximity, would be first. Still with his hands by his side Ant rocked back on his heels flexing his body slightly before snapping his head forward smashing his forehead into the bridge of the big man's generous nose.

The man spun around hunched, grasping his nose. As he bent down, Ant, in a fluid movement, drove his fist up into Hooknose's jaw. It was a searing uppercut that left Hooknose slumped unconscious against the bar. It happened so quickly Shaved head barely had the wherewithal to raise his hand up before an adrenaline-enhanced Ant was upon him.

The first thing he felt was that he was losing his footing, then he was flying through the air before crashing down onto his back. Shit, he was lying on the floor and he could see Ant again coming towards him. Shaved head tried to move but couldn't as the fall had winded him badly.

Ant knelt on the man's neck and grabbed his hands quickly breaking the middle finger on each hand. The last three men had just witnessed the clinical dispatching of their two mates. The perfectly-executed hip throw on the shaved-headed leader was enough to demonstrate that this guy could fight and at the end of the day he was only protecting an innocent mate who was now back up on his feet as well.

'Hey, hey, enough' said the tall skinny man, 'You've made your point Super Mario, we don't want any more trouble'.

Lachie stood there surveying the damage. He had barely noticed Ant amongst his classmates until now. Ant may not have been one of the handsome rich kids that Lachie usually liked to hang out with, but Ant was clearly a loyal type who knew how to fight. If there was one strength that Lachie possessed it was an ability to spot talent and, when someone was worth knowing, he would leverage off their skills. Yes, he would come in handy in the future.

From that day on Lachie engineered it so that Ant would become his friend. They ended up in the same rugby team and, where possible, they worked together on military exercises. From that day on they would become mates.

'Yep, she is one of Lachlan's people for sure', he pondered as his mind drifted back to the present.

I wonder how Lachie the spoilt brat is going?

A soft voice interrupted Ant's thoughts, 'Hello, how are you?'

Ant looked up; it was the little smiling Japanese lady from the hotel. 'My name is Yumi, what is yours?'

'Antonio, but most people call me Ant'.

'Well Ant, I hope we didn't get you into any trouble this morning'.

'No, no I'm good. It was all my fault, I was out celebrating last night and I overdid it.'

'Oh really, what were you celebrating?'

'Let's just say I was celebrating starting a new life chapter'.

'Pffft', huffed the tall woman in the floppy hat who was now looking up and taking an interest in Ant and Yumi's conversation, 'New life chapter? Mid-life crisis more like it', she said.

Yumi frowned at her friend's cruel remarks, 'Ant, this is my friend Tatsu. She can be a little rude sometimes. She always starts off thinking the worst of people until she gets to know them, but deep down she is a generous and caring person', said Yumi, whilst beaming an infectious smile that straight away lightened Ant's mood.

'Yeah well I suppose I should apologize to both you ladies seeing a hungover naked furry guy standing in the hotel hallway is probably the last thing you wanted to see in the morning. Can I buy you ladies a drink or something as a kind of apology?' asked Ant.

Cute little Yumi looked at Ant and said, 'A little early for me Ant but you could do something for me if you like? You see I really want to have a paddle in the surf but I'm not a very strong swimmer. I would feel safer if a big strong man like you could keep an eye on me in case I get into trouble'.

Ant smiled, 'Well of course I can little lady. In fact, I'll do better than that, I'll come for a swim with you if you like?'.

'Great let's go Ant. Are you coming Tatsu?'.

'In a minute Yumi, you guys go ahead.' Ant and Yumi paddled out into the water. Ant told Yumi he was going to have a quick body surf.

The hangover was washing away as Ant ducked under the small waves like a porpoise. After a couple of minutes, he looked over at Yumi who just seconds ago, was splashing around in the wash. Now she was out behind the breakers thrashing around.

I'd better go check on her. He was over by her side within 30 seconds. 'You ok Yumi?', Ant enquired already knowing the answer.

'No!' she spluttered. 'I can't get back into shore'.

'Yeah there is a bit of an under-tow. Relax and I will help you back in.' He gently placed his arm around Yumi's little waist and started paddling her back into the shore with ease. Yumi immediately felt safe. She was in the arms of a big strong man who gave the impression of being completely at ease in the surf. If she wasn't happily married she probably would have fallen for the rugged Australian on the spot she thought.

Tatsu was now on her feet watching the events unfold. 'The hero type', Tatsu surmised 'That could be handy'.

Ant walked Yumi back to her sunbed. Now a little embarrassed but relieved, she thanked Ant. He smiled a genuine smile and told her not to worry about it. He thought it might be a good idea to leave the two girls alone so he excused himself and returned to the hotel.

He toweled himself off and changed into cargo shorts, No Fear T-shirt, and thongs. He put on his G-Shock watch, which was issued to him by the Army, and placed his black Oakley sunglasses on his forehead. He checked himself in the mirror. Not the most-trendy man on the planet he thought to himself. Nonetheless he left the hotel room for the small markets next door.

The markets were mainly clothing and food-related. A young Thai man approached Ant. 'Do you want to buy Oakley sunglasses?', the man said, holding up a pair that looked identical to Ant's.

Ant looked at the man with a confused look on his face, 'Why would I want to buy some when I already have a pair?'

The man held up the pair he was trying to sell, 'No these not like yours, they are same same but different'.

Ant laughed at the explanation of 'same same but different'.

'Yeah that's a nice term for they are fake. For $4 they aren't going to be polarized like my ones'. Ant told the man no thanks and headed to a stand and bought two chicken satay sticks for the equivalent of 50 cents. He stood there stuffing down the delicious snacks whilst looking at a nearby T-shirt shop.

There hanging out the front was a white T-shirt with 'SAME SAME but different' printed on it. Ant chuckled to himself, 'I got to have one', so he purchased an XL and returned to the hotel.

Ant flopped on the bed and turned on sky sport. Daniel Ricciardo was happily thrashing all-comers in his F1 car. 'Ah, the other good-looking Aussie Italian', Ant chuckled to himself. I will relax and watch this, then I will go to a bar later get pissed and call it an early night.

KNOCK KNOCK KNOCK.

What now thought Ant, rolling off the bed and walking towards the door. He opened his door to find a stunning-looking Tatsu still in her bikini, covered only by a light partially transparent beach rap. Wow, thought Ant eyeing the fit, toned yet curvy body.

'Hi Ant', said the smirking Tatsu. She knew Ant was checking her out, which was her intent.

'Hi', stammered Ant, 'How's Yumi?'

'She's fine thanks to you, big boy. She wanted me to thank you again. I think she might have a little bit of a crush on you Ant'.

'Well who could blame her Tatsu? I'm a mountain of Aussie muscle', said Ant, flexing his bicep.

Tatsu shook her head at the display going on in front of her. 'Anyway Ant, unlike Yumi I am a footloose fancy free woman so it's up to me to take you out for a drink tonight.'

'Grass cutting poor little Yumi hey? Well who could blame you? Still you're only human, alright I'm in', said Ant. Tatsu shook her head and walked off calling back over her shoulder as she disappeared towards the lift, '7 pm at the beach bar down stairs, oh and wear pants'.

'Cheeky bitch', thought Ant. 'She couldn't be interested, could she? A hot sort like that. Still why else would she invite me out? It's not like Yumi was definitely going to drown and to be honest I didn't even raise a sweat bringing her back into shore. Anyway, a nice night out in Phuket with a hot girl, who cares what the reason is.'

THE DRAGON AND THE TIGER

AT 1855 HOURS Ant was down at the bar enjoying a Pina Colada in the hotel's beach bar. Suddenly the bloke next to Ant snapped his head around whilst letting out a sigh. Ant followed the direction the man was staring to see Tatsu entering the bar.

Her long black hair had been tied back and was held in place by a jade hairpin. She was clothed in a long skin-tight red silk dress that had a split in either side of it that ran up to her thighs. Her elegant shoes had a modest heel on them for which Ant was glad, as she was already taller than him. The soles of her shoes were interesting as although they were clearly dress shoes they look like they had a rubber sole.

'Hmmm', thought Ant, 'Must be a new fashion, graceful and you could still dance in them'.

She strutted over to Ant with the eyes of everyone in the bar upon her. She looked great and she knew it.

'Can I buy you a drink?' asked Ant.

'Definitely not, I'm already taken care of', replied Tatsu as the bargirl placed a bottle of Bollinger in a bucket of ice with two glasses on the bar. 'Can this girl get any cooler?' Ant thought to himself.

Ant and Tatsu sat there, sipping champagne whilst watching the sun go down. The staff lit the lanterns on the sand that covered the ground of the bar's outdoor seated area. They both soaked up the tropical paradise scenery over general conversation.

Tatsu told Ant she was a Japanese trade delegate and that Yumi was here to support her in her duties. She came from a well-to-do Japanese family who lived in the traditional district of Kyoto. Her father was Japanese and her mother was mixed race, Japanese and Norwegian, which is where her height and unusual eye colour originated from.

She spent a lot of time abroad. She had been to Australia several times, but usually to Canberra for work with the Japanese Embassy. She enjoyed skiing, Tai Chi, motorcycle racing and, like many women, was in love with former MOTO GP winner Valentino Rossi and actor Jonny Depp.

Ant told her he was currently taking a break after serving in the Australian Army as a logistics officer. He too loved motorcycles and Valentino Rossi although maybe not quite in the same way. He loved adventure and always appreciated returning home to his house in Brisbane.

After an in-depth discussion on motorcycle racing, Tatsu suggested that they go into town to escape the beautiful sanitized resort for the vibrant and chaotic party town of Patong.

They walked out through the back entrance of the Mövenpick Resort onto the beach road. Instead of taking a safe and comfortable taxi for the ten-minute trip they elected the noisy, slow, and unregulated 'tuk tuk'. The 20-something grinning driver turned around in his seat.

'Hey welcome chief and boss lady, I am Mr King. Where do you want to go? I can organize anything for you, skin painting or maybe jiggy jiggy. Boy or Girl anything you want'.

Ant smiled at Tatsu, 'How about we keep it simple Mr King? Just take us to the center of Patong and we will find our own way from there'.

Mr King pretty much ignored Ant and instead of taking them straight to Patong he took them on a small detour through the village slums. Tatsu and Ant didn't complain, it was fairly interesting seeing how the locals live. Observing people living in dilapidated buildings with bare earth floors reminded Ant how few problems we had in the modern world.

Night had fallen and the village took on an unfamiliar, almost medieval feel–to their left in the muddy alleyway two men were gutting a goat to prepare it to hang in the meat locker–small groups of men and women sat around in the street having evening discussions–the air smelled of exotic cooking and raw sewage.

The smells were completely at odds with each other and took turns in dominating the senses as the tuk tuk passed through the village. One minute their mouths would water as they passed by some huts with spice-laden meals being prepared, just to be followed by mild revulsion a moment later as they passed rotting waste.

The village was soon left behind as they entered the tourist strip that started with some hotels and restaurants. They then entered the center of Patong where the throng of tourists from Asia and the western world commenced. The place was colourful, noisy and very alive, a stark contrast to the primitive village Mr King had taken them through.

They cruised past a large building that had a lady-boy cabaret show advertised. Mr King dropped them off at the Komma Pub & Restaurant. They tipped Mr King for his guided tour.

The village turned out to be where he grew up and he offered to act as their tour guide whilst they were in Phuket. They politely declined, partly because they didn't want to be tied down but secretly because of the state of disrepair of his tuk tuk.

They walked into the bar that had an inviting a tropical setting with traditional Thai decor. They decided to have a refreshing drink after the ride in the non-air-conditioned tuk tuk. They both went for a guava juice laced with a dash of white rum.

They sat there for a while talking about family and friends. The conversation shifted to the subject of Tatsu's home in Kyoto. She described the Japanese traditional streets and how amazing the place looked in the cherry blossom season. Ant made a mental note to visit the place in the not too distant future.

He felt as though Tatsu was a little distracted as if she was scanning the bar for something. 'Everything alright?', Ant said.

'Yeah fine, just people-watching. Hey I tell you what Ant. I know this cool bar two streets from here that is wedged in amongst some night markets that I wanted to go to, to pick up some Thai silk scarfs. What do you say? Should we check it out?' said Tatsu.

'Yeah sure', said Ant. 'Just give me a few ticks, I've got to go have a snake's'.

'A what?', asked Tatsu.

'You know a snake's. Shake hands with the unemployed, drain the lizard', Ant said, getting to his feet.

Tatsu screwed up her face and laughed, 'What language is it that you Australians speak? It certainly isn't English'.

Ant laughed and headed for the dunny. When he walked in there were two tall, muscular Asian men engaged in conversation. As soon as Ant walked in the conversation stopped. Ant walked over to the trough very aware that he had interrupted the conversation.

While he was hanging a leak he also felt as though they were watching him intently. Ant zipped up and turned around to see one of the men washing his hands while the other one started the hand dryer. They were still discreetly watching Ant.

'Strange', he thought, 'I might leave them to it and get back to my date'.

He noticed a small tattoo on one of the men's arms. An anchor with a dagger through it. Kind of looked like a military style emblem. It was familiar but Ant couldn't quite place it.

Tatsu had seen the two men enter the bathroom. She recognized one of them straight away–an Indonesian gun for hire. He was an ex-Indonesian Special Forces Kopassus soldier and was so brutal during the East Timor campaign that the Indonesian military, known as the TNI, had discharged him. He was in his late 40s but was in exceedingly good shape.

If it were to go down, he would be a handful—a psycho capable of anything from acts of terrorism through to running small-scale military operations. He referred to himself as the 'Lone Tiger' that no doubt in his mind added to his reputation for being one dangerous dude.

The man that was with him was much younger and with a more solid physique. At 6ft 1in, she surmised he wouldn't go down easy. They were no doubt tracking her informant who she was due to meet at the night market in ten minutes.

Inviting the stocky Australian along for drinks might come in handy for more than just a cover.

The men entered the toilet no doubt to plan their next move after identifying her. She had planned to duck out while they were in there but the pea-bladdered heavy-drinking Aussie had scuttled that idea by heading to the toilet himself. Oh well, this was going to be interesting.

She was now glad she had slipped a precautionary payment to the local police inspector so that if anything did go down tonight she was likely to at least end up on the right side of the law.

She paid the bill and was ready to go by the time the grinning Aussie buffoon walked out of the men's room. 'Shall we head to the next bar then?' enquired Tatsu.

'Yeah sure, I'll just settle the bill', Ant said.

'Already done, let's go', insisted Tatsu. grabbing Ant by the arm and dragging him to the door.

As they walked out into the warm night air Ant mused to himself about Tatsu's firm grip. It was strange that this slim, elegant woman seemed to possess the hand grip strength of a brick layer. The other odd thing Ant noticed was that her knuckles showed the signs of long-term scaring. He had that as well but his were from fighting and a misspent youth. 'How did a woman end up with them?'

They walked and talked for ten minutes. Although Tatsu was smiling and bubbly, he sensed a degree of tension in her mannerisms. At one stage, she stopped to do her hair, using her mobile phone as a mirror, but really using it to look at the street rather than her hair.

'Here we are', said Tatsu pointing to a vibrant bar, 'Why don't you go in and get us some drinks whilst I grab the scarfs? I'll probably stop at the bathroom so am likely to be about ten minutes'.

'Yeah no problems', shrugged Ant. He walked into the bar, shoving his way to the front after queuing for about three minutes. He ordered a beer for himself and a Mai Tai for Tatsu and set himself up at an outdoor bar table.

He sipped on his beer watching the comings and goings in the bustling night market. 'Gee I hope she has gotten those scarfs, it's been about 15 minutes since she walked off. Probably a line for the chick's dunnys', he thought.

Suddenly Ant heard a commotion in the market. He could see people looking towards where the noise was coming from. Looks like something is going down, maybe I'll have a quick squizz.

He got up and walked towards the crowd when he heard a woman scream. Slumped against a T-shirt stand was a Thai man clutching his stomach–there was blood everywhere. It was the next site Ant saw that concerned him more. He could see a man holding a knife pointing it at someone.

The realization hit Ant. The young man from the toilet was holding the bloodied knife and was pointing it at Tatsu. 'Shit, the older guy is here as well also brandishing a large blade.'

Rather than a panicked and hysterical Tatsu, what he saw was much less expected. She slowly circled the two men and had adopted a fighting stance. Her movements were fluid and she maintained perfect balance whilst circling the men the whole time fixing them with an intense stare that looked like that of a predator circling its prey.

Well stuff this, Ant thought. The young fella with the knife is going down first. Ant pushed past two people and approached the man from behind. Cocking his right hand, he targeted the base of the young man's cranium. There was a sickening thud as the young man fell forward to the ground. The bloodied knife shot out of his hand and slid under a market stall table.

The Tiger saw the hit but was not concerned. Two more of his accomplices sprung from the crowd to contain the solid Australian. Now he could focus on the Japanese agent.

With her contact dead, the only person who could compromise his plans stood in front of him. She looked competent in her fighting stance but she would lack his strength and ferocity. Yes, he would kill her quick.

Ant moved towards the older man who had his knife pointed at Tatsu. Just as Ant was about to strike his head suddenly jolted backwards. The flash in his eyes followed by searing pain indicated to him he had been struck in the left side of the head.

The hit temporarily stunned Ant. His eyes were watering and he could just make out two fit-looking Asian men to his left. Of a similar age and size as the man he had just dropped. Bloody hell, he thought one of those pricks just king hit me–they must be with these other two dickheads.

Before Ant could react, one of the other men kicked him in the solar plexus, knocking the wind from him. He bent over slightly just in time to be kicked in the face. It was a hard hit and caught him in the mouth and nose. Now his eyes were really watering. He instinctively knew that the next blows would be to the back of the head or to his knees. It is what he would do to render his opponent helpless.

Meanwhile some nutcase was probably going to kill Tatsu with a knife and then he too would set upon Ant. He had to do something fast. With all his remaining strength Ant shuffled to the right. The attacker's punch aimed for the back of his head missed its mark and clipped Ant's left ear. He continued to stumble backwards away from his attackers to try to gain his composure and then counter-attack.

It was not to be, as one of the attackers immediately closed in on him while he was moving backwards. *Yoko Otoshi* throw Ant thought, as he grabbed the man's left arm and right collar.

Ant lowered his body height, doing a half split, and using his attacker's forward momentum, pulled the man forward and to the right over Ant's left leg. The attacker was now off balance and his momentum was about to be used against him.

Ant pulled with his left hand and pushed with his right whilst simultaneously twisting to his left and falling backwards. The attacker was now at Ant's mercy. He was off his feet and floating through the air to his front right. He was unable to break his fall due to its accelerated speed courtesy of Ant's polished technique.

The attacker hit the ground hard stunning him. Ant spun around on the ground and locked the man's left arm in his legs quickly bending the man's elbow backwards and shattering the joint.

Ant stumbled to his feet to look for the next target. Instead the only person in front of him was Tatsu. She looked unhurt. On the ground were the other two young men. Their necks looked twisted and they weren't moving. The only one moving was the one whose arm Ant had broken. Despite his arm the man got to his feet and fled through the crowd.

The older man was missing but Ant could see Tatsu was holding his knife. There was also a finger, laying on the ground, that looked like it was missing its owner. The crowd had grown. Some were screaming and crying and some were cheering, clearly having liked what they had seen.

'Tatsu are you okay?' 'I'm fine thanks Ant, but you have a fat lip, bloodied nose and a cauliflower ear. In fact, you are uglier than a shitsu's arse.'

'No Tatsu, you friggin smart arse. I meant are you okay emotionally? That was quite a scrap and I'm a little in shock myself.'

'Yes Ant, I am fine. Listen I want you to do something for me. I want you to go back to the bar and have a drink. The police will be here soon and I need to explain to them what has happened. I think it is smart to keep you out of it.'

'Bullshit Tatsu we should both get the fuck out of here.'

'Ant listen to me. I am well-connected and known to the police. I will be able to clear this up. Running on an island this small is not an option.'

'Yeah righto', said Ant, who could hear a police car closing in. He walked back to the bar and got himself two rums, picking a table where he could observe Tatsu talking to the police.

Before too long, two ambulances and eight police had descended on the market place. Tatsu was talking to them obviously explaining her version of the events. She handed the knife to the police and a card. After 20 minutes, she walked back over to Ant.

Ant had downed his two rums and had stopped shaking now that the adrenalin had left his body. His nose had stopped bleeding. His lip and ear weren't too swollen.

All in all, given the circumstances, he and Tatsu had gotten off lightly. Their attackers had not gotten off so lightly. The screaming man whose arm Ant had broken was carted off to hospital. The two lifeless corpses were loaded into the other ambulance. The police bagged the finger and recovered the knives that were used by the attackers.

Tatsu approached Ant smiling, 'We are good to go. I explained to the police what happened and where to find me if they need a more detailed statement'.

'Really?', said Ant, 'Do you mind telling me what just happened'.

'No not at all. It was a simple mugging. I was talking to a market storeowner buying scarfs, when four criminals attempted to rob the storeowner. He wrestled the knife off one of the attackers cutting one of their fingers off in the process. The older attacker fled the scene leaving his finger behind. Unfortunately, the stall owner was then stabbed and killed by one of the other two attackers. The crowd set upon the attackers disarming them. The crowd must have beaten two of the attackers to death. There were plenty of Thai spectators stepping forward claiming they helped save me', said Tatsu.

'Yeah well what about the ones that are still alive? They are likely to implicate me', said Ant.

'Yes, I thought of that', said Tatsu. 'I told the police a stocky blonde American man stepped in and helped. He broke the attacker's arm. The police are now looking for a large American to interview and probably congratulate. You however are off the hook.

You white guys all look the same anyway'.

'Yeah okay Tatsu. That sounds like a good cover story so what now?'

'Well I don't know about you Ant but I'm a bit pumped. I feel like a drink and a spa to wash this muck off me. I think we should take the party back to the hotel in case that fingerless bastard is still lurking around with a new gang of thugs.'

'Yeah sure, sounds like a good idea', mumbled Ant, still a little taken aback by how cool Tatsu was, given what had happened. He hailed a taxi to take them back to the hotel.

Once back at the hotel Tatsu said give her fifteen minutes to clean up and then catch the elevator to the top floor. She gave him a key card and explained he would need that to get to her floor. Ant told her he would see her later and went to his room to clean up.

He stripped off his shirt which was covered in night market ground gunge, blood and sweat from the fight. He examined his face and apart from a throbbing left ear which had cauliflowered up a little, and a slightly swollen lip, he didn't think he looked too bad. He just looked like he had played a hard game of rugby.

Still there were questions still needling Ant. Why does she want me to come up to her room? How did she survive that attack? Maybe some people from the crowd stepped in and helped her while Ant was scuffling with the other three. How did Tatsu end up with that guy's knife? Why was one of the attacker's fingers laying on the ground? What's more, Ant was pretty sure two of those attackers ended up dead with broken necks. WTF?

But she is one hot chick who wants him to come up to her room. She is way out of his league and possibly a psycho, but Ant thought he should give it a decent shot. God knew he could do with a root. He hadn't had one since he left to go to Afghanistan.

Ant shook his head. A year-long dry spell, 'I'm practically a monk', Ant mused, 'Yep, I should have a quick scrub and groom the old bowl of fruit just in case it sees some action'. On the off-chance she rips his pants off he didn't want her confronted by a furry sweaty baby's arm holding an apple.

The buzzer in the room announced Ant's arrival at the penthouse floor. Tatsu opened the suite door to find a freshened Ant standing at the elevator in the hall. Tatsu lead him by the hand from the top floor elevator to the door with Penthouse One written on it. As they walked through the front door of the suite, soft blue mood lighting activated with soft Euro-lounge music drifting in the background.

Ant was aghast, this was the single most luxurious place he had ever seen in the flesh. The huge apartment was sparsely populated with Norwegian-design furniture.

'Why don't you pour us a glass of champagne King Kong?'

Ant looked where Tatsu was motioning and saw a bottle of Cristal champagne chilling in an ice bucket. Ant walked over and realised the cork had already been popped by the hotel staff which meant this was probably all anticipated by Tatsu who had now disappeared into the bathroom.

Holy crap he thought, this girl is one tasteful smooth operator. Ant continued to survey the room and took in the impressive coastal view that stretched back to the main tourist beach some 2kms away.

Mounted on the wall was a huge plasma screen that rolled through a series of tranquil photos from Japan. Some of them had Tatsu in them surrounded by blossoms, temples, and Zen gardens. Ant walked out on the viewing deck and there was a personal spa and plunge pool.

This place must be worth thousands a night.

Tatsu walked out on the deck behind Ant. 'How rich did you say you were?', handing her the glass containing the exclusive velvet French champagne.

'I didn't say', she replied with a dismissive look.

'Alright then, how far in debt are you?'

'Haha, you so funny!', she replied in a comic reply.

Ant and Tatsu continued to talk for hours whilst taking in the view and washing it all down with expensive champagne.

As the first bottle was finished Tatsu sent a text and within minutes the hotel staff delivered another, this time with a platter of chocolates, dates, and tropical fruit.

Tatsu walked back onto the deck with her glass of champagne, sensually nibbling on a piece of dragon fruit. She then undid her dress and it fell away revealing a snakeskin-looking G-string bikini. Ant gulped down the glass of champagne more to calm his nerves than anything else.

Tatsu lowered herself into the spa, 'Care to join me Ant?' Ant took his shirt off a little self-conscious, as he wasn't in the best shape of his life, especially compared to Tatsu's pert figure.

Once he sat down in the spa Tatsu leant across and stroked his arm examining his tattoos, 'I take it these all mean something'.

'Not all', he said, 'Some of them I got to make me look more like Beckham'.

Tatsu laughed, 'Ant rugged and manly you might be but a pretty boy you ain't. Tell me about this one?', she said, pointing to the Lest We Forget tattoo on his forearm.

'I'd rather not at the moment if that is ok?'

'You're right, enough talk.' She leant across and kissed him on the lips. Ant kissed back and then recoiled, 'Honestly Tatsu don't think I'm not grateful but I head back to OZ soon and I would've imagined you to have ended up with a better sort than me'.

Tatsu fixed Ant with a wicked stare and hissed, 'I don't want Beckham, the pretty boy, I want to be ravaged by the jungle ape with the pet anaconda'.

Ant had given it his best shot and during that night had done his country proud. He had given Tatsu the pounding of her life and she was now deep asleep purring next to him.

He smiled to himself as he replayed the night's events in his head. He figured that if she looked like an elfin princess then he must have looked like a furry Orc climbing all over her. Still good on me he thought as he drifted off to sleep.

Before long, Ant's subconscious replaced the reality of the comfortable embrace of the climate-controlled apartment with the memory of searing and swirling dust. As his dream took effect, the comfortable bed he shared with Tatsu morphed into a much less-comfortable armoured truck seat. Ant scanned the dusty dasht (Persian word for a plain used by Aussie Diggers). His desert camouflage uniform now sported a Major's crown. It had been four years since he had returned from Iraq and, in that time, no one had shot at him until now. He was the Officer Commanding an Australian Army logistics company in Afghanistan.

He was out driving in between Patrol Bases running resupply. This was a dangerous part of the world. The Australian Task Force had been pushing hard up through Uruzgan into the Chora Valley to drive the insurgent force back to enable stable governing bodies and infrastructure to be established. It was a completely different environment compared to Iraq.

The desert camouflage uniform they had been issued suited Iraqi's white, sand and gravel environment, but not so good for Afghanistan, which had a combination of light-coloured dust, dark mud and a foliage-covered green zone that followed the rivers and creeks flowing through the valleys and villages.

The melt was underway as the snowcaps liquefied and flowed into the waterways. The air was crisp and the sky blue. Ant's truck convoy was moving slowly along the dirt tracks across the dasht. The dasht was featureless terrain that stretched for a kilometre in width and was framed by stunning, sheer, snow-capped mountains.

Running at the base of the southern range was a fast-flowing river. 'Fuck it's fucking beautiful isn't it Sir? I'd bring my missus here to show her except for all the fuckwits trying to kill ya.'

Ant turned to face the driver who was addressing him. The driver's name was Private Bob Anderson or Ando as he was known within the unit. He and Ant had shared the cab of this truck together for the last four days. They had in that time told each other their life stories, swapped jokes, shared their dreams and were now down to small talk to relieve the tension and the boredom.

Ando and Ant were halted by the engineer vehicle that had detected some disturbed earth on the track. 'Another flipping IED [Improvised Explosive Device] buried underneath the road', Ant said.

'Yeah but still a beautiful place', Ando responded.

Ant thought to himself, 'Seven-months in to a nine-month tour. Just two more months and I'll be back in Brisbane having a beer at SUNCORP Stadium watching the rugby and all of this shit will be a long way behind me'.

'Yeah Ando, it's a picturesque place, but I wouldn't hold my breath waiting for it to be safe enough to bring your beautiful Lynda to visit it on your holidays.'

'Hey boss', said Ando looking in the vehicle's side mirror, the load is coming loose and I want to tighten it up. How long do you think we are going to be stopped for?'

'Only a couple of minutes before the escorts find a safe route around the IED.'.

'Stay in the truck Sir, this is a one-man job and I don't trust an officer to do it.'

With that, Bob Anderson leapt from the truck onto the deadly landscape that was littered with mines. He sprinted along the side of the armoured truck and climbed onto the back tray where the offending loose load chain was hanging. It only took him a minute to tighten the chain. He knew he should get back to the relative safety of the truck cab but he had been cooped up in that stale cab for four days and the landscape was so beautiful. He sat there for a moment allowing the crisp fresh air to enter his nostrils. 'Yeah, this place is beautiful', he thought, staring at the snow-capped mountains.

Up in one of those snow-capped mountain some 800 meters away from the convoy in the valley, Talzere and Amere Khalid lay on their stomachs shivering under the camouflaged blanket. They had been there for two days in the freezing remote location just waiting for the opportunity to ambush the infidel invaders. They peered through the scope, scanning for targets.

'The Kangaroo crusaders', Amere said.

'Pity', said Talzere who had been hoping for an American target.

'No, that's good, the Australian Special Forces kidnapped Eluseff two weeks ago, so it is God's will that they pay.'

'Yes', Talzere thought, cradling the stock of the DShKM. This Soviet heavy calibre automatic weapon with a range of 2000 meters would be perfect for this job. Talzere wasn't confident that the weapon would penetrate the Kangaroo soldiers' armoured vehicles, so he focused on the four soldiers that had ventured outside of their vehicles.

The IED they had forced the farmers to bury had done its job and had halted the convoy. Those soldiers working the IED were on their stomachs, presenting a small target. But here on his own was a soldier on top of a vehicle nice and high in the air fixing a load.

Yes, even if Talzere missed him, which was very likely, the rounds might still strike the vehicle load and ignite the ammunition they were carrying.

The soldier was a difficult target scurrying across the back of the truck as he set about his task, but then suddenly he stopped. The soldier was now still. He looked like he was staring directly at Talzere. He felt as though they had a connection, like a hunter does when it meets eyes with his prey. This is God's will he thought as he squeezed the trigger. Six large, deadly rounds spat from the machine gun's barrel.

It was as much as a surprise for Talzere as it was for PTE Anderson when one of the rounds found its target. The impact flung the digger from the back of the truck to the ground.

In that instant, a young man's life was snuffed out. His dreams would now not be realized. He had planned to marry Linda his fiancée as soon as he got back. Her engagement ring was still nestled in his pocket, having remained in his possession since he purchased it in Dubai a month ago. His fiancée's and his parents' hearts would break when they heard the news of his death and yet again when they saw the ring.

The media in Australia would briefly report the incident that night during the commercial break of the latest crying chef reality TV program. The media would fail to explain to the public why PTE Anderson was there—that his was a precious life, and that his loss would be felt by his family and 775 of his Army unit mates.

His name would appear on a plaque at his Battalion's memorial wall at Amberley and on the honour role at the Australian War Memorial in Canberra. Every Anzac Day thousands of Australians would gather to remember his sacrifice. But for family and friends he would always be on their mind.

Ant would think of him almost every day for the rest of his life. In his mind, Ando was his responsibility and his death was now his cross to bear.

Tatsu started shaking Ant as the Uruzgan dust dissipated. 'Ant, Ant, wake up!', said Tatsu.

Ant lay there for a moment trying to make sense of the familiar environment of the penthouse suite. He could feel his elevated heart rate. He began breathing slowly and deliberately to return it to normal.

'Ant, where were you just now?'

Ant propped himself up in bed to face Tatsu who was leaning over him with a look of concern on her face. 'Oh, I was just having a dream Tatsu, that's all', replied Ant still trying to focus his mind.

The look on Tatsu's face changed from concern to mild annoyance, 'It was a little more than a dream Ant. Whatever you were dreaming wasn't imaginary. Your breathing was erratic and it sounded like you were trying to scream, then you started sobbing. Does it have something to do with tattoo on your arm?', said Tatsu, gently rubbing Ando's name.

Ant paused for a moment before a nervous smile crept onto his face, 'Alright Tatsu if you must know you are right, I was reliving a traumatic event. Watching that last game between the All Blacks and the Wallabies would have made any Aussie man cry'.

Tatsu slapped Ant playfully, yet hard, 'Ant this isn't funny. I have seen people with PTSD before. If people ignore it, it can be a killer', she said in a serious tone.

Ant looked into Tatsu's beautiful blue/hazel eyes, 'Yeah, well, so can be going out on a date with you'.

Ant's repeated attempts at humour lightened Tatsu's mood. 'What kind of a name is Ant anyway?', asked Tatsu. Relieved the topic of conversation had changed Ant happily responded, 'Oh it is short for Antonio. My mum is Australian and my dad Italian, though he now refers to himself as an Aussie that can cook.

The guys in the Army liked to call me Ant which they said was short for "ant dick", said Ant chuckling. 'Now, what about your name, Tatsu?'

Tatsu smiled, 'Well I don't know. I wouldn't say you have an ant-sized dick Ant, but my name has a true meaning. Tatsu means "dragon" and is given to girls who possess certain traits', she said.

'What, like fighting off thugs with knives?', asked Ant. Tatsu turned to face the ocean and gazed out towards the horizon 'Tiger', she muttered drifting off in deep contemplation.

Tatsu got up out of bed and went to the bathroom. Ant heard the shower turn on. It was now his turn to lie there looking out the window towards the ocean. He smirked as he thought about the dragon lady having a shower. She's beautiful, athletic, sharp-witted and I suspect has more money than god. He had to admit to himself that she was well out of his league. Still why not enjoy it while it lasts.

In the shower Tatsu was likewise thinking of Ant. She was fond of this Australian. He was a real bloke, masculine and capable of being brutal yet with a kind soul. Yes, she thought, it was a pity her life wouldn't let her settle down. Life with Ant would be great. He made her feel like a real woman. He made her feel safe, not that she needed a man to protect her but it felt nice regardless. On top of it all it was his humour and energy that drew her to him.

After another couple of days frolicking with Tatsu in the surf, Ant was relaxing by the spa when his phone rang. It was a video call. Ant opened the app to see a neatly-preened Lachlan calling from a sun-drenched marina full of yachts.

'Antonio, how are you sport?'

'Hmm', thought Ant, 'I wonder where the posh twat is calling from?'

'Lachlan, I am fantastic now I am a long-haired, fat civilian enjoying life. How about yourself?'

'Yes, yes good. Ant, listen, when are you back in Brisbane?'

'Well, I'm due to fly out in a day's time but I've met a girl, a *bela splendido* girl and I was thinking of staying on in Thailand for a few more days with her.'

'Well Antonio, enjoy yourself mate. We have something on the boil that has a paycheck attached to it and for a change we would actually be helping people. So it's a win-win. When you get your arse back to Brisbane I will meet you there and discuss details over a few beers'.

Ant knew that Lachlan had recently been involved in some private security work in Iraq. He screwed up his face at the prospect of heading off to some dangerous third world country.

'Listen Lachlan, I plan on getting a legitimate and very average life once I have a few months off. I'm not a bad bloke, so I don't think I deserve to be shot at anymore. I'm going to ring a friend of mine who reckons he can get me a job in a transport and logistics company. I'm going to marry a girl, maybe even two. I'm going to drink beer, get fat and boring'.

'No need to worry Ant, you are already fat and boring. You just got to hook up with some chick and grab a beer and you are there mate.'

Lachlan leant forward towards the camera and sneered, 'Fuck me Ant, I'm offering you a fantastic opportunity and all I'm hearing is waaa fucking waaa. Now stop friggin whining and while you're at it put some sun screen on your face you're turning red and your head is starting to look like a fucking pumpkin.

Enjoy the rest of your trip and I will see you back in Brisbane when you have finished bumping uglies with your new little girlfriend'. With that Lachlan hung up.

Ant flung the phone back onto the towel. 'I wonder what that prat is up to', Ant pondered. 'Still, it will be good to see the self-centered egomaniac again. As painful as he is, I do miss him.'

A door slid open as Tatsu walked out onto the deck with a cold beer and some freshly-cut fruit. Her smooth skin glistened in the sun as she placed the beer next to Ant. 'Then again, fuck Lachlan', thought Ant.

HIS BREATH FORMED VAPOR CLOUDS as he trudged through the mud that clung to his Hunter Wellies. It was a beautiful crisp morning in southern England. To the southeast he could just make out the huge white horse carved below the Ridge. The carving made by the ancients in 500 BC was almost glowing in the dim light as the early morning rain had washed clean the limestone in which it was etched.

The man stared at the eerie carving, musing at the contrast between the landscape of his father's farm in the Cotswolds of the UK and their farm in Clermont, Central Queensland, Australia. His attention was suddenly focused by the shouting of beaters and the occasional bark of a hound eager to retrieve the prey. Like a veteran hunter, he stood clutching a Purdy shotgun scanning his arcs.

Two large game birds leapt from the thick damp foliage. From their squawking, he knew they were pheasant and they would be moving fast. One broke to his right and the other flew straight at him. He lifted the ornate shotgun to his shoulder and fired to his front.

The velocity of the pellets halted the bird's forward momentum causing it to drop like a stone 18 meters to his front. He swung the barrel to his right tracking the second bird now 25 meters away. With one shot left in the gun he squeezed the trigger in a slow, controlled motion whilst smoothly tracking 20 cm in front of the bird. The gun barely bucked as the shot scattered from the barrel. The large colourful pheasant flapped several times and drunkenly fluttered to the ground. At that moment, the hound was released and it set about its retrieval task with vigor. '

A left and right! That is some fine shooting Lachlan. I see you haven't lost any of your skills from your days in the Aussie Army'. Lachlan cleared the gun of the spent shells and placed it in the back of the old Series 3 Land Rover. '

Yes, some things stay with you forever regardless how much you try to forget them.' The gamekeeper called out to Lachlan, 'I will prepare these birds and drop them off at the estate home kitchen for you then shall I sir?'.

'That would be great Colin thank you.' At that, Lachlan climbed into the vehicle and lurched off.

He drove up the tree-lined English country road sipping from a leather-bound silver flask that containing a concoction of gin mixed with sloe berries that are indigenous to the area and popular amongst the country gent set.

Lachlan was an interesting blend of Australian and British culture and could seamlessly transition between the two. As a good-looking, lean-built man who stood 6ft 3in, with golden wavy hair that was slicked back, and piercing blue eyes, he had always had very little trouble attracting the attention of the fairer sex. He had fair skin and a posh accent that he had developed as a youth in the English boarding school system. He was convincingly English gentry, although the Antipodean twang from his time spent in Australia was ever present.

He pulled up out the front of his family's home. The home was a large two-story stone house perched on top of a rise and surrounded by a well-kept lawn and manicured topiary bushes. Curving around the front was a large circular stone driveway.

He examined the cars out the front. Sitting behind his Porsche 911 was a black Aston Martin. The black car signified the presence of a much-appreciated guest. Lachlan smirked to himself and muttered, 'Jonty'.

Jonty was Lachlan's school chum from Eton, which was a very exclusive school in England. Lachlan's family may have primarily resided on their cattle property in Central Queensland, Australia, but they had decided Lachlan should be educated in the UK at the school his father had attended.

This decision was based more upon the quality of contacts he would make than the standard of education that he would receive.

Lachlan hadn't seen Jonty in years. So, he was excited to see the car in the driveway. After school, Lachlan had returned to Australia and joined the Australian Army. Jonty on the other hand had joined the Green Jackets, a British Army unit whose commissioned officers were educated primarily at Eton.

Both Lachlan and Jonty had left their respective Army two years ago, and this was the first Lachlan had returned to England since discharging from the Services.

Lachlan walked not up to the grand entrance of his family's mansion, but rather to the side entrance where he could remove his mud encrusted wellies. Next to the boot rack was a pair of clean RM Williams slip-on boots into which he changed.

He removed his Barbour hunting jacket and flat cap and placed them on the hat rack. Underneath his hunting attire he was wearing tan trousers, a light blue shirt and forest green tie. Examining himself in the cloakroom mirror he determined his outfit from this season's 'Paul Smith' collection was not crushed or stained from the morning hunt so he could receive company without changing.

He drained the last of his sloe gin from his hipflask and placed it on the entrance table for the maid to clean. 'Alright', Lachlan thought to himself, 'It's 11 o'clock, so I bet Jonty is in the observatory drinking my favorite scotch'.

Lachlan sauntered through the house to the light-drenched glass-roofed observatory. Sure enough, Jonty had made himself at home, slumped in Lachlan's favorite armchair and sipping his favorite scotch. To his surprise, Jonty's 22-year-old cousin, Lucy, was also there sipping on a glass of Pommery Champagne. Lachlan had not seen Lucy for 5 years. The skinny, annoying teenage girl he remembered had now blossomed into a stunning curvy woman with dark flowing hair, piercing hazel eyes and a cheeky smirk that could enchant its male quarry.

She oozed confidence as she leant on the bar, looking stunning in a revealing light fabric summer dress. It was the type of outfit that made the statement 'I'm not dressed to impress. I am merely dressed for the season, but now try and look away, cause I bet you can't'.

"Hello Mr tall blonde and handsome', said Lucy, lecherously eyeing Lachlan up and down.

Lachlan fixed Lucy with a stare and replied, 'My how you've grown. Not little Red Riding Hood anymore are you?'

'No, you're right darling I am not a little girl anymore, I'm more like the big bad wolf come to drink your champagne, huff and puff and blow your house down', she said.

Fair enough Lucy, however I see you're not the only unsavory character that has broken into my house to consume my top-shelf booze. No, there appears to be two of you bludging Poms in my house helping yourselves.'

Jonty looked up from the chair and sporting a bored look responded with, 'Oh how droll, yet another tiresome display of your colonial upbringing'. With that Jonty made a sudden movement hurling a long slender steel object he had stashed next to the armchair at Lachlan.

Lachlan's reflexes took over as he caught the fencing foil by the handle. In a single fluid movement Jonty was on his feet brandishing an identical foil. 'On guard!', he yelled.

Lachlan regained his composure and raised the hilt of the foil to his top lip before slashing it away to his side in a ritual fencing salute. Jonty mimicked the gesture before both men entered an appropriate combative posture.

The two men glared at each other in a way that would have convinced a naive onlooker that they were mortal enemies. 'May the best man win', called Lucy. She was in a frenzy, induced partly by a champagne glow and partly by the spectacle of two elegant men poised to engage in a form of combat from a bygone era—she was rich, but this scenario evoked images which made her feel more than ever like an aristocrat.

Jonty attacked at a lighting pace, thrusting the tip of the foil at Lachlan's torso. Lachlan parried the thrust to the right hence defusing the attack. It was only now that Lachlan realized that the rubber tips of the foils had been removed, upping the stakes. Personal injury and a visit to the emergency ward were now real threats.

The two men circled each other, which added an extra dimension to their experience as schoolboys fencing at Eton where they were required to stay on a competition mat. The competition mat limited the combatants to much more linear attack options. Jonty attacked again. Yet again it was fast but his thrust was to the right of Lachlan's midriff and was easily parried.

'Hmmm', thought Lachlan, 'he's not as precise as I remember. He is either out of practice or my scotch has started taking effect. You wombat Jonty. Fancy starting this if you are pissed. I will have you done in thirty seconds'.

Lachlan faked a thrust that caused Jonty to react slashing his foil through the air. It was then that Lachie shuffled two paces towards his drunken prey, making his true attack. Jonty avoiding the attack clumsily shuffled backwards towards the open door of the atrium.

He glanced around him and, realizing he now had little room in which to move, stepped backwards out of the house onto the well-manicured lawn of the courtyard, which was the size of a tennis court. This relieved Lachlan–here was now less chance of damage to the Chesterfield couches, the bar's crystal or the much-cherished citrus trees that sheltered within the conservatory's glass walls from the wet and cold British climate.

On this day, the sun was out and shining now that the early morning mist had burnt off. Lachlan coolly followed Jonty into the courtyard whilst reaching into his pocket removing a pair of Ray-Ban sunglasses that he flicked open and placed on his face.

'Yet another indication of your antipodean heritage. A true English gentleman would not wear sunglasses during a duel', taunted Jonty.

Gentleman or not, Lucy was impressed. She had always had a crush on Lachlan and here he was engaged in combat and maintaining a very cool demeanor whilst clearly taking control of the fight. 'Yes', thought Lucy, 'as long as he doesn't lose his manhood in this tussle I think I will make use of it this evening'.

After another couple of failed attacks by Jonty, Lachlan decided to launch a premeditated five-stage attack. After all, fencing is a combination of sport and chess. After one has the measure of their opponent a series of moves and counter-moves can be planned to defeat one's opponent.

Choices are made in split seconds and would have resulted in a death in past centuries. Lachlan observed Jonty squinting in the sun. 'Yes, I will keep him facing the sun. Should slow his reaction time just that little bit further.'

Lachie shuffled forward and made a thrust at Jonty's torso. Lachlan never planned this thrust to defeat Jonty–it was merely the first phase of the attack. Jonty parried the attack to the left. Lachie followed the energy of the block and parried Jonty's counter-thrust, which had immediately followed. Jonty prepared to parry

Lachie's next counter-attack but he faked a thrust and instead slapped Jonty's foil downwards with a vertical slap that was then followed by a thrust at Jonty's right arm.

Jonty again stumbled backwards to avoid the inevitable wound to his arm. Lachie had him but just as the foil was about to destroy Jonty's beautiful pink Ralph Lauren shirt he slipped, falling backwards. Instead of the arm, the foil stabbed Jonty's right hand.

He felt cheated until he looked down at Jonty and realized that what had saved his prey from a decisive defeat was a big steaming pile of hunting dog shit which was now smeared on Jonty's back. Lachie positioned the foil on Jonty's neck and shouted, 'Submit or die, shitbag.'

'Oh, bloody hell,' cried Jonty. Lucy howled with laughter and danced around taunting Jonty, 'You're not coming home in the car covered in dog poo!'

Lachie called for the housekeeper, Laura, and after berating her for the staff having left a big pile of his hunting dog's shit on the lawn, had her escort Jonty to the bathroom and set him up with a change of clothes. He suggested that she might also take a look at Jonty's hand which was oozing blood from the stab wound.

The housekeeper rolled her eyes, 'Of course sir', she replied whilst thinking 'Do these rich, posh kids ever grow up?' Laura then disappeared to the downstairs bathroom and returned with a triangle bandage that she placed over Jonty's wound before leading him away to the visitor's suite upstairs to clean him up. The house was well-stocked with first aid items as Lachlan's family and friends were often injuring themselves in their boys' own adventure pursuits.

Once Jonty left the room, Lachlan looked across at Lucy who seemed to have a further button on her dress undone, exposing an extra hint of breast. 'So, I guess we have an hour to kill whilst Laura sorts out Jonty'. said Lachlan.

'Yes', replied Lucy, 'Shall we go for a walk?'

The pair walked back out into the courtyard and took a path through a modest-sized wood down to the estate's 'Water Garden'. The water garden concept was popular back when the house was built, inspired by the ancient Roman concept, which consisted of a series of ponds and fountains, which were powered by gravity. In this case the water features were fed from a large pond also on the estate.

The water garden extended for some 60 meters and was the perfect place to sit and engage in casual conversation whilst supported by the tranquil background noise of trickling water and chirping wildlife.

Lachie enquired what Lucy was doing these days. Lucy explained that after school she went up to Oxford where she studied psychology. At the completion of her studies she undertook a role within the family business and now managed the family's prestige car sales business.

'Car sales?', enquired Lachlan, 'Doesn't sound like the type of business Lord Erskin-Stamper would associate himself with.'

'Oh, but my father does,' replied Lucy, 'You should come out and have a look tomorrow, it is not what you think and it is by appointment only', she said.

'Alright then it's a date Lucy, where and when?' asked Lachlan.

Lucy tapped on her phone for a moment, 'There you are, I have texted you my home address, which is where we run the business from. I will see you there at 10:30 am'.

Lucy continued to explain the family business and investments that ranged from property management, import export and, more recently, mining exploration. She also spoke about how much money and asset the family businesses had accumulated over the previous five generations and how they were expanding their philanthropic activities as a means of giving back to their fellow man.

Of course, such activities also enhanced the reputation of the family as well as enticing the 'ethical investors'.

They were currently working with some of the subsidiaries of DFID [the Department for International Development] to support victims of natural disasters.

This piqued Lachie's interest. 'There is an opportunity for ex-military in that field', he thought. 'In fact, I know a fat ape that has commanded a disaster relief team. I wonder what Ant is doing now he is out of the Army. Yes, I think I need to touch base with Lucy's dad', thought Lachie.

They chatted away for a little over an hour before Jonty appeared, all freshened-up and no longer covered in shit. He proudly pulled back the bandage to reveal the wound, which Laura had cleaned and mended with butterfly clips.

She had suggested he should go to the clinic to get it properly looked at—a suggestion that Jonty promptly dismissed. In truth, he was hoping for a messy dueling scar, not a well-mended almost invisible scar.

'So, Jonty you smell better', said Lachlan.

'Just tell me Lachlan, was that your dog's or your excrement that I fell in? After all I know you Aussies love your outdoor dunnies', taunted Jonty.

Lachlan winked at Lucy and responded, 'Well I don't know Jonty. Did it smell like dog meat or lobster and Fosters?'

'Thankfully dog meat', Jonty sniggered.

The trio sat outside in the sunny but crisp afternoon often encountered in southern England. They talked about their past exploits and what the future might hold for them.

What became evident during the conversation was that Lucy and Jonty had their futures mapped out but Lachie didn't. He elected to leave the Army as he had reached a level where he would have had to develop some sort of political acumen—something in which he had no interest, not to mention the thought of an office job made him want to self-harm.

Nor was he a farmer like his father, so joining the family business was out. He wanted the adventure of the military but without the bureaucratic politics and compromise that haunt the senior ranks. He also wanted more money than the military would allow so he could gain some independence from the family.

What did his strengths make him suitable for?

He was a handsome and charming man which made him suitable for acting, politics or sales. He was very fit, lethal with most weapons, fluent in several languages and possessing a flair for small-team tactics. What did these skills make him suitable for? Security, mercenary or a contractor of some sort?

Jonty looked at the sun disappearing behind the trees, 'It looks like it's going to get cold this evening–let's go to a warm pub and partake in some pints of Guinness'.

The house caretaker offered to drop them off and pick them up as cabs were rare in the British countryside.

They piled into the Land Rover and headed to the King and Queen Pub in Longcot. The centuries-old pub itself was a trip back in time. White-washed walls with a shingle roof gave the old pub a traditional look as it sat comfortably in the middle of the quaint village of Longcot. The front of the pub gazed out at hedgerow and green pastures leading-up to the mesmerizing limestone white horse carved along the Ridgeway.

In addition to the aesthetic appeal of the pub, the meals were well-prepared by Mark the owner-operator. Mark's wife, Sally, looked after the vast beer and gin selection.

This pub was referred to as a 'free house', meaning that a commercial brewery conglomerate did not own it, and could therefore choose its own local beers, set its own menu and source local produce. It was amazing that pubs like the King and Queen remained off the tourist trail, but if it were, the constant stream of coach tourists would likely ruin it.

Its patrons were predominately regulars that Mark and Sally knew well. As with many small villages in the English countryside it provided the social hub of the community.

As they walked into the pub Lachie reflected just how much he missed the English pubs like the King and Queen. It was before meal service so Mark was manning the bar. He looked up at Lachie with a smirk that crept across his rugby-battered face, 'Lachie, Jonty, great to see you chaps again.

There goes our quiet evening'. Sally, who took over the bar to free Mark up for two hours so he could prepare some meals, joined the four of them.

He rejoined them after meal service and the five of them chatted into the evening drinking several pints of extra cold Guinness before switching to the King and Queen's featured ale. It was 9:30 pm in the evening and the light outside had well and truly faded.

The pub was full with locals enjoying the pub's warmth and the ale. In front of the fire two hounds lazed. Every now and again they would look over towards their master to make sure all was well.

One of the locals caught Lachlan's accent and said, 'Is that a little bit of an Aussie twang I detect?'

'Well yes, it is. I spend most of my time in Oz, but I am a dual national and sometimes I reside in Great Britain', said Lachlan.

'Sounds perfect', replied the man, 'Wish I was so lucky. Is it true the Aussies don't drink Fosters?', he said motioning towards the blue-labeled beer tap.

Lachlan thought to himself, 'This is a commonly-asked question that most Australians travelling through the UK or the US have posed to them. The temptation is to respond with "God no, we don't touch that piss we just sell it to silly POMs and Yanks". But over time he had realized this just made people feel foolish. After all what was their crime? To try and enjoy an Australian product?

At the end of the day as far as a lager goes Fosters isn't a bad one'. So, instead he explained that Fosters is typical of an Australian lager and many Aussies drink it. Most however tend to drink their state brew like VB in Victoria, Tooheys in NSW or XXXX (Fourex) in God's country. For this reason Fosters has concentrated on the export market throughout the UK, US, and Europe.

The man seemed satisfied with this answer and insisted on buying Lachie and his friends a round of the stuff.

By 2300 hours there were still eight people in the pub. Although no one could remember how it started they were all standing around the bar drinking Fosters and singing merrily.

'Okay', announced the barman, 'You have five minutes to get out of here or you will be locked down with us'. Two people quickly made their escape. The remaining six, which included Jonty, Lucy, and Lachie, let out a cheer as the publican locked the doors.

'No more selling of alcohol, it's the law. So, for the rest of the night it's on the house. But no more of that Fosters you heathens, its back to ale for you lot', Mark said, slapping the King and Queen's finest ales down in front of them.

The others in the bar were involved with the local racehorse stables– were some 40 top-level stables in the village of Lambourn, a 10-minute drive from Longcot. They regaled the others with tales of early mornings, late nights and the highs and lows of racing.

Lachlan expressed an interest in their line of work so they offered to show him around the Jamie White's stables, which predominantly trained 'Chasers' but with some 'Flat Trackers' as well. The terms referred to horses competing in steeplechase or flat race track events.

The passion they shared for their trade reminded Lachlan of what was missing in his life. Mateship, the challenge and adventure, aspects of life intrinsic to Service life that he experienced in the Australian Army.

As the tight-knit group continued to share tales and discuss their future dreams, a strange feeling swept over Lachie. He felt empty, alone, very much a foreigner in his childhood home.

A feeling of nostalgia swept over him. It was clear to him now. He craved the warmth of the southern sun. He wanted to stand on a sparsely-populated white sand beach. He wanted to watch the orange sunset over the dry Clermont farm. He wanted a girl to love him as much as he loved himself.

He looked at Jonty. He was a good friend and his charm, good looks, and family money complemented Lachlan's perfectly. He was the ideal friend for the English gentleman to cut about town with. But deep down Lachlan wasn't an English gent even though he imitated one beautifully.

His heart was in Australia. He felt a connection with the land and the genuine, tough, 'what you see is what you get' Aussie Digger. He missed their humour and resilience that he had experienced in Iraq as they willingly exposed themselves to danger time and again, in an attempt to live up to the ANZAC legend. But above all else, Lachie missed his one true mate on the planet.

It was an unintended consequence of a casual relationship that Lachie had formed with one Antonio Lucciano. Ant didn't complement Lachie's image like Jonty did. Ant was crass, and although not badly-off, was not from family money.

He was not elegant or well-spoken; not well-connected nor overly ambitious. Yes, they shared a lot of interests like fast cars, motorbikes, hunting and mountain biking; but this didn't explain the longing Lachie felt to be in Ant's company.

Ant had settled in Brisbane purchasing a charming Queensland cottage in the highly-desirable suburb of Petrie Terrace near the party district of Caxton Street. Lachie loved the area. Near Suncorp Stadium for ease of watching the rugby, Ant's beautifully-situated house had cost him nearly every cent he had, but it was a fantastic investment.

Whilst visiting Ant a year ago, the house next door came on the market. Ant and Lachie were sitting on Ant's tranquil deck enjoying a beer when an estate agent followed by two wide-eyed couples wondered out onto the house for sale's balcony.

On a whim, Lachie yelled out to the real estate agent while she was running an open house, 'How much do you want for it?'

'$950,000', she replied, with a tired look as she figured he was curious rather than a potential buyer.

'Done, bring over the paperwork' Lachie replied.

This stunned the estate agent, the two couples waiting to view the house and most of all Ant, who spat his beer out at the thought of his new neighbor.

It had the desired effect; Lachie proved to Ant that he had loads of money and at the same time he trusted Ant's judgment. But there was more to it than that. It gave them something else they had in common, another enduring link.

'God, I hope I'm not in love with the fat fuck', Lachie thought to himself as a smile crept on his face for the first time in months.

'It's good to see you smile', Lucy said intently staring at Lachie. 'Maybe it's time we call it a night whilst you are still in a good mood? I've got something to show you', she said intently gazing into Lachie's eyes.

Sally drove Lachie and crew back to his estate as the offer of the pick-up from Gerard, the caretaker, had long since expired. Lachie pointed out the rooms that had been set up for Jonty and Lucy to stay in. Lachie then walked through into his room.

He opened the door to the huge room. The room was about four times the size of a normal main bedroom. Its space was dominated by a large four-poster bed that sat on a low set stage. There was a lounge set facing the bed. A TV could be lowered from the ceiling when required; otherwise it remained hidden. The room was fitted with surround sound and mood lighting.

When Lachie had stumbled through the door the lighting that was on dusk setting so as not to be too bright was triggered. Soft classical music swam around the room.

Lachie stripped and headed for the en suite. It was again another large room that contained a rainwater shower, a steam room and a large spa bath that accompanied the other essential facilities. He freshened-up and headed back into the room towards the bed.

Suddenly he heard the door quietly open. He turned around to see Lucy confidently strut into the room clad in a silk dressing gown. She smirked as she looked at Lachie standing there naked in the impressive room.

She let the gown drop to the floor exposing some very expensive lingerie she had recently purchased from the Rue Saint-Honoré in Paris. Her purchase gave her an extra boost of confidence. It was like a costume that helped snuff out the memory they both had of her being an awkward teenager.

Standing there in the dimly-lit red and black colour-schemed room she looked more like a beautiful and sexy woman that was very capable of getting what she wanted. In this case, what she wanted was Lachie and he was now ensnared by her femininity.

The alcohol coursing through his veins had dulled Lachie's senses. 'I'm not sure how much good I will be to her tonight but I will give it a go', he thought to himself.

Lucy kissed Lachie. In his drunken state, he was clumsily pawing her. She took control pushing him back towards the bed. He collapsed backwards onto the mattress virtually spread-eagled. She grabbed the waist tie from her gown and lashed his hands to the bed posts.

'Ooh I didn't realize you were so kinky Lucy', said Lachie.

Lucy left Lachie and headed towards the en suite fetching a glass of warm water. She then walked towards an ice bucket that was on a drink stand. It had been filled by the housemaid on the off chance that Lachie would need a night cap. She filled a glass with ice and then returned to the bedside.

'What are you up to?', chuckled Lachie. 'I want to make sure in your drunken state you can perform', purred Lucy. She sipped some warm water and then went down on Lachie. The extra sensation of the warm water cut through the drunken haze causing an immediate stirring in his loins.

After a minute or so Lucy pulled her head back and took a sip from the ice-filled glass. She repeated her previous performance. This time the cold sensation Lucy applied to his old fella really woke him up. It still felt good but settled him back down again.

A minute later Lucy repeated the warm water performance, which drove him wild.

She kept up the hot and cold treatment until she was convinced she had his attention and there was little risk that Lachlan was going to lose his hard-on. She decided to leave him tied up as she climbed on top and started to ride him.

He was so drunk his hands would have just gotten in the road, not to mention she was enjoying dominating this over-confident man. She continued to thrust against Lachie. The alcohol was now having a positive effect in providing Lachie with some staying power. She bumped, ground and thrashed about for 20 minutes, achieving an orgasmic climax twice before Lachie's grunting confirmed she had finished him off as well.

After Lucy, had untied Lachie they cuddled and joked about Lucy's creative technique in getting some performance out of him despite his partially-inebriated state. They soon fell asleep content with how the night had progressed.

Morning came far too early and the three friends sat at the kitchen table trying to force down some coffee and a bacon sandwich, or bacon butty as the British call them. Jonty was going to head back to London on the Oxford to London train to help him avoid the Sunday afternoon traffic nightmare as hundreds of thousands headed into London ready for the working week.

Lucy and Lachlan were going to head to her home in England's Peak District to see her used car sales business. Lucy suggested to Lachlan they both travel in the Aston Martin so they could chat along the way. She said she would loan him a car to drive back so he could try something other than his Porsche.

After breakfast Lucy and Lachlan climbed into the Aston Martin. Lachlan was impressed by the quality interior. It had the same feel of quality as the exterior displayed and the car's looks inside and out were sublime. Lucy placed the Aston Martin Swarovski Crystal key into the ignition.

There was a loud whirring noise that sounded like a Spit Fire starter motor. Suddenly the huge six litre V12 engine burst into life with a deep masculine growl. The sound sent chills through Lachlan. Two B&O speakers rose from the dash, along with a previously-hidden GPS.

The car truly was like something out of a James Bond movie Lachlan thought to himself stroking the leather-clad dash.

'The whole interior is hand-stitched and four cows died in the making', proudly stated Lucy. 'In fact, even today Aston Martins are largely hand-made. Huge attention to detail is given to every aspect of these cars', Lucy explained as she edged along Lachlan's 600-yard drive way. Once at the main road Lucy let the V12 beast off its leash throwing Lachlan back into his seat.

The car's advanced electronics fought the 470 bhp to keep traction on the wet road. The howl of the engine was incredible, causing Lachlan to fall in love with the vehicle. Once on the highway Lucy sat on 80 mph and the huge engine quietened down, as running at only 1500 rpm it was under no strain at all.

They cruised along in comfort for the next few hours. Lucy told Lachlan how her business made three million pounds' net profit last year, which staggered him. He couldn't imagine how she had managed to achieve this through a used car yard.

He explained to her that he was looking to establish his own business in regards to assisting government agencies in austere environments and that he could tailor his multi-disciplined team to meet any requirement, anywhere and anytime. He needed his first big contract to get his idea off the ground, and there lay the challenge.

After a while Lucy and Lachlan pulled up to a huge solid timber gate that swung open as the car approached and they drove down a fifty-yard driveway to a large newly-built house. To the side of the house was a twenty-car garage cum showroom.

'Bloody hell', exclaimed Lachlan as he climbed out of the Aston Martin.

The large property was fully fenced-in with stone walls which were topped with razor wire. He spotted a number of CCTV cameras and even some infrared motion sensors set up along the driveway.

'This way', said Lucy as she walked Lachlan towards the show room.

A tall well-groomed man approached them, 'Hello Lucy did you have a good trip away?', the man queried.

'I did thank you Charlie.

Charlie, this is my friend Lachlan, Lachlan this is my Head of Sales, Charles Wellington.'

The two men shook hands as they exchanged pleasantries. Lachie said 'Wow, working on a Sunday Charlie, that's dedication'.

'We never stop here Lachlan, in fact you must excuse me as I have to get back to my customer in the showroom.

Lucy, I will need to introduce you as I think we are about to make a big sale.' The three of them walked into the showroom and Lachlan was stunned. He didn't know where to look first. In front of him was a Lamborghini, a GTO Ferrari, a convertible Bentley, a pristine E-type Jaguar, a spotless Porsche 356 roadster, and the true James Bond car, the Aston Martin DB5.

In the corner of the showroom was a Bugatti Veyron that had an Emirati in traditional dress leaning in through the window. Charlie approached the man, 'Sheik Al Rashid may I introduce to you the business owner the Honourable Lucy Erskin-Stamper?'.

'But of course', responded the Sheik, removing his gold-rimmed Ray-Ban Aviator sunglasses that seemed to never go out of style in the UAE.

'Hello Sheik Al Rashid, which of these beautiful cars are you interested in?' The Sheik looked up at Lucy,

'Well I don't know, which one do you think? This will be a car for my UK estate. In the UAE I have a custom Humvee and a Ferrari 458.'

Lucy smiled at Lachlan, 'For you Sheik it needs to be something that is, above all else, masculine. So unfortunately, that rules out Porsche and most supercars'.

'Bitch', thought Lachlan, 'She's having a dig at my 911'.

Lucy continued, 'The Bugatti you are looking at is very masculine and is quite exclusive. You will turn heads on the UK roads. Problem is this particular one is 990,000 pounds' sterling. So maybe there is another car here you would prefer to look at as most of the others are below the 400,000-price point?'

The smile left the Sheik's face, 'I like this car and this price is not a problem for me. I do however want a special gift to show me that you respect this business transaction'.

Lucy thought for a moment, 'Actually Sheik, I may have something that would be a once in a lifetime opportunity.

A very good friend of mine is the Commanding Officer of the Queen's Household Cavalry. He has provided me with four tickets to his marquee at Royal Oaks Race Day. I would be happy to pass on two of the tickets to you and offer to host you and your guest, if you buy this rare high performance car today. I will even organize VIP parking so you could drive it to the race day'.

The Sheik's eyes glistened. He had money and power, but the opportunity to rub shoulders with the Royal family and the British elite was a rare opportunity. Maybe he could woo a British girl with his charm, money, and a promise of adventure.

'Miss Erskin-Stamper, we have a deal.'

'Excellent choice Sheik may I please leave you with Charles to organize the paperwork and any other necessary arrangements?'

The Sheik nodded his concurrence so Lucy and Lachlan took their leave.

Suddenly, Lachlan understood how Lucy had made so much money last year from selling second-hand cars. She had a niche market and a unique business model to access it. Her social contacts meant she could lay her hands on their prestige vehicles, as they got bored of them.

She would either sell them on to the British 'Young Turks' who were climbing the social ladder or she exported them to the 'new money' in places like the UAE, USA, China and even, on the odd occasion, Australia.

Lucy dealt mainly with European cars but her passion was British cars so she proudly showed Lachlan the collection of Aston Martins, high-spec Jaguars, and the silly fast McLaren.

Lachlan could feel himself being impressed by her passion. Lucy took Lachlan for a drive in a number of her vehicles. His dream cars ended up being the Ferrari and a McLaren, but the cars he would like to own were the Aston Martin DB9 or the Maserati, due to their usability in the real world.

Lucy took him to the house for a late lunch. It was a completely modern contemporary-styled house with a networked and minimalist interior.

Lucy prepared them some tea. She then potted around the kitchen and assembled some sandwiches to keep their hunger at bay. 'So, Lachlan when are you heading back to Australia?'

'Soon, but I need to work out where my next adventure is going to be,'

Lucy nibbled on one of the sandwiches whilst she contemplated what she was about to suggest, 'You know Lachlan, my father is looking for someone to manage his aid abroad programme. You would be perfect for it with your ex-military background. He's looking to pay well and sometimes the aid team will be contracted to various government agencies such as DFID. There are some surprisingly big opportunities for investment return in this field and it has the added feel-good factor associated with this line of work. You also would have the added benefit of maybe occasionally shagging the boss's daughter.

Well at least until I get sick of being with an old man'. 'Yeah good on you Lucy, but tell me more about this business your old man is running. I certainly know plenty of people in this field that may be of use'. They spoke for hours about the present and the future.

After the Sheik and Charlie left they walked back over to the cars to look at them more closely. At 4:00 pm Lucy suggested they go back to the house and crack a bottle of Champagne.

This time Lucy went all out on the snacks to accompany the 2004 Dom Pérignon. She handed a small bag of ice to Lachlan and asked him to crush it with a small kitchen mallet for her. While Lachie crushed the ice, Lucy fetched a fine crystal bowl. She placed a fine glass cone and a mother of pearl spoon next to it. On a silver tray, she laid out some blinis.

Once Lachie had finished crushing the ice, Lucy placed it into the bowl. She then nestled the cone into the bowl into the crushed ice. Lucy opened a tin of Russian Beluga caviar and emptied the precious content into the chilled glass cone. Lachie was impressed by the whole set up, which looked quite elegant with a degree of theatre to it all.

'Shall we take this in the sun room?' she said picking up the silver tray.

'Sounds like a splendid idea', replied Lachie as he picked up the ice bucket containing the Champagne and two crystal flutes.

The next morning Lachlan woke up in Lucy's bedroom. The light streamed through the curtains but lacked the warmth of the Australian sun.

He walked down the stairs to find Lucy on the phone. A maid came from the kitchen and asked if she could fetch Lachlan something.

'Tea', replied Lachlan.

Before long Lucy ended her phone call with, 'Thanks daddy. Kiss, kiss'. Lucy looked over at Lachlan,

'Well hello sleeping beauty', she said in a childish tone.

'That was my father. It looks like you might be leaving England earlier than we anticipated. My father wants to discuss a business proposal with you. He is in Monte Carlo and wants me to book you a flight and a hotel room. Here it is Lachlan, your big break. Don't blow it. Oh and by the way you owe me. Big time!', she said with a devilish grin.

After brunch, she took Lachlan out to the lot to let him choose a car to drive back to London. Lachlan gazed at the colourful sports cars in front of him. He looked at Lucy and said with a smile 'The Englishman in me wants to drive a refined British car and the Aussie bogan in wants a big thumping V12 engine. Better give me the Aston Martin'.

THE JOB

LACHIE ARRIVED AT AÉROPORT NICE CÔTE D'AZUR and got the helicopter transfer to the LZ that linked Nice to Monaco. He had to meet with Lord Erskin-Stamper in Monte Carlo. What a wanker, his estate was only 30 miles from his in the UK. Rich people!

Lachie's family was rich but the Erskin-Stampers were one step off Royal rich. More important were the connections the family had. It was rumoured that Lord Erskin-Stamper was a good friend of Prince Albert II of Monaco. He, like many others, laundered their money here to avoid tax.

His yacht *British Elite* was moored in the harbor in front of the Port Palace Hotel. Lachie was to meet Lord Erskin-Stamper at the top of the hotel in the rooftop Michelin-star restaurant that sits at the top of the hotel.

Like most of these tourist havens the place bordered on annoying during the day as the tour bus and ocean cruiser crowd infested the dockland. At night it was a different story. Only the polite and entitled evening crowd consisting of the locals and the well-heeled tourists who can afford to stay in Monte Carlo walk the streets.

It transforms into an elegant setting where an Audi or a beautiful BMW is not noticed. It is the home of the Italian and British super cars such as the Ferrari, Lamborghini, Aston Martin, and McLaren. An expensive Porsche or AMG are considered to not be exceptional, just sensible.

Lachlan was collected from the heliport by Erskin-Stamper's Bentley. Lachlan studied the driver. Well-built with a swagger, he looked more like a body guard than a driver. sHe picked up Lachlan's bag and put them in the boot. Few words were exchanged in the five-minute drive from the helicopter pad to the Port Palace.

Lachlan climbed out of the Bentley and was met by the doorman who grabbed his bags and guided his guest, skirting around two Ferraris to get into the front doors of the Hotel.

As he approached the desk a smiling man and woman greeted him, '*Bon soir, Monsieur* Webster I presume?'

'*Oui*', replied Lachlan.

'Sir welcome, can we interest you in refreshment on this hot day?'

Lachlan smiled to himself, funny how Europeans think 28 degrees Celsius is hot.

'Sure, a glass of champagne will be fine.'

The man disappeared and fetched Lachlan a glass of Veuve Clicquot. The women at the front desk introduced herself as Veronica and explained to Lachie that the room had been paid for and that the contents of the bar fridge were free. She asked him to register and fill in his details, handing him a pen.

'No that's ok I have my own pen', he said, reaching into his jacket pocket, and removing a silver and carbon-fibre Mont Blanc fountain pen.

Using a fountain pen is a common affectation amongst Army officers. It also acts as a preventative measure against forgery; if someone claims they have your signature and it is not from a fountain pen then it can be treated with some suspicion. Handy for those whose role requires them to authorize more documents in a week than they can likely remember.

Veronica then offered to show Lachlan to his suite on the sixth floor.

As he entered the door Lachlan was distinctly pleased with the room Lucy had booked for him. It was a large modern room with a large plasma screen TV mounted on the wall.

The room had a well-stocked bar fridge and large windows that looked out over the Port of Monte Carlo.

Lachlan dismissed Veronica and peered out the window at the huge yachts and cruisers that lined the Port. He could see the *British Elite* from where he was standing. It wasn't the biggest private boat at the Port but it was still impressive.

Lachie decided to have a shower and use the Port Palace's posh toiletries. He then placed out on the bed his evening outfit. This dinner with Lord Erskin-Stamper was essentially a job interview. Therefore, a nice Hugo Boss suit would be appropriate.

He decided that a blue Italian cotton tailored shirt would be a good match with the grey suit that had a very discreet blue pinstripe through it. He then expertly selected the appropriate tie that said I am a competent go-getter.

He dressed in a well-rehearsed format that suggested a touch of OCD.

He placed on a pair of traditionally-made Cotswold woolen socks before fitting his Hugo Boss shoes. He fixed the cuffs of his shirt with a pair of hand-crafted silver cufflinks that bore his initials. He stood there perfectly dressed staring at his suit bag.

'Which watch shall I wear to complete this outfit. I think it is a choice between my classic Submariner-styled gold Rolex or my limited-edition Steve McQueen Tag Heuer Monaco.'

Lachie was the type of man that believed a book should be judged by its cover, and he assumed that he himself was always being judged. So detail in regards to watch, tie and even sock selection were important.

This was yet another behavioral trait he had picked up from the elite UK schooling system.

He decided on the Tag Heuer as there was less chance that he would be wearing a watch that Lord Erskin-Stamper would be wearing, as he was no doubt a Rolex man.

Lachie caught the lift the one floor to the restaurant and walked past the large tanks of lobsters and crabs into the main dining room of the Michelin star establishment.

The view from the glassed wall dining room was stunning and Lachie was shown to a table that looked out over the Monte Carlo Port. The maitre d' explained that his fellow diners had not arrived yet but asked if he would like a drink in the mean time?

Lachie ordered a cold Peroni that was served in a tall elegant beer glass. Lachie gazed around the dining room. It was a silver-service seafood restaurant with an Italian-styled cuisine. Before too long, two men walked in through the door; one was tall in a bespoke Savile Row suit, a gold Rolex watch and with grey disheveled hair hanging below the collar.

He was the typical Cotswold English gent. Gifted with a sharp intellect and raised to be confident, charming and ruthless, he was the product of a classical formal education and firm guidance in developing his business acumen from his family who had been involved in the ruling of England for centuries. He was in his 60s with a booming, confident voice as he announced his arrival.

The man that accompanied Lord Erskin-Stamper was clean-cut and well-dressed. By his subservient body language Lachie guessed him to be an executive assistant of some sort.

On the arrival of the two men Lachie stood up from his seat to greet them. After all manners cost nothing and first impressions count.

'Well you must be Lachlan, the lad that my Lucy has been telling me about?', boomed the big man.

'Lord Erskin-Stamper thank you so much for meeting up with me. I very much appreciate your charming Lucy's introduction', replied Lachlan shaking Erskin-Stamper's hand.

For a country gent, his hands were callused and sported several twisted fingers that had endured numerous breaks–undoubtedly a polo player thought Lachie.

'Lachlan, this is my business assistant Prescott. He is not family and is somewhat of a sniveler, but he is extremely well-organized and a very capable man so I keep him by my side to assist me with my business dealings.'

Lord Erskin-Stamper's assistant, unaffected by the jibe, leant forward and shook Lachie's hand. 'Pleasure', he said.

Lord Erskin-Stamper unbuttoned his jacket and took his seat, 'Lachlan, I must confess Lucy and Jonty both speak highly of you. Jonty has briefed me on your military background and associated skills. Lucy has informed me of your family-owned businesses and your desire to be independent of it'.

Lachie smiled awkwardly taken aback by the lack of introductory small talk.

Lord Erskin-Stamper perused the menu barely making eye contact with Lachie while he had addressed him.

'Well Sir', Lachie replied, 'Your background on me is correct. My military skills, although useful in times of war, have limited application in peace and I am no farmer. I have a craving for adventure and I am good with people'.

'Yes, so my Lucy tells me', Lord Erskin-Stamper said looking up and fixing Lachie with a look so intense that it sent a chill through him. The waiter appeared, '*Buona Sera Signori*, can I get you gentlemen anything?'

Lord Erskin-Stamper looked at the waiter, 'The squid carpaccio for starter and the grilled swordfish for main'. Lachie and Preston nodded at the fine selection and indicated they would have the same.

Preston went on to order Lord Erskin-Stamper's favourite Chablis to accompany the meal but Lord Erskin-Stamper stopped him.

'Preston, don't be so insensitive, let's honour our colonial friend here by selecting a wine from his homeland. Now normally I would order a white variety but I have never found an Australian white to my liking. Usually too heavily-oaked you see. So, if you don't object to accompanying your dish with a red may I suggest Hill of Grace which is my favourite "New World" wine.'

Although staggered by the bottle's €2000 cost, he nodded in support of the decision. *Bravissimo*, announced the waiter in support of the decision.

Lord Erskin-Stamper's phone rang so he excused himself to answer it. Lachlan scanned the room. It looked like a scene from a show on the rich and famous. He recognized several people in the restaurant. There was a young pop star and a pill of a celebrity chef who was regaling the guests at his table with cooking techniques that he would use to improve the courses they had received.

It was the guests on the two tables behind where they were sitting that interested Lachlan the most. They were well-dressed middle-aged Italians who were covered in gold bling. They had a very distinct rank structure. The bloated old guy dressed in a black suit, with his much younger wife and their poorly-behaved children, on the closest table appeared to be the boss.

The other table was full of subservient hard-looking men. Every now and again the older guy would get up from the table with his family and sit down with the men. He would help himself to the wine on their table and bark what appeared to be directions at them. He would down his wine and head back to his family's table. It looked to Lachie that he was using the regular ten-minute table swaps as a means of getting a few extra drinks in under his wife's nose.

Erskin-Stamper suddenly tossed his phone to Prescott and said, 'Be a good chap and go and sort this out'. Prescott excused himself from the table to take the telephone conversation outside.

'Well Lachlan, the reason I wanted to meet with you is that you might be able to assist me in my philanthropic pursuits. I am well-connected with the UK's Department for International Development or DFID as it is commonly known. I would like to assist some of their humanitarian and disaster relief operations amongst other things.

I plan to fund a small but very capable team to act as first respondents to natural disaster and humanitarian support efforts. I plan to show how agile a commercial organization can be in cutting through red tape and deploying quickly. My group will be able to insert into a disaster zone and commence operations without any external infrastructure or logistical support. The organization will be called Global Angel.

My parent company will organize permissions for entry, international clearances et cetera. I need a Global Angel Team leader to assemble and train a team of tough and capable people that will achieve mission success and make me look good. My long-term plan is that organisations such as DFID and AusAID will become so dependent on Global Angel to provide an immediate response that we will be contracted long-term and get the jump on any other competitors in the future.'

Erskin-Stamper sat back in his chair pausing so as if to offer Lachlan the chance to give his thoughts.

Lachlan smiled at the idea of being involved in such a venture before replying, 'Great idea, you charge big money for a service within say 48 hours that most other organisations would take a week or two to able to deliver. On top of it all it has a massive feel-good factor to it that would no doubt appeal to the ethical investor. Once everybody is hooked on the Global Angel concept, you jack up the price as you know that government organisations such as aid agencies love certainty in regards to contracted support. You remain the prime contractor possibly for the next decade and, in the meantime, you make a killing and come out of it smelling like roses.'

'Yes Lachlan, like roses, a beautiful English rose to be exact', said Lord Erskin-Stamper.

'Global Angel eh? It sounds a little like an International Rescue type organization', chuckled Lachlan.

Lord Erskin-Stamper smiled at Lachlan's humour. He already liked the lad, although he still had a deep-seated desire to flatten him for defiling his innocent and beautiful Lucy.

'Yes Lachlan, kind of like international rescue except without the vulgar thunderbirds', responded Lord Erskin-Stamper.

Lachlan and Erskin-Stamper spoke of concepts as to how the team might function that inevitable led to a discussion on budget.

'Lachlan, I leave the team size to you, but obviously the bigger it is, the less money for you. I am prepared to allocate a set-up budget of no more than 3 million pounds' sterling and a further annual budget of 1.6 million for salaries and upkeep. I will pick up the costs of the aircraft and its fuel, but the rest is up to you and comes from your paycheck.

Lachlan, understand the opportunity here. My business partners and I are looking to start up an organisation that fills the gap between the military and nationally-based emergency services. This organisation could do good and react quicker than government-based support as there would be no bothersome politics to be sorted through. This is in effect a trial to test the validity of this idea.'

Lachie sat there staring at Lord Erskin-Stamper. He wasn't sure what it would take to set up an organisation like this. 4.6 million pounds in the first year sounded like a lot of money but without knowing what equipment and facilities they would need he just wasn't sure. One thing he was sure of was that it beat the shit out of anything else he had going.

'Sir that sounds like an excellent opportunity. May I have two weeks to sort a proposal?', responded Lachie.

Lord Erskin-Stamper reclined in his chair, 'I'll give you four weeks, but at the end of it I want your team signed to a retainer contract and I want a complete cost breakdown of all setup equipment and infrastructure costs'.

Lachie approached the front of the Monte Carlo Casino. There were half a dozen exotic cars parked out the front. Looks like Lucy's place he thought.

He was greeted as soon as he walked through the front door. 'Here for the casino sir?', enquired a staff member dressed in a smart black tie dinner jacket.

'Yes, of course', said Lachie. 'Very well Sir, please head over to the counter. The entry fee is €10.

Flashing a cheeky grin, he responded, 'Hang on, it's not good enough for you that I come in here to drop my money on your tables. Now you want me to pay for the privilege of losing my money to you?'

'Well you see sir, we use to give free entry but the tour buses started traipsing through the casino bothering the gambling clientele. Of course, they would spend no money themselves. As soon as we implemented the €10 levy the tour bus spectators stopped coming.'

'Genius', said Lachie. 'Alright I will pay the €10, but rest assured I am going to win this back'.

The doorman grinned at Lachie, 'You didn't really come here to win did you Sir? Much better to come here to enjoy the opulence and the games. For the experience itself. That way one will not be disappointed when he leaves'. Lachie huffed and headed to the reception desk to pay the entry.

Upon entering the main gaming room, Lachie had to agree with the doorman that it was opulent. Probably even worth paying €10 just to see it. There were frescos and paintings everywhere with a well-stocked bar in the middle of the room. The only aspect of the environment that seemed at odds were the obligatory poker machines at the entry of the gaming floor.

As Lachie rounded the corner an adjoining room revealed gaming tables as the main feature. He exchanged €500 for chips and started checking out the punters. There were punters from all around the world. Some North Americans occupied the closest Black Jack table with Russians on the Roulette table. They were all dressed relatively formally, some elegantly and some quirkily.

The Russian males were dressed in expensive and colourful open neck shirts. Big, chunky, gold chains and rings were definitely the order of the day. The Americans were probably the shabbiest-looking of the gamblers. One guy looked quite the character dressed in a tucked-in loud shirt with a Texas-styled string tie. His outfit was topped off with a fine pair of Thomas Cook snakeskin boots.

Lachie smirked to himself as he headed to the Roulette table. Time to win my €10 back, he thought. He sat there and watched three spins come up red. He couldn't believe the amount of chips the punters were bleeding. One punter placed two hundred on 0 and didn't even blink as the chips were scraped away after the red spin.

Lachie thought let's keep this simple. He placed €100 on red.

Black 33 called the dealer.

Bugger, thought Lachie as his chips disappeared. He doubled his bet this time placing 200 on red. He watched intently as the croupier spun the small steel ball around the roulette dish. The ball ran for what seemed an eternity before it dipped down into the spinning wheel. The ball bounced in and out of the numbered black and red slots. It almost looked like it was going to stop in the green 0 at one stage but skipped out.

'Red 14', announced the croupier.

'You little beauty. I am back in front', thought Lachie.

He took 300 of the €400 away and let 100 ride on red, with his original 500 now safely off the betting table.

Red 23 was called, 'Excellent!', thought Lachie, 'I'm now 200 up'.

He shifted the pile across to black.

Black 24 was the call.

'I might just let that 200 ride. If I win I will walk away and pocket my €400 winnings. I might then go hit Black Jack. If I lose I start my system again.'

Black 31.

'Terrific', thought Lachie, 'I am now 400 up. I think I can afford a drink now'.

He chuckled as he walked towards the bar at how tight he was. The bloke next to him had done €2000 in the time he had been at the table.

'Ouch!', thought Lachie.

Lachie ordered an eighteen-year-old McCallans Scotch with one ice cube in it and sat at a bar stool sipping his expensive drink bought from his winnings. 'Thank you, Monte Carlo Casino', he toasted to himself.

He sat there reflecting on what he had discussed with Lord Erskin-Stamper. Certainly, he had some of the skills needed for this line of work. He certainly had the contacts. He would need a logistics guy, well that's a no brainer, it's got to be Ant.

If things went tits up he wanted people like Ant that he could trust to keep their cool and defend themselves if need be.

He needed a doctor. He considered an ex-Army mate they called FOT. He was a big man with scrubby red hair and a gruff demeanor; as tough as old boots with a keen intellect.

As is often the case with highly-functioning individuals he was cynical in his view of his less-talented fellow man and their commitment to society. He often expressed his views on the inadequacies of organisations and the individuals within them that he cleverly disguised as humour. His favourite whipping boys were the government and public service organisations, including the clumsy antiquated military bureaucracy.

His competence and his humour made him a popular member of any group. He had been at the top of the pile in Special Forces as a corporal within the elite SASR. Upon becoming a father to two beautiful little girls he decided he needed a career change and left SASR to become a doctor of medicine.

As soon as he could, he left the military and was now a civilian-contracted doctor. He was called FOT by Lachie as it stood for 'Fucking Orange Thing'. He didn't particularly like the nickname, mainly because it was unimaginative and he thought he deserved a clever nickname that was more complimentary. As a result, only those he considered mates or in the inner circle were permitted to call him by that nickname.

Lachie looked at his watch, should be 0900 hours in Australia he thought to himself. FOT should be awake by now I might give him a call he pondered.

In fact, not only was FOT awake, he was already seeing his first patient at the Royal Military College Duntroon Medical Centre. His patient was a fresh-faced 18-year-old staff cadet. He crouched down and examined the embarrassed cadet's flaccid penis.

FOT looked up at the cadet. 'You see, what you have there my boy is a non-specific urethral infection or NSU as we call it'.

'What', asked the confused cadet.

'The clap my boy, you have earned yourself a dose of the clap by being a stupid dirty little bugger', said FOT in a tired tone.

The cadet smirked, excellent, he was another step closer to being a hardened soldier. He now had a story, a man's story he could tell his friends—evidence of his exploits—FOT could read the kid's mind.

'Yeah well you won't think it's funny when I give you the umbrella and a shot of penicillin', said FOT.

The smirk left the cadet's face.

'The, the umbrella?', asked the cadet.

'Yeah you're going to love it. We are going to scrape the infection out of the inside of your old fella', said FOT, just as his phone range.

He pulled it out of his pocket and squinted at the phone to read the screen like an old wino squinting to read the alcohol content on a *goon*.

His sight had stared to degenerate now that he was in his 40s. The rest of him was a perfect physical specimen—it was just his eyesight and his tolerance for his fellow man that weren't what they used to be.

He answered the phone, 'Lachie, how are you mate? 'I'm great doc, how are you?', asked Lachie. The ever-cynical doctor looked menacingly at the terrified cadet as spoke into the phone, 'Oh I'm great Lachie, except for working in the most boring medical centre in the world.

All of these cadets are extremely healthy. If it weren't for the need to pop their infected blisters they get from marching and disinfect their rotting shaved genitals I wouldn't have a job.' Lachie laughed into the phone. The FOT always had a way with words.

'No honestly', responded FOT, staring it the nervous cadet's crutch, 'What is with kids today and their fascination with manscaping? I'm staring at one of these bald, shriveled viral super spreaders right now', said FOT.

Lachie, still laughing into the phone, caught his breath and replied, 'Listen you grumpy prick. If you are bored I might have some well-paid contract work coming up that will need a person of your skill sets. Skills, present and past, if you know what I mean?'

'Well, Lachlan I must say I am interested, send me the details and I'll let you know. Right now, I've get to get back to work and euthanize a cadet for being a stupid, dirty little waste of my time.'

'Righto mate, take care and I'll send you more details', Lachlan said prior to hanging up. 'Well that's a positive start', thought Lachlan.

'Good, that's medical and logistics covered, time to turn my attention to communications'. In an austere environment, communications would be essential. He might also need to do research including cyber-snooping. Although these skills weren't directly related in the professional sense, Lachie happened to know a communications specialist that knew back to front how to exploit every communications device from the radio, to mobile phone, to satellite connectivity through to computers, and their search programs and hacks.

He thought straight away of an ex-military Signals warrant officer he knew named Wayne. His nickname was a straightforward one. He was known as 'Crazy Wayne' or 'Crazy' for short. Crazy got his nickname from the various predicaments he had found himself in. He was a Kiwi who now occasionally lived in Fiji and did contract work for a resort cum cult retreat of the American motivational speaker Anthony White. He had himself attended White's seminars and saw a great deal of merit in focusing to achieve his goals while always maintaining a positive outlook.

For Crazy his life goals were all about money and women—Crazy Wayne loved money and women. He would do anything for them, from communications work, hacking, through to contract work. He had an infectious smile, whitened teeth, and a perfectly-managed tan. He always dressed smartly and applied a series of techniques that he had learned from White's workshops to make people he met feel special.

He had paid big money at the workshops but they had enabled him in five-years to transform his image from a shady womanizer into a charming, attractive, and likeable guy. For those that had known him for longer than five-years, his new persona was false. His fake tan, whitened teeth and elocution lessons still didn't change the fact that when it came to hacking and setting-up communications he was very good and always available with no questions asked if the price was right.

Lachie rang Crazy Wayne but the call wasn't picked up and went straight to voicemail. He was greeted with, 'Hi Wayne here, CEO of Super Charged Solutions. Web-based research, network, and communications specialists. We also offer a one-on-one life coaching service for business people whose lives are stuck in a rut. Sorry I can't take your call at the moment, I'm out living each day like it's my last. So, leave a message and I will return your call'.

Lachlan smirked and left his message for Super Charged Crazy Wayne to give him a call when he returned from doing what he was doing. In truth Wayne was lying next to his phone desperately wishing he could answer it but he was unable to move. He was lashed to a bed in an unfamiliar house in Auckland. He had been left there by a girl called Lisa who he had met in a bar the night before.

The attractive Lisa had promised to let him do naughty things to her if he satisfied her kink first including cuffing him to a bed. Wayne agreed and thought it might be fun. After all he wasn't called Crazy for nothing.

When they arrived back at Lisa's house, the silly bitch had lost her house keys so she asked Wayne to help her break-in. Wayne obliged by breaking a small panel of glass in the back door allowing Lisa to reach in and unlatch the lock for a relatively quiet entry into the house.

Lisa, after freshening up, had led Wayne into the bedroom. Wayne was drunk but still was starting to get a little suspicious of Lisa's behaviour. They had to break into the house and here in the bedroom was a series of photos of a girl around Lisa's age but none of them had Lisa herself in them.

Wayne looked at Lisa 'Um, who is this girl in all the photos? Is this even your house?', he asked. Lisa dropped her cloths on the ground and stood naked in front of Wayne.

'That girl is my best friend Kylie. I took those photos of her. Now Wayne, let's not focus on the photos of Kylie, let's focus on us. I want you to ride this', Lisa said pointing to her backside. 'But first I want to chain you to the bed posts and give you a blow job tease', she said.

'Sounds great', said Wayne, removing his clothes, and jumping on the bed spread-eagled. Lisa reached into her big handbag and removed some zip ties that she used to fasten his hands and feet expertly to the bed's cast iron frame.

'Wow they're a little tight Lisa', said Wayne, feeling the ties biting into his wrists. Lisa crouched down over Wayne and took him into her mouth. Suddenly Wayne cared a little less about the pain in his wrists. He was just starting to get into it when Lisa reached back into her handbag and took out a small screw clamp which she placed over Wayne's knob. Unable to move his hands or feet, Wayne was powerless to stop Lisa fitting the clamp and screwing three twists till it started to hurt his dick.

'What the fuck?', protested Wayne.

Lisa smirked and reached back into her bag and pulled out a whip. 'Now', she said, 'We are going to play a game. If you behave you get this', and she bent down and licked Wayne's still enlarged penis for, despite the pain and his anxiety level, the clamp wouldn't allow the blood to escape hence maintaining a painful erection against his will.

She continued, 'If you scream or piss me off you will get this', and with that she whipped him across his stomach. The stinging sensation brought tears to his eyes as he sobbed a subdued protest.

'I know baby, mummy's sorry', said Lisa as she sucked on his knob again.

'Fuck', thought Wayne, 'This chick is nuts, I'd better play along until she unties me. Then I'm going to get the fuck out of here and report this bitch to the cops'.

'Yeah ok Lisa I'm into this, yeah I'll be good. You are so beautiful. I can't wait until you untie me so I can hold you in my arms and make love to you'.

With that the woman sat up with a cheeky grin on her face.

'Make love to me? Oh Wayne, that sounds so much nicer than what you said to me in the club, which was if I recall correctly, that you wanted to pound my hot ass'.

Wayne grimaced.

She continued, 'I will let you go Wayne, but first you must answer some questions for me. You see the way you behave leads me to believe you don't have much respect for women so I'm going to give you the opportunity to prove me wrong'.

Wayne was now sobered up and genuinely concerned for his well-being. Lisa sat up on his legs and said, 'Now my fake tanned, pretty boy, when did women get the right to vote in New Zealand?'

Wayne clenched his eyes and thought for a moment. He opened his eyes and fixed her with his best puppy dog eyes, 'I think it was around the time of WWI in 1913.

Can I just say way too late? Women should have been able to vote from the outset'.

Lisa looked dreamily into Wayne's eyes and said, 'Oh Wayne, how nice of you to say. Unfortunately, you are not even close. It was in 1893 that the sisters were finally able to have their say legally.

1913? Really, even the Aussie girls could vote before then, and you know what chauvinistic bastards their men are. Now you must be punished for your wrong answer'. She bent down and started sucking him off again but with her right hand tightened the clamp another notch. Wayne again grimaced as the pain shot through his penis.

'Wayne, I feel bad about the pain you are in. I tell you what since you have spent so much time with the Aussies if you can tell me the names of the first female prime ministers of Australia and New Zealand I will let you up'.

Wayne wracked his brain–he could still picture them both. The Australian one was some ranga lawyer from Wales and the New Zealand one looked like a bulldog eating porridge, but stuffed if he could remember their names.

Wayne protested, 'Hey that's not fair Lisa, I'm not into politics. I couldn't even tell you what the male ones since those talented ladies were called'.

Lisa glared at Wayne, 'That's not good enough my little whitened-teeth Ken Doll'.

With that she turned the screw another notch. Wayne cried out in pain and frustration. Lisa snarled and whipped him for his insolence.

'Okay Wayne, this is your last chance. I am going to give you the benefit of the doubt. After all I have to be sure you are a misogynistic moron and not just a moron. So, I am going to ask you questions which you were given the answers to earlier this evening.

What is my full name? What star sign am I, what sport do I play?'

'Wayne smiled, 'Easy. Your name is Lisa Ingrid White, you play softball and you are that crab sign'.

Lisa glared at Wayne, 'My name is Lisa Ingrid Black, I play hockey and my star sign is Scorpio, you metrosexual fuckwit'. She got to her feet and whipped Wayne three times. When she finished, she looked at poor, sobbing Wayne with a look of loathing. She went for the clamp and Wayne winced with anticipation. But instead of tightening the clamp she removed it.

Out of relief Wayne cried out, 'Oh thank you, thank you, I am sorry for having been a prick. Now please untie me and we can just go our separate ways'.

Lisa glared at Wayne, 'I took the clamp off because it probably would have permanently damaged you if I left it on too long and I need it for the next chauvinist I trap. So consider yourself lucky. I'm not letting you up though and here is a memento of the hot ass you so badly wanted to fuck'.

With that Lisa squatted over Wayne and crapped all over his chest.

Lisa had left him six hours ago. He was still strapped to the bed covered in Lisa's crap and his urine. Staring at his ringing mobile phone. After a while the phone stopped ringing.

'Help me', he mumbled. Then he heard a new sound.

Fumbling in a lock and what must have been the front door opening. Footsteps made their way to the bedroom. A woman entered the room. Wayne recognized her straight away, 'Kylie help me'.

The woman shrieked and ran from the house.

In a small London apartment sat a hulking ex-British Army Staff Sergeant named Si. He sat there staring at the paperwork on the table in front of him. How had it come to this?

The bank statements and bills painted a grim picture. Eight months ago, his financial situation was completely different. He still owed £250,000 on his £500,000 apartment which he had hoped to be well on his way to paying off. Eight months ago, he had just returned from Afghanistan with no debt other than what was owing on the apartment and £50,000 sitting in his savings.

Or so he thought.

Unfortunately, upon his return he found that his partner and his £50,000 had gone. In their place was a stack of bills she had racked up on his credit card. He had been discharged from the Army shortly after on medical grounds due to a knee injury which prevented him from running.

Alone, in a melancholy mood, he stared out the window, watching people take shelter from the rain in the street below. Some of the rain seeped through the seal in the window frame forming a little puddle on the sill in front of him.

'Is this my life now?

I use to be well-paid and held a position of authority. Surrounded by my mates it was a great way of life. Now? But now, I'm nobody', he thought as he surveyed the cramped, virtually-unfurnished apartment. To make matters worse he was tired. The dreams visited him almost every night and were getting worse. He would often wake up drenched in sweat from the sound of gunfire.

Si got up out of his chair and walked to the fridge. Only two beers remained. 'Yes, things are getting grim', he thought reaching for one of them.

To add to his woes, he was facing assault charges after last Friday night's party. It was a fancy-dress party with a 'come as something innocent' theme. He hired a massive checked tunic that he wore with white bobby socks and a yellow pig-tailed wig.

After a good night and still dressed as a schoolgirl he left the party about 1 am to head home. Walking alone he was only three blocks from home when he happened across three drunken louts. The three men saw the big man dressed as a girl and started calling him a poofta. Before long a fight broke out that resulted in the normally passive Si decking them. One of the louts was unfortunately badly injured in the scuffle resulting in a police investigation.

Because of the comedy value of a man dressed as a schoolgirl beating the crap out of three thugs when the CCTV footage made its way onto the web it went viral. Once Si and most of the free world saw the footage he presented himself to police and was subsequently charged.

Now he was due to face court in six months.

'Shit!', he thought, shaking his head.

He was suddenly distracted from wallowing in self-pity by his phone ringing. He lurched over to the kitchen bench where the phone lay. 'Hello Britney', an Aussie voice boomed down the phone before breaking into a song, 'Oops I did it again, ha, ha, ha'.

Si smiled at the sound of the familiar voice of Jonty's good mate, 'Mister Lachlan, good to hear from you'. Lachie boomed down the phone, 'Look mate I don't have much time but Jonty tells me you might be interested in some work. Some rather high-paying work?'

'Would I!', responded Si enthusiastically.

'Problem is Si you might need to live in Australia for a while, would that be ok?'

Si looked through the window at the cold, bleak London night. 'Oh, I think I might be able to tear myself away for a while as long as I can be back for my court appearance', said Si.

'We'll talk about that tomorrow mate when I'm back in London. I'm sure we can work something out', said Lachlan.

Before long Lachlan hung up and Si just sat there for a minute grinning, 'Well isn't that just the dog's bollocks?', he said to himself.

An athletic-looking woman with red hair named Barbara Clarke sat on a commercially-owned Sydney ferry watching some steroidal, middle-aged man gyrating around on the stage in front of her.

To say she wasn't enjoying herself was an understatement. The same couldn't be said about her soon to be sister-in-law and her bogan friends who were having the time of their lives clawing at the male stripper.

She sat there silently judging the overweight, drunken, soon-to-be-bride as she jumped up on the stage shrieking. A sneer crept on Barbara's face as she noted the cheap bleached hair-do and the electric blue eyeliner combination.

'What is my brother thinking?', she pondered? Maybe she fucking sucks dick for Australia, Barbara thought as her sneer was replaced with a smirk in appreciation of her own joke.

She sat there quietly in the back of the room as far away from the stage as she could get. The boat was full of shrieking women watching what was one of the oldest strippers Barbara had ever seen. She didn't really know anyone there other than the peroxided, tangerine blob of her future sister-in-law.

It wasn't just that the woman didn't take care of her appearance; it was also that every time Barbara spoke to the woman she felt as though she had become dumber from the experience. Barbara reflected on a time when she had friends, back when she was in the Services. Of course, her friends in the Forces didn't call her Barbara, instead they called her Baz as a means of teasing her for her tomboy tendencies.

'What I wouldn't give to be having a few beers with those pricks instead of being here', she thought to herself, raising the straw of her drink to her mouth. Before she took a sip, she noticed the straw was shaped like a penis. She pulled it out of the drink and tossed it on the floor before gulping down the Jack Daniels mixer.

Worst hen's party ever she thought to herself as she saw her phone flashing in her bag. She picked up the phone and walked outside onto the rear deck so she could get away from the crappy 80s' music the stripper was doing his routine to.

Baz smiled as soon as she heard the voice. After brief moment, she cried out, 'You little farkin' ripper Lachie! Yeah, you bet I'm in. I'm not cheap though', said Baz, pausing waiting for the posh man's response. Baz's sister-in-law walked out and lit a cigarette in time to hear Baz say into her phone,

'Yeah OK smart arse, yeah I am cheap. I meant to say I don't come cheap', she said bursting into laughter.

The sister-in-law had never seen Baz laugh before. When Baz hung up the sister-in-law took a big drag on her cigarette and asked, 'Who was that Barbara?'

Baz smiled and pinched her sister-in-law's cheeks, 'That my little orange dough girl is my ticket out of here!'

In a modest gym in the Nerang commercial park off Queensland's Gold Coast stood a hulking man. His shirtless back was a canvas of religious and Gothic tattoos depicting scenes and scriptures from the Old Testament. On the man's chest was a large tattoo of the Angel Gabriel holding some demons at bay with a sword. Hanging around the man's neck was a large silver cross hanging from a leather thong. Threaded onto the thong was three Australian Army dog tags, none of which had the man's name, Julius Bligh, on them.

The big man stared at the 170 kilos in front of him with his menacing, piercing blue eyes that were set behind a broad, crooked nose. A smile which looked more like a grimace appeared on the man's face as he stared at the barbell perched above the bench. He had been working out for one and a half hours and this was his last set. His arms and shoulders were blown from physical exertion, but he wanted to finish this last set of reps for his chest.

He was sweating, as there was no air-conditioning in the building. It was not that sort of gym. It was in fact a hangar, originally designed to house a workshop. There were no cardio machines, just a vast collection of chin-up bars, sit-up benches, punching bags, barbells, and kettle weights. The gym was not designed for your trendy urbanite, it was for hard people. It was in fact owned by an organization known as 'the Syndicate', which was essentially a criminal gang. They had risen-up to fill the void created by the Government targeting of outlaw motorcycle gangs.

Like gangs from days gone by, they were into motorcycles and muscle cars. Unlike those gangs, they didn't overtly parade themselves in front of the general public in intimidating club colours. Instead they wore casual clothing that blended with the public. Some of them even wore suits. The only tell-tale that someone was in the Syndicate was a chunky titanium ring on each middle finger knuckle. The rings were etched with a black dagger piercing the words 'The Syndicate'.

The Syndicate liked to manipulate the construction industry and stand-over nightclubs. They had also taken over a string of brothels, strip joints and tattoo parlors. The only thing they weren't into was drugs. That market was a mess. Every prick was into it and they were all being tracked by the cops, which is what allowed law enforcement to bring down the motorcycle gangs and the mafia. They didn't need to be into drugs. If you wanted to sell in the Syndicate's clubs, parlors or anywhere near their establishments or clientele you paid them their cut and their cut was extortionate.

The core element of the Syndicate were largely cleanskins with no serious criminal records. They were all hard as nails, many of them returned Servicemen and Servicewomen who had served in the Middle East and craved adventure and comradeship. Many ex-athletes, plant operators, truck drivers, club bouncers and even a few accountants and lawyers adorned their ranks. The membership all brought certain skills to this sub-culture. Some managed finances, provided legal representation, were trainers, security, thieves, thugs, mechanics, drivers, programmers, front of house representatives.

All members ate well and trained hard. All learnt kickboxing and Jujitsu. The inner circle or 'the Directors', as they were known, planned and executed serious crimes. Their motto was 'We do bad things to bad people and profit from it.' Unless you were well-known by the membership it took a long time to join and even longer to be trusted.

Unlike mostly everyone else in the gym, Julius did not wear the Syndicate ring as he was only an affiliate member. In truth, he didn't desire to join the group. He wasn't the Underworld type, but he was the hard as nails type, and for now he and the Syndicate were benefiting through their arrangement. A bald, tattooed Syndicate member called out to Julius who was mustering the energy to complete his final weights set.

'Hey Priest, do you want a spot?'

Anger swelled in the pit of Julius's stomach. He glared at the bald man and growled, 'Keep your criminal scum hands away from me Sid you FINCL!', (pronounced finkel and standing for a Fucking Idiot No Cunt Likes).

With that, Julius aka Priest dropped on the bench and started pumping the 170 kg up and down in the air, growling as he went.

The bald man and his two mates shook their heads and laughed. 'What an angry prick', said Sid to his mates.

'Is he really a Priest?', said one of the men.

Sid looked at the man and replied, 'Yeah the boss served with him years ago, in the commandos or some shit like that. He reckons after serving in East Timor he studied to be a priest and even deployed to Afghanistan with his unit as their padre.

Imagine that prick giving spiritual guidance to the flock as they kicked the Taliban's butt'. They stood there watching the Priest aggressively punch through his weights set like a man possessed before slamming the barbell back into the rack.

'On second thoughts, I couldn't think of anyone better', said Sid.

After his workout, Priest sat on the bench chest heaving from the effort. Sid called out, 'Hey Priest, I might be a FINCL, but you're a FONC, that's right a Friend Of No Cunt!'

The three men burst out laughing. Glaring at them Priest leapt to his feet. The rapid movement of such a large man towards them caused all three of them to flinch. Priest let out a menacing chuckle as he turned and walked towards his locker where he put on a T-shirt with 'Heaven doesn't want me and Hell's scared I'll take over' printed on it. He then grabbed his crash helmet and walked out of the gym.

There in the car park was his custom Triumph Rocket in his favorite colour; black. It was another perk of knowing the Syndicate. They owned a bike dealership on the Gold Coast. They had pretty much gifted him the bike for services rendered.

Priest was just about to turn the key in the ignition when his ringtone from the Vatican Choir started playing. Priest took out his phone and growled into it, 'Speak!'.

Lachlan recoiled from the phone, 'I see the elocution lessons have been working for you Priest', he said in response.

Priest grinned as he recognized the voice, 'Lachlan you scaly little prick. I take it your soul hasn't been committed to the pits of Hell yet?'

'Oh Priest, that is just charming. I ring to offer you some well-paid work and all I get is you smearing my good character', said Lachlan.

'How much Lachlan and when. I keep 40 per cent of my fee and the rest goes direct to my orphans' fund, as per usual', said Priest.

'Yeah righto Priest, you may not be the most charming guy I have ever met but you certainly are the most generous', said Lachlan.

'Thanks Lachlan, children deserve our support and a good start in life, after all they can still be saved, unlike some adults. Besides the Lord provides me with everything I need and occasionally some things I want', said Priest caressing the tank of his bulky 2.6 litre motorcycle.

'Listen Priest we will discuss details in four days at my Brisbane house. Do you remember Ant? He lives next door and is in on this gig as well'.

Priest's mood lightened, 'Yeah I remember Ant, he's a bloody good bloke. We had a party at his place before he deployed to Afghanistan'.

'Yeah that's him. Hey I gotta get going Priest but I will see you in four days.'

'Roger, Priest out', he said to acknowledge Lachlan's instructions and to end the call. He turned the key and the Triumph fired into life. He revved the engine a couple of times and then dropped the hammer, screaming out of the car park and headed for the freeway.

Lachie finished his drink and threw the money with a tip onto the bar. With a drink under his belt, his win and looking great, Lachie felt confident enough to hit the Black Jack table. Maybe now it was time to make some real money.

He sauntered over to the furthest table that had a spare space at the table. His table had a Russian, two Chinese and a group of loud Americans huddled around the furthest player's spot. Lachie placed €50 on the table and the croupier started dealing cards. Lachie's first two cards were twenty out of a possible twenty one. The dealer drew a nineteen and beat all the players except Lachie.

Ha, fifty up already he thought. Lachie won the next four hands in a row and was already up €250. Lachie felt a presence behind him and glanced over his shoulder to see a short, medium build man dressed in an odd flared suit. The outfit looked like it was from a seventies film. Underneath the man wore an open large-lapelled shirt exposing a chunky gold chain. Oddly, the man was wearing Carrera sunglasses even though he was inside a casino at night. But this entire strange ensemble was not the most bizarre thing the man was wearing. No, that honour was bestowed upon the completely unconvincing Rod Stewart mullet wig he had on his head. 'You got to be friggin' kidding', thought Lachie.

Lachie was caught staring by the man who leant forward to Lachie and said 'You're having quite the night champ. Mind if I bet on your hand, I'm as crap at Black Jack as I am at fashion?'

Lachie smirked at the man's obvious humour, 'Sure be my guest', he said. Lachie, feeling the need to show off, placed a €100 bet but was surprised to see the man place 500 down.

'Shit, the pressure is on', thought Lachie. Lachie only got an eighteen and decided to sit. The Americans had a twenty-one and the Russian had a twenty. He had to hope that the dealer would go bust trying to beat the high hands. The dealer drew a six and a seven. He had to go for it. A nine, 'The house is bust', said the dealer.

'Yeh bra, you kick ass', said the strange man.

Lachie spun around 'It's kick arse not ass. An ass is a donkey like creature', stated Lachie, not completely sure why he was bothering to engage the strange man in conversation.

The strange man smirked 'Whatever bra, I'm getting a drink. Can I get you one while I'm at it? That way you can keep your spot at the table'.

Lachie eyed the man, 'Why thank you, but sorry, I'm at a loss as to whom I am receiving a drink from?'

'Oh sure, that manners thing, yeah I lack those. My name is Frank. I'm from LA in the United States'.

'Frank, my name is Lachlan, it is pleasure to meet you. I would like a McCallans Scotch with one ice cube in it if you are offering'.

Frank grinned, 'Sure a scotch for the Limey, one ice cube'. With that the man left the table, but not before Lachie spotted his gold-capped front teeth and a neck tattoo poking out from under the wig.

I must be mad accepting a drink from the strange gangster-looking American. Oh well, hopefully he doesn't Rohypnol me. With that Lachie turned around and placed a bet. This time it was Lachie who went bust. With €100 down the drain, Lachie doubled his next bet to €200. He lost again.

Damn it he thought. My luck is changing. He was considering his next move when he heard the LA twang behind him. 'Ouch bra. That must of hurt. Here have this and get back in the game', said Frank handing Lachie a scotch.

There you go, 30-year-old McCallans, Bit more expensive than my Jack Daniels, but whatever fluffs your feathers bra'.

'Thanks', said Lachie, taking a sip of the smooth, high-end scotch.

Frank let Lachlan take several sips of his scotch and sit out two hands. Frank questioned Lachlan as to how long he was in Monte Carlo? Where was he staying and what did he do for a crust?

Lachlan asked Frank a similar set of questions to which the American told Lachlan that he was staying aboard a small boat at the Marina and that he was an entertainer doing a little bit of work in Nice.

That is interesting thought Lachie. Even mooring a small yacht in Monte Carlo costs thousands per night. That is assuming you even gain permission to use a vacant mooring. The way he was tossing money around on the tables he can't be too skint.

After ten minutes, Frank felt as though Lachie had calmed down after his losses. 'Hey Bra it's getting late and I got to get going. What do you say we have one more big hand, say €1000?'

Lachie looked at Frank. Was he mad? €1000 on one hand. The very thought of it excited and scared Lachlan. It wasn't losing €1000. He had enough money that that outcome would not even come close to affecting him financially. It was more that he would feel down, a loser.

He had promised the doorman he would come out in front, which he currently was. But the excitement at the prospect of gambling the best part of thirteen-hundred Aussie dollars was too great for him to walk away from. 'Alright Frank, I'm in for a thousand, what about you?'

'Oh I'm in bra. I think ya going to make us some money. You know what they say, when you fall off the horse, just get straight back on'. They both returned to the table and slapped down a thousand each. The dealer accepted the bets and started dealing cards to the seven players sitting in front of her.

Lachlan's and Frank's bets weren't by any means the biggest she'd seen but they did display a degree of confidence in ability and luck. As the two cards were placed in front of him he couldn't believe his eyes. Two Aces that could equal two, twelve or twenty-two depending on how you take them.

There was another option thought Lachlan—play the hand as two separate hands. That way each Ace would be treated as an eleven and only the first card of each hand. Problem with this tactic is that he needed to double his bet. Screw it he thought as he placed another thousand next to the betting box.

Frank must have anticipated his move as his bet hit the table just after Lachlan's. With €4000 placed on the hand the dealer separated the cards and continued to deal. A four and a nine. That's a fifteen and a twenty. Right he though, I'll sit on the twenty but I'm going to hit that fifteen again.

As per his rule, anything under sixteen he hit again for another card. The dealer dealt a three of hearts. Eighteen, I'm not confident but I'm in the game, I'll sit on these two hands.

Of the seven punters, two had already gone bust. There were still six hands in front of the dealer, two of which belonged to Lachlan. Of the six hands, all except one were over seventeen. The dealer was going to have to go for it. The dealer drew six of clubs, ten of diamonds and the final card Jack of clubs. 'The house is bust', said the dealer.

Lachlan calmly turned to face Frank who, unlike Lachlan, was not maintaining a calm demeanor. Frank was pumping his fists in the air followed by a little moon walk.

Lachlan and Frank collected their chips, both tipping the dealer €25 as they left the table. 'Bra that was brilliant', drooled the American to Lachlan. 'If ever you are in LA and bored look me up', Frank said, handing Lachlan his business card. They chatted excitedly about their winnings. Frank was up four thousand and was particularly chipper.

He was sorry he had to go as it was only 11 pm but he had a prior engagement to get to. Lachlan wished him luck but declined Frank's offer of a lift as he was going to have one more drink and then enjoy the fifteen-minute walk home.

Lachlan fetched a gin and tonic but drained it fairly quickly due to the excitement. He changed his chips into cash rather than a cheque as he had one more thing to do before he left. On his way out, he had to flash his cash roll at a certain doorman!

After his win on the tables, Lachie was completely wired. He felt like partying but he didn't want to go to a club. Instead he grabbed a bottle of beer from the room's bar fridge and wandered down to the wharf. He leant against the rail on the public walkway sipping his beer in the moonlight watching the party rage on aboard one of the large cruisers. Security guards guarded the gangplank to stop unwanted people crashing the party. From what Lachie could see that seemed to include anyone male. Nearly everyone at the party were beautiful young women in bikinis. 'Yeah, pity I can't join that party,' he thought, taking another pull on his beer.

In his tipsy state, Lachie had stood there gawking for about ten minutes, looking slightly disheveled in his suit minus the tie. 'Hey you,' said one of the security guards, 'Time to move on, these people deserve their privacy.'

'Sorry,' replied Lachie. 'I was just enjoying watching people have fun. I'll move on'. Lachie turned to walk away when a figure moved out of the shadows behind him. 'It's alright Bob he's not bothering anyone and it's a free world. Right pal?', the figure said as it emerged from the shadows.

Lachie could just make out the face of the man now that had been smoking a cigarette in the shadows watching Lachie drink his beer and the party aboard his luxury vessel. The figure was a familiar-looking man. Like Lachie he was in his mid30s. He looked like he had some Hispanic blood in him but had a thick LA accent. He was wearing Banana Republic shorts and a Tommy Bahama shirt with a Hawaiian-style pattern of palm trees and surfboards. He had a little pork pie hat, which had become popular with some rappers. To top it all off he was sporting some serious tattoos up his arms and neck.

Lachie eyed the man having his cigarette. 'Your boat I take it mate?', asked Lachie. 'Yeah', responded the man, 'What can I say, I enjoy a spot of fishing'. Lachie laughed at the thought of the vessel being a massive overkill for fishing. The size and the radar system suggested this was an ocean-going luxury vessel that few people in the world (even Lachie's family) could afford.

'Hey pal, where is your accent from?' the man asked Lachie. 'Well, largely from Australia, but I was schooled in England'. 'Hey half kangaroo, half Limey', the American drooled. So, what are you doing in Monte Carlo? Holiday?'

'No work meeting with the owner of that boat', Lachie said pointing to the *British Elite*. 'I see', said the man. He looked at Lachie and said 'I'm Pit Dog, what's your name bra?'.

'Ah', Lachie thought, 'Now I know why this guy looks familiar'. Pit Dog was a popular rapper who had released a series of video hits of him cruising the Mediterranean partying with hot girls ten-years younger than him. Lachie thought this guy was an inspiration to men everywhere, living the dream even though he was a middle-aged, short, bald guy with mediocre talent.

'G'day Pit Dog, my name is Lachie, but you can call me Scooby Doo if you want to keep the dog nickname thing going'. Pit Dog laughed. 'Yeah well Lachie, my real name is Eugene so I had to come up with something with a little more street cred than that.

So, what are you doing now Scooby?' Lachie drained the rest of his beer, 'I don't know, bed I guess'. 'Fuck that Scooby, as long as you're not media come and join the party, I got more girls than I can handle anyway. Just leave your phone with security and climb aboard'.

Lachie beamed. 'Party on a cruiser full of expensive grog, celebrities and hot birds? Why not, it'd beat the shit out of going to a club or hitting the sack.'

Lachie handed his phone to security and followed Pit Dog along the gangway onto the vessel. If the boat looked impressive from the outside it was absolutely jaw-dropping on the inside. They walked straight past a plush downstairs lounge area into a hallway, past some bedrooms to a small glass blue neon-lit lift that they caught to the second deck.

The doors of the lift slid open and it exposed a party that was well underway. There were some sixteen people in the room. Straight away Lachie weighed up the staff. Dressed in black trousers and polo shirts, one of the men was working the bar, and there was a heavy-set man with an earpiece who was clearly there for security purposes.

There was a girl serving and collecting drinks that appeared to consist primarily of champagne and cocktails. The revelers were primarily young women that were varied in ethnicity but they all appeared to be wearing light, revealing summer clothing.

There were several men dressed in relaxed island wear like Pit Dog. Everyone looked relaxed and like they were enjoying the party. There were even two girls sitting in a big hot tub on the back deck.

'Yep, this is going to be fun', Lachie thought, 'I wonder why a famous rapper would invite some bloke off the street onto his boat on which he was holding his private party. Hopefully he's not hot for me he thought'.

Hey Lachie, I don't know half the people here and I don't know you, so forgive me for not introducing you to everyone, but help yourself to whatever you like on the party deck. Just leave the tall redhead over there alone, she's kinda my travel buddy for this trip if you know what I mean', Pit Dog said, motioning towards an equally tall beautiful, olive-skinned woman.

With that Pit Dog excused himself and left Lachie to socialize. The first thing Lachie did was grab a champagne off the bar top from one of the two opened bottles.

Hmmm, Dom Pérignon or Louis Roederer Cristal Champagne. 'Ohhh, definitely the Cristal', said Lachie to himself as he poured a glass.

'While you're at it handsome', a dusky voice said from behind him.

Lachie spun around to see a stunning woman with short black bobbed hair. She looked a little like Uma Thurman out of *Pulp Fiction*.

'Well hello', thought Lachlan, who immediately turned on the charm, more out of reflex than a conscious decision. Lucy might be pretty, sexy and wholesome-looking, but this woman was an elegant and unobtainable-looking creature. Lachlan poured the woman a champagne and introduced himself. He had detected a French accent so he referred to himself as an Australian instead of as a Brit as he thought that might give him an exotic image.

The woman introduced herself as Natasha. She was French, but her mother, who she took after, was from Belarus. Lachlan thought to himself that explained the French chic and the alluring yet almost menacing undertone typical of women from the former Eastern Bloc. In this package the mix was almost irresistible. In her left hand, she held what appeared to be a diamond-studded silver and black e-cigarette that looked something like an old-styled slender-stemmed holder for a traditional cigarette common place in the early 20th Century.

Lachie asked the stunning woman what she did for work to which she replied acting. She had just finished a role in a gangster movie where she played the mob boss's girl. That was why she was sporting the 50s-styled bobbed hairstyle.

She had also kept as a souvenir the authentic-looking e-cigarette that had cost the set designer €10,500 to have made. Lachlan was impressed at the generosity of the set designer and the studio letting such an expensive set prop go.

Natasha gave a sinister smirk, 'The set designer didn't give it away Lachlan, I earned it', said Natasha while seductively rolling her tongue around her lips.

Lachlan gulped as he contemplated what Natasha's deal must have involved.

Lachlan was pouring Natasha another champagne when there was a commotion in the main entertainment space. The partygoers were crowding around as some loud music started. He recognized the rap that ensued as one of Pit Dog's famous party tracks.

He and Natasha moved closer to see the performance but when they got there instead of seeing Pit Dog dressed in his colourful Tommy Bahama shirt and pork pie hat, he saw Frank. Lachlan shook his head as he realized he had been hanging with the hip hop star in the casino and didn't even know.

Pit Dog paused and said 'Ladies and gentlemen, introducing the man that helped me break the Monte Carlo Casino Bank, Lachlaaaaan.'The crowd turned to face Lachlan and started clapping.

Pit Dog returned to his rap. 'Broke the bank did you Lachlan?', purred Natasha into his ear. Lachie smiled, 'Hardly Natasha, I only won a few thousand Euro'. Natasha stood close to Lachlan and discreetly caressed his penis, 'For a few thousand Euro, you could have an under-paid actress for the night'.

An hour later Lord Erskin-Stamper's supposed driver spied Lachlan walking back to the hotel Lucy had booked for him. The security man cum driver had been tasked to keep an eye on Lachlan by Lord Erskin-Stamper to see what he got up to.

Lachlan looked like he was calling it a night, but he wasn't alone. Accompanying him back to his room was a stunning woman who looked like Uma Thurman. He would need to report this to his boss who was already unhappy with Lachlan's relationship with his daughter.

This might complicate things.

#

VIVA BRISVEGAS

EARLIER IN THE MORNING Ant had flown back into Sydney Airport from Phuket. He would have liked to have gone straight back to Brisbane but first he had to do some family time. He had been away for so long in war zones that he was virtually a stranger to his niece and nephew. The nephew was young enough to accept his absences but the niece, now aged seven, didn't seem to want to connect with her uncle.

'Why should she', Ant thought to himself? 'I'm just someone her mother and grandmother talk about. I make an appearance every second Christmas and expect them to bond with me. I wonder if the kids can sense the things I've done? No, BrisVegas will just have to wait until tomorrow so I can make my nephew's party'.

As the car rolled up in the driveway of the house in the leafy suburb of Turramurra, Ant could already hear kids screaming. He grabbed two presents from the boot of the hire car and walked up to the front door.

As he rang the bell frenzied excitement, followed by heavy footsteps, signaled that the inhabitants were aware of his presence. Before long the door opened to reveal Ant's sister and brother-in-law. After a kiss and a few handshakes, Ant was in the house.

Once inside his face displayed a look of abject horror as a tribe of screaming children now surrounded him. His nephew emerged from the crowd to give him a hug. His niece reluctantly waved at him and disappeared back into the fray.

Ant's sister Renee started laughing at the look on Ant's face as he surveyed the children's party. Come on Ant, let's get you set up outside where it is quieter', she said, leading him out the back to the relatively quiet pool area.

Ant's brother-in-law gave him a cold beer and the three of them sat there chatting for fifteen minutes.

'Good to see you again Ant', said Renee. 'I don't think you've been to our house in years', she said taking a sip of her chardonnay.

No, I guess not', said Ant. 'It must have been just before I left for Afghanistan', he said.

'No, it was the year before that, I remember because you had been back from Iraq for two years', said Ant's brother-in-law Adam. Just then a loud crash and some crying interrupted their conversation.

'Excuse us Ant. You sit here and enjoy your beer, we'd better go check on that', said Renee, grabbing her husband's hand, and leading him inside.

Ant sat there alone sipping on his beer. 'Had it been that long since he had been here', he thought to himself?

'Had it been that long since Iraq?'

His mind drifted back to his past as the warm Sydney breeze blew through his long hair. The pool and the greenery faded from his view to be replaced by a stark, dry, and dusty landscape.

Captain Antonio Luciano surveyed the scene. It was a stinking hot day in Baghdad. The temperature was reaching 50 degrees outside the armoured Humvee–it was more inside. His vision beyond 80 metres was obscured by the airborne dust particles which formed a haze typical in the Middle East. They were stuck in slow-moving traffic.

This was a situation the US soldiers of the six-vehicle convoy did not want to be in. They were now vulnerable to ambushes and VBIEDs (vehicle-borne improvised explosives devices).

Ant was in the passenger front seat of the vehicle communicating with the American Army Convoy Commander. He was relaying orders and directing the US driver and the gunner who was manning a 50 calibre machine gun mounted on the roof of the vehicle. A 50 calibre gun fires a big round that can rip a person apart.

In a built-up area like Baghdad a stray round can travel well over a kilometre with enough kinetic energy to penetrate objects such as buildings and the human body. Therefore, rounds in built-areas are used sparingly in an attempt to reduce collateral damage.

The main reason behind using such a destructive weapon was as a vehicle stopper. It could tear through an engine block and stop a vehicle dead in its tracks.

There was a US Army element running the convoy that referred to themselves as 'the Rough Necks'. Ant was an Australian Army Officer on exchange with the US Division. His air of calm made him a welcome member in missions that tended to degenerate into chaos within the blink of an eye. The US Brigadier-General particularly liked to hand-pick his protection team and Ant was always on the list.

Ant and 'the Rough Necks' were near exhaustion. They had been in Iraq for five months of their twelve-month tour. They had barely slept in the last three weeks. The best they could hope for was four hours down time in a twenty-four-hour cycle. There were no weekends and no set hours.

The absence of a sleep routine combined with the heat and inevitable dehydration had created a jet lag like haze in the minds of many of the soldiers. Their immune systems worked hard to battle the new bugs and diseases to which they were being exposed.

Added to all of this was the stress.

In the last week, two of their 180-strong unit had been killed. Another had been evacuated to a hospital in Germany and was now missing his right leg. Most dreamt of home. The ones that didn't had either already totally accepted their fate or they came from such a shit hole that they had nothing much to look forward to when they got home anyway. By now for almost all of them it felt like they had been there forever and their minds had started playing tricks on them.

Did the loved ones that they spoke to on the phone actually exist?

Did their countrymen back home know about or give a shit what was going on in Iraq.

The only thing that mattered was to look after your mates and try and survive. To this end, Ant was vigilantly staring out through the dust haze scanning his arcs of vision for anything out of the ordinary.

Ant wiped the dust-encrusted sweat from his eyes to improve his vision. Suddenly his attention was drawn towards a silver Mercedes vehicle swerving through traffic towards the convoy some 60 metres away. Ant gave an immediate target indication to the Convoy Commander. The Commander responded from his front vehicle that he couldn't see the potential target.

'Your call sir, if they get too close you know what to do'.

The suspect vehicle broke free of the dense traffic and headed straight for the middle vehicle of the convoy. Ant watched as the Mercedes seemed to zero in on the vehicle the General was in. Ant relayed directions to the gunner,

'If they get within 20 metres I want you to put a three-round burst into the engine block with the 50.

When the suspect vehicle got to within 40 metres the vehicle behind Ant's fired some warning shots from a small calibre 5.56mm rifle in front of the Mercedes. The vehicle reacted with a series of erratic movements and rammed cars in an attempt to get closer to the convoy.

This was strange behavior even in Baghdad so Ant gave the order to engage. Time suddenly seemed to slow.

Sparks spat up from the road surface in front of the attacking vehicle as the first round missed the fast moving car. The second and third rounds were expertly marched into the engine block of the car, bringing it to a stop.

Flames licked around the vehicle as the petrol ignited.

The passenger doors burst open and four occupants sprung from the vehicle.

The traffic had now come to a complete halt as innocents hid under the dash of their cars or attempted to drag their children to safety. The air was suddenly filled with indiscriminate, automatic AK47 fire coming from the four occupants of the Mercedes.

The gunner engaged the men dressed in their traditional dishdashas. Ant's vehicle was now at a crawling pace next to the men. One of the attackers sprayed rounds at Ant's car. Three rounds slapped into Ant's bulletproof window. This all happened half a second before the shooter exploded into pink mist.

Private First Class (PFC) Santiago took aim again from his gunner position above Ant. He was no longer scared, nor excited. Training had taken over and he business-like set about his task of engaging two more targets before the gun stopped firing.

'Stoppage!', yelled the gunner.

'Fuck', Ant thought. There was still a remaining shooter firing at their vehicle. The shooter had switched his attention to PFC Santiago who was attempting to rectify the gun's stoppage whilst ducking behind the tiny gunner's shield.

Ant thought to himself, 'I have to act now or this kid is going to die'.

Ant kicked the heavy armoured door open and surveyed the scene. He had lost situational awareness once his window was shot.

The driver yelled, 'Fuck what are you doing you crazy Aussie bastard?'

The driver's words were in vain as Ant was out of the vehicle and on his own. It was chaos. People were running and screaming everywhere. He could see the remainder of the convoy to his right. They were stopped and had formed a hasty defensive posture, no doubt forming-up ready for a counter-attack on the shooters.

Ant could see the burning Mercedes between them and the remainder of the convoy. The fourth shooter came sprinting from behind the burning vehicle at Ant. The shooter seemed oblivious to the fact that his long loose-fitting traditional cotton gown was on fire. The shooter focused his attention on Ant. He was so close that Ant could see the deep hatred and murderous intent in the man's eyes.

Ant knew it was now down to a one-on-one fight for survival. The man was within 10 metres. This was up close and very personal. The man swung his weapon towards Ant. At the same moment, Ant dropped to one knee, which reduced his profile and steadied his weapon. He placed the butt of his Steyr rifle firmly into his shoulder just before squeezing off two rounds that struck the shooter in the chest, flinging him backwards. Ant could see the impact of the rounds causing little puffs of dust and blood as they entered the man's body.

Ant was trying to regain composure scanning arcs for another target when he heard a yell, 'Target two o'clock, black vehicle....'.

All went white. Ant was on the ground slumped up against his Humvee. His ears were ringing. He was having trouble breathing. Brief panic set in. 'Am I fucking dying? What the fuck hit me?'

Ant suddenly became aware of a presence. The Brigadier-General was knelt over him.

'God damn boy, that was some crazy shit! You smoked those sons o' bitches. Thank God you're OK, I would have hated to have had to explain your getting killed to the Aussies'.

The oxygen returned to Ant's lungs and he eagerly gulped the hot smoke and dust-filled air. 'Fuck yeah, you little pisser, you are OK, you're just winded and looking more like a bag of shit than normal.'.

The Brigadier-General told Ant to lie there for a moment while he got the medic, 'Medic come and check out this little pisser. Make sure he is all right. I love that furry little Aussie son o' bitch!', he boomed as he strode off.

The dust, the noise of gunfire and the burning smells dissipated. Ant looked at the swimming pool and took a large gulp of his beer. 'God man, get a grip on yourself—it's just a memory', Ant thought to himself.

He opened his clammy palms and stretched out his fingers. His breathing was fast and erratic. His sister looked at him and said, 'Ant are you alright, where were you just now? Your eyes were completely vacant'.

'Listen, I just need to go to the bathroom for a minute', said Ant excusing himself so he could go and wash his face and get control of his breathing so as not to give himself away.

'Ant, on the way back out stop and talk to your nephew, will you? I know kids aren't your thing but he thinks the world of you and it is after all his birthday party.'

Ant smiled, 'Sure sis but you have it wrong, I love the little yard apes'.

Ant went to the bathroom and cupped the cool healing water in his hands to splash on his face several times before running his wet hands through his hair.

The stimulation of the cool water on his skin brought his mind back into the present and the dust of Iraq faded from his thoughts. Staring at his reflection in the mirror he went through the breathing exercises the psychologist had taught him. He watched as the colour returned to his face. His heart rate was lowering. The tightness in his chest and the nausea in his stomach faded. 'Good, now I can go out and socialize with my nephew and his horrid little friends'.

He walked out of the bathroom and into the living room that was slowly being reduced to rubble by a sugar-frenzied gang of five-year-old carpet baboons. No sign of my nephew as he scanned the room right to left. Suddenly Ant heard his nephew yell, 'Uncle Antonio!' Which was followed by a loud bang. Ant leapt into the air, 'farrrk!' he bellowed.

Some of the children cried and some giggled at the naughty word Uncle Antonio had just let out.

'Antonio, are you all right? We try not to say that word in front of the children mate,' said Adam.

Ant looked down and his nephew and saw the burst balloon in his chubby little hands. He was giggling. He loved his crazy Uncle Antonio and the reaction he had just gotten was way beyond what he had hoped for. Ant apologized to his brother-in-law and disappeared back to the bathroom.

The next day Ant sat in the cab gazing out the window at Lang Park Stadium as he made his way home to Petrie Terrace from the airport. 'God it's good to be home', he thought as the cab crawled its way down the Caxton party street. It had been a long time since Ant had spent any real time in his beloved Brisbane or even Australia for that matter.

Within two minutes the cab pulled up in the narrow street in front of Ant's beautiful old Queenslander house. Ant paid the cab driver and grabbed his bags. Petrie Terrace is one of Brisbane's original suburbs, nestled in between the exclusive suburb of Paddington and the city CBD parklands.

He chose this house as it had outdoor balcony spaces, was quiet, a five-minute walk from the rugby stadium, and was surrounded by trendy bars, cafes, and restaurants. He could walk into the CBD in fifteen minutes. The narrow streets were designed in the days of horse and cart and the houses are close together, giving it a village feel.

Due to the suburb's characteristics the residents knew each other and predominately comprised of well-heeled couples and single professionals. 'Hi Ant good to see you home', two female voices chimed from the balcony across the street.

Ant spun around to face the two beautiful young ladies. Their athletic bronzed bodies were clad in skimpy summer clothing. Both beautiful blonds beamed infectious smiles. 'Ladies, you two are a sight for sore eyes. Any chance you have decided to bat for my side while I've been away?', asked Ant.

'Sorry Ant, we still drink from the furry cup', one of the girls giggled.

'Can't blame you ladies, so do I. I will catch you later', Ant said, walking through his house's front door.

'See you Ant', they chorused, raising their wine glasses in a sort of a toast.

Once inside Ant opened the windows to let the cool afternoon air into the stuffy house. A light breeze swept through the house providing an instant improvement. He carried his duffle bag down to the laundry and dumped his clothing straight in the wash. He then headed upstairs to the top floor of the three-story house to the main bathroom to freshen up.

After a quick shower and a snakes, he headed to the kitchen. He picked up his Bose controller and activated his wired-in surround sound system. *Black Crow* by Angus and Julia Stone started playing through the speakers. Now, Ant thought to himself, 'Is it too early for a beer? 4 pm, no it is not', he mumbled, reaching into the fridge and fetching a XXXX Bitter.

Drinking XXXX as opposed to any other beer always seemed like the way to go given the Milton Castlemaine Brewery was only a kilometer from his house. Sometimes in the evening from the front deck you could smell the hops.

He wandered out onto the back deck and collapsed on his day bed. He lay there sipping on his beer admiring the palm trees and bamboo surrounding the house and giving it a tropical feel. It was just going on to 6 pm when Ant decided he was getting hungry. Since he had no food in the house yet he decided to head up the road to grab a bite to eat.

He got changed into his cargo pants and one of his many Hawaiian shirts. He traipsed twenty metres up the street before he heard a voice call out.

'Hey, are you back cuz? There goes the neighborhood. Just what this neighborhood doesn't need, another fat Aussie bogan slothing around'.

Ant stopped in his tracks and looked up to the house on his left. Leaning over the balcony railing was a young man with blond dreadlocks.

'What do you want Jarred, you bludging Kiwi fucktard?'

Jarred laughed, 'Just wondering how many more Kiwis you are going to recruit into the Queensland Reds to try and win the rugby this year'.

'Well, I don't know, but if we don't let them play rugby they just end up on the dole anyway'.

'Oh Ant you are so witty. Where are you off too? I'm at a loose end'.

'I'm going up to the Paddo for a feed and beer. Do you want to tag along?'

'Yeah cool bro I'm in', said the dread-locked man running down his back steps to the street. Despite his constant sledging of Jarred and Kiwis in general Ant liked him. He was carefree and the eternal optimist. Jarred was well-heeled but was no professional executive type like most of the residents in Petrie Terrace. No, he was the classic CUB (cashed-up bogan). He was a wizard machinist.

He had moved to Australia five-years earlier after his apprenticeship, taking up a job with a custom performance car company. He could make anything from scratch, from a drive shaft for an antique car through to a custom-designed grill. It wasn't long before he gained a reputation as a hard-working and very talented tradie. He now ran his own business blinging cars and fitting performance packages. He did everything from engine upgrades to custom vehicle interiors.

Ant wasn't sure how much he was making but he had moved into Petrie Terrace a year ago and bought his own home. Sitting in his driveway was a 100k custom Holden ute so he couldn't be too poor!

As the two men strolled up the road to the Paddington Tavern they discussed aspects of Ant's recent trip to Thailand. Ant only mentioned the resort, meeting Tatsu and his heroics at the beach. He stayed well clear of the fight and his possible involvement in the manslaughter of several hoods.

It was still sunny, beautifully-warm with a bit of humidity. Perfect drinking weather. They walked into the Paddo to a table next to the south-facing window that looked-out across Brisbane City.

The Paddo Tavern had been around for a long time but had gone through many renovations and now had a bit of a Northern Queensland rodeo feel about it. Some of the bar stools are saddles and the barmaids wore cowboy style hats. The food was cheap and cheerful with a relaxed environment and some of the best views in town.

Ant and Jarred hooked themselves up with a steak and several ice-cold

XXXXs. After a relaxing hour or so chatting, two of Jarred's mates turned up to join them for beers. The relaxed drinking pace suddenly increased to the rapid rate as Jarred's recently-arrived mate, nicknamed 'Bath Tub' suggested ordering jugs of beer was a better idea than buying glasses.

'You know, we don't have to go to the bar as often if we get jugs', had suggested Bath Tub. But all it really meant was they were still going to the bar as frequently except now they were having two glasses instead of one.

After an hour of rapid-rate drinking they were all having a great time looking out at the view over Brisbane and telling funny stories. The nickname Bath Tub intrigued Ant. He had asked where it came from but Jarred, Bath Tub and their other mate Don just looked at each other and smiled, refusing to bring Ant in on the joke.

Ant could take no more, the curiosity was killing him. Why did this jovial well-built fireman, who seemed like a good bloke, have the nickname of Bath Tub?

After a while Bath Tub's shout came up. He disappeared off with the empty jugs to the line at the bar. By the look of the line he was going to be some ten minutes before returning from the bar. 'Yes', thought Ant, 'It's my time to strike'.

'OK you two shitbags!' said Ant, 'Why is ol mate called Bath Tub. That is the most bizarre nickname I have ever heard'.

Don smirked at Jarred, 'Alright Ant, Jarred tells me you are a good bloke so I will tell you as long as you don't tell Tub I told you. As you can see he is a big guy and sometimes he can get a little stroppy if we tell people. Believe me Bath Tub cracking the shits is not good for anyone'.

Ant nodded his acknowledgement. Don continued, 'Well you see Ant, Bath Tub and I went to school together. Back in year 10, Bath Tub was just known by his name Peter Richards. Peter was a popular kid, vice-captain of the rugby team, in the cool group and was going out with Samantha Thompson who was the hottest girl in school. Yep the world was Richard's oyster. He was even getting well above average marks in his subjects.

Anyway, one day our economics teacher decided the class should see this ABC documentary on the shifting of global investment. He of course left us unattended and we thought it was as boring as shit so everyone started clowning around. Richard and Sam found a dimly-lit corner and decided to use it as an opportunity to make-out.

After the half-hour program the teacher still hadn't returned so we stayed where we were, rather than going back to the classroom. The next ABC program was *Playschool*.

'*Playschool?*', mimicked Ant. Jarred said, 'Yes Ant, you remember *Playschool*. That kids' program with the song There's a bear in there, and a chair as well. We have games to play and stories to tell.' Don joined in the singing, 'Open wide, come inside, it's play school...'.

Ant started to chuckle at the sight of two grown men carrying on like children. 'Okay you two I know what you're talking about. Keep going.'

'Well', continued Don, 'You probably don't remember this Ant but *Playschool* used to have a little feature story. On this day, it was a look inside an average Aussie family to follow their evening routine. I guess it was ahead of its time in that it was essentially reality TV.

The family kids got home from school, had dinner et cetera. None of us really paid much attention to what was going on with the show as we were all too engaged in our own conversations.

Suddenly Sam starts laughing hysterically. We all look around to see Sam with Richard's hand still up her top, looking at Sam with a quizzical look on his face. Clearly, he had no knowledge what had triggered Sam's hysterical laughter.

She then started pointing at the TV screen, screaming 'Look, look it's Richard's mum'. Sure enough, a younger version of Richard's mum was on TV bathing what looked to be a five-year-old boy.

The poor kid was on TV completely stark naked. It would have been must see TV for a pedophile. Suddenly Sam cried out again not only is it

Richard's mum, that's Richard in the bath, 'Ha Ha, it hasn't grown much since then has it Richard?'

Suddenly the penny dropped with the rest of us in the room. By pure coincidence we happened to have stumbled across video footage of the coolest dude in the school naked as a child. I knew Richard had had some minor acting roles as a child but this was gold.

'The poor bustard', laughed Don.

By now Jarred was in stitches. Ant was still digesting what he had just been told. 'Poor bastard is right', laughed Ant, 'It must have been like that nightmare where you turn up at school in your pajamas and then suddenly you are standing in front of the class naked'.

'Damn right', chuckled Don, 'From that day on he ceased to be known as Richard and from that day forth was called Bath Tub Boy'.

The three sat there chuckling away at Richard's misfortune. Being a teenager was tough enough without such an episode. It's the type of thing that could scar someone for life. Don wiped the tears from his eyes,

'As one would expect Richard dumped Samantha, hot or not. Probably was a good thing as she was a bitch anyway.

It also created a strain on his relationship with his parents as they could only see the funny side of the situation and couldn't understand his anxiety in regards to being nude as a child in front of his classmates.

To this day although he accepts his name of Bath Tub, he still hates new people finding out. Shit, anyway here he comes, mum's the word Ant!'

Bath Tub returned with two jugs of beer in hand. Grinning away at his achievement of retrieving the beer he placed them down on the table 'Help yourself fellas', he said.

Ant looked up at Richard, 'Well thanks Bath Tub, it's a pleasure to be shouted a beer by a famous child actor'. The three men at the table burst out laughing. The smile suddenly disappeared from Bath Tub's Face.

'Fuck you guys!', he said visibly upset. 'Fuck you Don you weasel, and fuck you Jarred, you Kiwi prick.'

Ant, still laughing, said to Bath Tub, 'Oh come on mate don't get the shits, sit down and have another beer with us, as we have games to play and stories to tell'.

The three men chorused, 'Open wide come in side, it's Play School'. They continued chuckling, partly because in their drunken state they thought they were funny and partly because of the sour look on Bath Tub's face who looked like he had just been made to lick a baboon's arse.

Ant thought it might be best to take the focus off Bath Tub. After all, he was a good bloke whose only crime had been to go fetch them some beer. He decided to take the piss out of himself to lighten the mood so he regaled them with the story from his recent trip to Thailand where he ended up in the hall of his hotel naked. He included the bit about him waking up pissing in the cleaning closet. The story went down well and got a laugh from his three friends.

The stories and the beer kept flowing for another hour as the men sat there looking out at Brisbane City's night lights. 'Anyway fellas, thanks for the company, but I might head off and hit the sack. Still a little tired from travelling', said Ant.

Ant wondered home enjoying the warm evening as the bats played in the trees overhead, fighting, fornicating, and gorging on fruit. His Petrie Terrace village was sleepy now. Many of the houses had their lights turned off. The occasional house was dimly lit, signifying the occupants were still awake relaxing in the warm evening air.

He walked past one well-appointed house where relaxing music was drifting from the balcony. Through the balustrade he could make out, by the candles and oil lanterns, a middle-aged couple sharing a wine and enjoying each other's company—the woman was giggling at something her partner had said. They looked happy and completely in love.

Not wanting to be a perv Ant continued on his way. To be honest he wanted to keep watching. 'Why?', he thought to himself. Was it to get lost in their happiness for a moment or was it he, like a child wanted to study them to understand how to obtain for himself their degree of contentment. Seeing two people so happy had given him a feeling of well-being but as he walked on he began to feel a little empty and alone. He walked up the stairs to his beautiful but empty house. He walked through the house to the kitchen. He pulled out his phone and connected it to his sound system selecting his Enigma album which was essentially chilling-out music.

He grabbed a short tumbler and added ice, a slice of lime and Bombay Sapphire gin, topping it off with tonic water and moved out onto his balcony. He lit the citronella oil lamps to keep the mozzies at a distance. He lay on his sunbed sipping his drink and gazing up at the palm trees.

He continued to reflect on his life. He was relatively successful–he owned a great house–had a sound shares and savings portfolio. He already had enough super and savings to support himself in his retirement very comfortably and he was still only in his thirties. He has his physical health. He had travelled the globe with good prospects for the future. He'd just scored a great root with Tatsu so why was he feeling sad after seeing the happy couple on the way home.

He took another sip on his drink and watched two translucent geckos chasing each other on the pergola. The humidity finally gave way to the rain. As the heavy drops struck the tin roof the rhythmic patter sent Ant into a further trance, reviewing moments of his life captured in his memory. He remembered key events that had led him to his current life circumstances.

Other than his sister and his aging parents he had only ever deeply cared about a few people. He thought of some of the mates he had lost as he again rubbed the remembrance tattoo on his forearm. His belief was that if you spent too long dwelling on the loss of good soldiers then eventually you only felt sorry for yourself, but only their family and loved ones had that right.

So what was it that was bugging him? Loneliness? Uncertainty? He thought of giving a more routine-based life a go. An office job and a white picket fence might crush his soul or it might help him connect with the community. Completely confused, Ant took a big swig of his drink and stared off into the night.

Fuck it, time to do something to improve my situation he thought taking his phone out of his pocket. He opened a new message and typed Hi sexy...

Seven thousand kilometers away Tatsu was walking through the Kyoto streets on her way home. It was a beautiful time of year as there was a light dusting of snow over the city. Much cooler than Thailand last week she thought, pulling her fur-lined collar closed.

She smiled as she thought of her time with Ant. He was the first man she had let near her in two years. He was so different to anyone she had ever dated before. Dated? She hadn't dated him, she thought. You used him as a cover, that's all.

You don't have time for men. You're about to board a boat in four days' time, and then you'll be at sea for a month. Her phone signaled an incoming message.

Hi sexy, it's Ant the love dynamo here. Hope you settled back into fast paced Japanese living since our time together swanning around in Phuket? Thinking of you, it would be good to catch up again sometime. Regards Ant the Stud.

She started laughing. What a dag she thought to herself starting to type a response.

'Stop!', Tatsu said to herself putting her phone back into her bag, 'Let him go, don't drag him into your life. He's a good guy and deserves better. You should never have given him your number. Silly girl, you might have to speak to work and get them to issue another one'.

Thirty minutes later Ant lay there still listening to the rain on the tin roof. He had nearly drifted off to sleep a couple of times which he wanted to avoid as there was a real risk that the local semi-tame possum would curl up next to him on the outdoor bed.

He had nicknamed the possum Mad Max. He knew Max used the bed to sleep on, as he would see its dirty little footprints on the mattress some mornings when he went outside for his coffee.

Ant looked across at the empty house next door. By some cruel twist of fate the closest thing he had to a life partner was his occasional neighbor. Now, he was off gallivanting around the UK and Europe. Ant tried to recall where he last said he was. Monte Carlo or some bullshit like that.

Who does the jerk-off think he is? James Bond I suppose. Toffee-nosed Pom. Still try as he might to dislike Lachie for being what could only be described as a self-centered cad, he couldn't help but like him.

Hell, he even missed his company if he went away more than three months without seeing him. Well, Ant thought to himself. He will be back here in a few days and then the peace and quiet will no doubt be shattered. Time for bed mumbled Ant as he dragged himself to his feet.

Tiger Tears

THE COUNTRY OF EAST TIMOR sits in the north of the Timor Sea, approximately one hour's flight from Darwin, Australia. The largely Catholic population speak the indigenous Tetum language deriving from Malayo-Polynesian. The country had had a turbulent history as it was host to a Portuguese colony for centuries.

The East Timorese were separated from their West Timor brothers and sisters so that the Dutch could stake their claim to the western half of the Timor Island. In the early 1940s, the people of Timor were dragged into WWII by the Japanese and the Australians. An Australian and British Commando force sought to deny this land mass to the Japanese as, given its proximity, it was seen as a staging area for an attack on Australia.

The several hundred Australian Special Forces soldiers gained the support of many of the Timorese who supported their fight to deny a Japanese occupation. The small Australian force fought hard and although eventually overwhelmed, as they were vastly outnumbered, they achieved a strategic victory due to their ability to delay the Japanese advance.

Unfortunately for the Timorese, it was estimated that some 40000 to 70000 Timorese, men, women, and children were killed as the conflict raged. Tragically the heartache was to continue after WWII when the Portuguese gave East Timor its independence.

Shortly after, Indonesia invaded the country. Suddenly the largely Christian people had an Islamic ruler. This act of aggression brought condemnation from some Christian countries.

Australia remained silent. Maybe the Australian Government held the view that Indonesian was a desirable ruler, uniting small countries that could otherwise fall to Communism. It appeared that the 1975 Australian Government had long since forgotten the sacrifice the Timorese made in support of Australian troops in WWII.

By 1976, after the invasion and the murder of five Australian journalists who were reporting the atrocities being committed by the occupying military forces, East Timor was annexed as part on Indonesia.

The Timorese looked across the Timor Sea waiting for its old friend to help them repel the invader. The help never came; Australia had a new and more strategically important friend in Indonesia.

It was a typical hot, humid November morning in 1998. The village of Liquiçá, found on the coast of East Timor, was quiet. The only noise to be heard was that of fishermen returning from their early morning ritual.

An Indonesian soldier named Pramana looked across the sandy beach out to the clean blue sea. 'Yes, it is a beautiful place', he thought to himself. He looked at his rifle that he had just finished cleaning. 'Pity about its primitive indigenous population', he thought to himself as he slapped a full magazine into the weapon.

Today he was going out on patrol. Hopefully they would find the scum that had killed 7 of the Liquiçá Company's 12-man patrol from two days previous. Sergeant Pramana belonged to the elite Indonesian Army Special Force called Kopassus. They had been choppered from Dili this morning to hunt down the FALINTIL rebels.

The FALINTIL were an armed group of East Timorese who were sick of waiting for a foreign power to grant them independence. They were prepared to fight and die for freedom. Any Indonesian soldier in their eyes was fair game. At any given time, they had over 15000 Indonesian targets for them to hunt. That number was duplicated by Timorese militia who were armed and pro-Indonesian and they, like their masters, were also fair game.

The FALINTIL were a relatively small tight-knit and effective group of hardened jungle soldiers. They largely had the support of the indigenous community and they were ruthless and relentless in their pursuit of freedom.

Through trial and error the FALINTIL survivors, some of which had fought the attritional battle in 1975 against Indonesian forces, were now very good at guerrilla warfare. Many a young Timorese boy fantasized about joining the FALINTIL ranks but only the tough and brave did so.

The average Indonesian soldier hoped not to come across them on their patrols. For the Kopassus soldiers, they longed to encounter them. The Kopassus were better-equipped and better-trained than the other Indonesian soldiers. They were far superior in every way than the local militias.

Certainly, the FALINTIL knew when they were in a fight with the aggressive Kopassus units. Today Sergeant Pramana was going to lead his patrol and get some pay back. He hated the Timorese.

He was from the tough and deprived streets of Jakarta. He had killed his first man at age fifteen in a robbery before he joined the forces, had a reputation in the Kopassus for being ruthless and was on a warning for being too brutal. It was rumored that he had murdered civilians in East Timor over his black-market businesses that he ran on the side.

He planned to retire rich so as not to return to the poverty-stricken Jakarta streets he grew up in. Sergeant Pramana was a loner and a mystery to his men, but they knew enough not to mess with him.'

Let's go!', he called to his seven-man squad.

They leapt to their feet and headed to the two waiting Toyota utes. A young, fit and feminine-featured soldier lined up alongside Sergeant Pramana.

'You stay out of harm's way today Susanto my darling. I think we might find trouble and I don't want to see any scars on that beautiful body',

Sergeant Pramana said patting Susanto on the backside.

Private Susanto giggled and grabbed the Sergeant's hand as they ran towards the waiting vehicle. The distinct lack of women available to the occupying force had encouraged rape of East Timorese women and homosexuality amongst the Army members. This suited Sergeant Pramana as his preference was for men anyway.

He had found someone he truly cared about in Private Susanto, forming an eight-month relationship with the young man. He was a junior member of the squad and not as battle-hardened as the others. Sergeant Pramana planned to keep him near the vehicles so that he would not be in direct contact with the enemy and could make a quick escape should anything went wrong.

The vehicles set off up the steep single track, which climbed the mountain linking Liquiçá to Ermera. The numerous villages along the way were surrounded by a mix of fruit trees and thick jungle. They drove through the first of the villages containing a mere eight huts. There was no one to be seen as they had hidden five minutes earlier when they first detected the Indonesians driving up the road.

The potholed-road twisted back on itself as it wound up the steep jungle-lined mountain. The poor road surface and the encroaching vegetation make it slow going. The locals didn't have much in the way of vehicles so any vehicle noise was treated with suspicion.

As they passed through the deserted village, Pramana made a mental note that in two more villages they would arrive at the village of Batiguado, a 15-minute walk from the ambush site of the Indonesian patrol yesterday. The FALINTIL were not the type to necessarily hit and run. Sometimes they would lay in wait and hit the response force as well.

They would not normally seek to ambush Kopassus unless they thought the odds were in their favour. Sergeant Pramana had a trump card up his sleeve to encourage a confrontation. He had dressed his troops in standard Army unit uniforms. They used run-down vehicles to mask their true identity.

The enemy could have no way of knowing that in their rucksacks they carried three times as much 7.62mm ammunition as a standard soldier with two M79 40mm grenade launchers not normally in an Indonesian patrol's arsenal.

Yes, if the FALANTIL were around, they would see a small squad of poorly-trained and equipped standard infantry with low morale, lost in the jungle–not a well-equipped, super-fit squad of experienced killers itching for a fight.

The vehicles pulled up in Batiguado and the disheveled-looking soldiers climbed out of the vehicles. Sergeant Pramana shook his men out ready for the patrol. He instructed the two drivers and Susanto to remain and guard the vehicles. He headed for the largest hut in the village and walked in without waiting for an invitation.

The village chief and his family were in the one-room hut. When Pramana walked in the chief motioned to his wife who had already prepared coffee. The coffee in East Timor is extraordinary. It is organic and the bushes cling to the sides of the steep hills. The plants are nurtured and harvested by hand.

The once Portuguese-owned plantations now have the look of naturally occurring vegetation that is free of interference. Nothing could be further from the truth. Coffee is as good as currency and the Timorese take the preparation of it very seriously.

With no modern appliances or even electricity in the village all the preparation was done by hand. The final ground beans, suspended in a piece of old but very clean stocking, are soaked in a pot-full of hot water. The strong beautifully bitter coffee is served black in small glasses. It can be served with or without sugar, but if one does request sugar it will result in an extremely sweet beverage.

The offering of good coffee extends to every visitor, even an uninvited potential enemy. The chief's wife approached with two coffees on a tray. She tried her best not to look at Pramana through fear of provoking the man.

Pramana eyed the cowering woman and removed a coffee from the tray. The chief motioned for Pramana to take a seat on the mat in the corner of the hut so they could take their coffee and discuss the purpose of Pramana's business—the Chief surmised it would involve the FALANTIL's successful ambush of an Indonesian patrol.

Pramana took a sip of his coffee and muttered, 'Do you speak Bahasa Indonesia?'

The chief nodded cautiously.

'Good', said Pramana, 'Your chances of survival are increasing Chief. Now what can you tell me about the FALINTIL?' The chief looked down at the dirt floor.

'Chief if you don't tell me something I will kill your family.' The chief looked up at the Indonesian sergeant. He could see the hatred in the man's eyes.

'They come and go as they please. They were hunting a militia group that raped a local girl. She was only 12-years-old. Instead of finding the militia they ran across your patrol. They weren't alone. They had white men with them.

They were like ghosts. One minute they were there and they and the FALANTIL worked together killing every one of the Indonesian patrol within minutes. They then faded back into the jungle like ghosts.'

Pramana's eyes widened, 'Who were they? Where did they go?', he demanded. The chief steeled himself returning Pramana's stare, 'I don't know', he said.

'Chief, you are making me annoyed. Let me make this very clear to you. I am going out to get these bastards. I am leaving my two drivers and one guard in your village to protect the vehicles. If anything happens to my men or my equipment I am going to kill everyone in your village.'

Pramana got to his feet and hurled the empty coffee glass across the room. He stormed out of the hut. The Chief looked at his wife who was shaking with fear. 'Darling, as soon as he leaves the village, you and the children run into the jungle to the cave under the waterfall. I will send for you when everything calms down.'

The chief's wife nodded her head in reluctant compliance.

Pramana placed Susanto and the two drivers in a defensive position to guard the vehicles. He then gathered his remaining six men and headed for the jungle. He would track along the river to see if he could find any sign of the FALINTIL and their foreign friends.

He and his men patrolled silently. This was more than just revenge now. He had to find out who the foreigners were. White men—Not many of those in Timor–Probably the Australians–It couldn't be them as they were Indonesia's allies. He had even trained with their Special Forces in a training exchange.

He had heard that the Australian people were slowly getting behind the East Timor pro-independence campaign, but to attack an Indonesian patrol, that's insane. Indonesia outnumbered the Australian troops ten to one.

They would lose the war even if they won a few battles. They were arrogant though, with a love for war. They regularly travelled the globe attacking other countries—Germany, the Turks, the North Koreans, the Chinese and the Vietnamese. Yes, they have form in this regard.

He needed to find these ghosts and report on them. After fifteen-minutes of disciplined patrolling he reached the ambush sight. The sight was tranquil and dark from the reduced light that struggled to penetrate the thick tree canopy. He shook his men out in all-round defence and examined the sight. There was blood and scattered equipment everywhere. It looked like the patrol had been down by the river cooling off in the natural pool when they were attacked.

He looked up to his right and saw a ledge on the cliff above them. He grabbed two of his men and signaled to them to follow him up the steep embankment to the ledge. When they got up there he found several grenade pins and scattered 5.56mm cartridges.

Bloody hell he thought. He could just envisage the scene in his head. The Indonesian patrol bathing in the pool. They must have let their guard down and not thought to secure the high ground. This gave the FALINTIL and the white ghosts the opportunity they needed.

They crept up to the ledge pulled the pin on half a dozen grenades and tossed them down on the soldiers bathing below. They then stood back and machine-gunned the survivors. Murderers!

Suddenly, he heard shooting off in the distance. It wasn't intense fire, just half a dozen shots ringing out from the direction of the village. Susanto, please god, don't let anything happen to him.

'Let's go men. Quick! They are attacking our rear security team in the village.'

The elite soldiers broke their disciplined movements and started hastily moving towards the village in fifteen-metre running bounds. Even at this accelerated pace it will still take the best part of ten minutes to get back to the village.

'Speed it up men', cried Pramana.

What Pramana couldn't know is that he would have been better to take his time and maintain patrol discipline. His men in the village, including Susanto, were already dead. Professionally executed by four FALANTIL fighters who had already disappeared back into the jungle.

The FALANTIL leader, Romero, was now patrolling back down to the gorge. From there, they would circle back around to the track to ambush the next convoy that would undoubtedly be sent to find out what happened to the two vehicles they had just confiscated from the now three dead Indonesian soldiers.

He had also dispatched a small force to ambush the only close clearing on top of the mountain range on the off chance that the Indonesians send an elite chopper force. They would use a series of command-detonated mines for the road, which required his force to be on the ground to initiate the explosives. These mines were used to ensure they could effectively target the enemy force and weren't accidently initiated by some hapless local going about their business.

For the potential helicopter landing point, they would use the reliable and cheap rocket propelled grenades or RPGs as they were commonly known. They can be devastating against rotary wing aircraft that slow down enough to offload their troops—a technique they had learnt from the Somalians in Mogadishu who used them to great effect against US Black Hawk helicopters.

The Indonesians were 300 metres from the village when Romero spotted them moving at speed. He motioned to his patrol to spread out and go to ground. Romero couldn't believe his good fortune—no time to set up explosives, but then again, he wouldn't need them. His fighters were more accurate with their weapons and were battle-hardened.

Romero and his FALINTIL patrol were in position. He would initiate the ambush to ensure the element of surprise once the Indonesians were within range. His targets must be untrained he thought. Moving at speed like they were was clumsy, making them vulnerable. They were close now.

The shabby state of their uniforms was another indication of their lack of discipline. This was going to be another massacre Romero thought. He searched for a rank slide through his binoculars. He liked to pick off the leader first to add to the chaos of the encounter. He scanned the approaching men but could make out no rank slides.

That's odd? Something else that wasn't making sense was that although they were moving fast instead of patrolling, they were doing it in formation. Well-rehearsed bounds? Half the men took up fire positions whilst the other half moved.

Another thing, they were moving fast and their physiques suggested they were very fit. Two of the men had grenade launchers strapped to their patrol packs. Although their uniforms looked crap their weapons were immaculate.

'Shit, these guys aren't standard troops. They're a Special Forces hunter killer team probably sent to find us. This could go bad but it's too late to escape. Better to get the first hit in and hope for the best!' Romero took aim on the man in the middle of the advancing Indonesians who were now within 20 metres.

A loud crack, crack, crack sounded in front of Pramana followed almost instantaneously by a thump, thump, thump as the supersonic rounds whizzed by his head.

The man next to him dropped as the rounds struck their target. The remainder of the patrol went to ground and started crawling forward at pace.

The FALANTIL fired at the moving foliage but failed to hit the Indonesian soldiers moving towards them. The Indonesians could see the muzzle flashes. The two men with the grenade launchers had moved to slightly higher ground. They launched their M79 grenade launchers into the middle of the attackers.

Two of the FALANTIL were killed outright as the grenade fragments tore through them. Of the remaining two, Romero was badly wounded. The other fighter returned fire and dropped another Indonesian Kopassus soldier before he was shot repeatedly by rifle fire.

The Indonesians moved fast and one of them was now standing above Romero with his rifle pointed at his face. Romero knew what was going to come next. 'Pity', he thought 'I would love to have been around to see what was going to happen next year. The Australians said they were coming'.

Pramana fired a single shot into the FALANTIL rebel's face. Odd he thought, he could have sworn the man was smiling. They quickly searched the dead FALANTIL, collected their dead and then continued onto the village. The whole altercation from start to finish was over in five minutes.

As they got to the village they placed their dead down on the outskirts of the clearing with two guards that would also act as concealed security as he and the remaining soldier entered the village.

Pramana and his remaining squad member exited the jungle and marched into the village clearing. The ground was a light brown hard-packed dirt which was in stark contrast to the lush, green jungle wall that encased the village. The huts in the village were small and basic. Constructed out of a mixture of corrugated iron, wood, and sticks, with palm tree frond roofs, the huts were arranged around the edges of the clearing. They wrapped around the chief's slightly larger, concrete hut located next to the village's meeting place cum parking area.

Pramana glared at the clearing. The vehicles were gone. In their place were the mangled lifeless bodies of the two drivers and the once beautiful Susanto. Rage swelled in the pit of Pramana's stomach. From this day forth he would operate without constraint.

He could see the shell casings from the FALANTIL's weapons lying on the ground. They must have already been in the village hiding when he arrived. That lying traitorous chief knew they were still in his village lying in wait. Now the FALANTIL were dead he would exact his revenge.

He would make an example of them starting with the chief pig and his disgusting family. He didn't have enough ammunition left to waste on them all and the FALANTIL had stolen the weapons and ammunition along with the vehicles from his dead men. He glanced down at his thigh.

The blade it is then. Good, that's all this pig deserves.

He barked at his counterpart to go into the hut and round up the chief and his family. After a short period of yelling, the soldier emerged.

'Sergeant, I've got the chief but his family are not here'. Pramana's eyes narrowed. 'You crafty little pig', he thought to himself.

He pointed at the hut next to the chief's. 'Fetch me whoever is in that next hut.'

The Indonesian soldier snapped to attention and headed towards the next hut. Pramana was now alone with the chief. He unsheathed his knife and grabbed the defiant man by his shoulder-length hair.

He held the knife to the chief's face. 'I'm going to kill you now, you pig. Then I'm going to kill three more people in the village in the place of your family. I'll hunt them down and kill them eventually. Know that I will take love from you like you have from me today'. Pramana plunged the heavy-bladed knife into the chief's stomach.

The chief grimaced and then stared back defiantly at Pramana. 'The FALANTIL will kill you too', mumbled the chief.

Fueled by rage Pramana stabbed the chief three more times in the torso.

'What are you doing Sergeant?', cried the Indonesian soldier who had emerged from the hut with two young males in tow.

'Shut up trooper and bring those two scum over here.'

'No, this is wrong, we are soldiers, not murderers', protested the Indonesian.

Pramana turned his back on the soldier and stared at the chief who was now slumped on the ground. He was in his final throes of life as he coughed blood and gasped for air. His diaphragm and lungs were punctured and he would be dead within minutes. Just enough time for him to witness the killing of two more of his people.

Still glaring at the chief Pramana yelled, 'Bring those two here now Private'.

Pramana heard movement behind him and assumed the private was corralling the two villagers towards him. Instead he felt a hard blow to the back of his head.

Still stunned and face down on the ground a new voice speaking to him in Indonesian said, 'Pick yourself up and get to your knees Sergeant'. Pramana scrambled to his knees and looked up to where the voice came from.

He immediately recoiled as he focused on the source of the voice. The figure was not that of an Indonesian or a Timorese as he had expected. Instead, looming over him was a foreigner dressed completely in a green camouflaged uniform. Even the man's face was completely green and black except for two piercing eyes that glared at him. He would have been almost invisible in the foliage. He had a silenced weapon pointed directly at Pramana's head.

Pramana looked to his right. He could see two stunned Timorese frozen with fear and his Indonesian counterpart who had been stripped of his weapon and was now on his knees with his hands on his head. He was under guard of another green-clad foreigner.

'The ghosts', gasped Pramana.

The foreigner closest to Pramana smirked and said in English, 'Priest, have you got those other pricks yet?'

There was a rustling in the foliage on the edge of the village as the remaining two Kopassus patrol members emerged with their hands on their heads. There were two more green men behind them. One was the biggest man Pramana had ever seen. He was about six and a half foot tall and his shoulders were a pickaxe-handle wide.

The big man responded, 'Yeah Bossman we got them and their two dead buddies', he said as he dumped a dead body that he had been carrying over one shoulder on the ground.

The foreign boss spoke again, 'Good work Priest. Starlight get over here, we have a badly-injured Timorese. See if there is anything we can do'.

Another ghost sprinted from the bushes to the wounded chief. After a brief investigation, he plugged the wounds with a pressure bandage and injected the chief with a painkiller. The ghost called Starlight looked up at and reluctantly shook his head that signified to the boss that death was imminent.

The chief looked up at the boss and said, 'Aussie ghost, save my family. Don't let him kill them....'. He then looked across to the two East Timorese villagers, 'Tell my wife I love her'. With that the final breath left his body and the man died.

The boss looked down at Pramana and frisked him. He found the sergeant's wallet and searched through it. He removed his identification card and knelt-down next to his captive.

He whispered in Pramana's ear, 'Sergeant, we have not yet harmed an Indonesian soldier, but understand me, we can. We know who you are now and we will be watching. You are Sergeant Pramana of the Kopassus and you are a murderer'.

He pointed at the chief lying dead on the ground.

'If anything happens to this man's family, I am going to take it out on you and trust me, you won't know when retribution is coming, but it will'.

The boss's glare and his intimidating message delivered in near-perfect Indonesian, spooked Pramana. He knelt there frozen.

Bossman stood back up and looked about the village. Some twenty-three Timorese were peering from their huts at the goings-on. 'Now this is for the Indonesian soldiers', said the boss. 'Leave your weapons, collect your dead and piss off out of this village. Now!

Oh, and don't come back here'.

The Indonesians loaded their two dead into a rickshaw and started down the road. 'Hey, pay the village for the use of that rickshaw', called one of the ghosts.

The Indonesians turned around to see only the Timorese standing there. The ghosts had melded back into the jungle.

Pramana never did take retribution against the chief's family. He was strongly reprimanded for his brutality against a civilian by his peers and superiors. The adverse reaction of his superiors and his fear of the ghosts caused him to leave the family be. Instead he focused his anger at the FALANTIL. He became an accomplished fighter, surviving many skirmishes.

He became known over the next year as the 'Lone Tiger' due to the single-man reconnaissance missions he would conduct, and his ferocity in a fight when he was cornered. He was training himself in every fight, preparing himself for the next time he encountered the ghosts.

He didn't know it at the time but he would encounter them again soon. They would be back with the remainder of the Australian Defence Force that would form part of INTERFET, the UN-sanctioned intervention force deployed in October 1999. By December 1999, Tiger and his team had withdrawn across the East Timorese border into West Timor.

The UN had approached the Indonesian military over war crime enquiries. His brigade commander wanted him interviewed in relation to the chief's death, which had been brought to the UN's attention by his family.

'I should have tied up that loose end', Tiger thought. 'I need to disappear off the grid before I get tried for murder.'

The night before his interview, he chartered a local fishing vessel and left the island. As the boat pulled away from the island he stared at the ever-decreasing coastline, bathed in the moonlight and took stock of his life. He had lost his love and lost his humanity on that island. He was a man without a future and now he needed to be a man without a past or risk international prosecution. Sergeant Pramana was no more; he was now Tiger, a gun for hire.

The Sub-Culture

Ant woke at 0800h the next morning after drinking with Don, Jarred, and Bath Tub the night before. He wasn't completely hung-over, but he wasn't feeling great either. He headed down to the kitchen to make a coffee.

Like a lot of well-travelled people, Ant was a coffee snob. He had spent a small stint in East Timor as part of a peacekeeping mission. The Timorese are coffee fanatics and by the time Ant left there so was he.

He had been able to source some organic fresh Timorese coffee from a supplier in Brisbane. It was strong stuff and gave you a hit that could wake a backbench politician during a sitting in Parliament.

Ant moved out onto the deck with his coffee. The weather was beautiful as per usual. 'The Beach, that will wash out the cob webs', Ant thought. He finished his coffee and wandered back inside the house.

The coffee might have woken him up but now his stomach was rumbling. He opened his fridge door, no eggs, 'Bugger!', he thought to himself. I know how to solve this dilemma, I will just wonder up the road to the Scout Café and get them to hook me up with some bacon and eggs.

When Ant arrived the Petrie Terrace café was packed as usual with hipsters sipping their lattes. Ant pushed through the trendy crowd to the counter and ordered some breakfast.

'Where are you sitting?', the lady at the counter asked.

Ant looked around for a spare seat and spotted one next to a man with his head buried in his hands. 'Over there, thanks', he said before walking over to the sick-looking man.

Ant took his seat and leant over to the man, 'Well, well, Jarred, you look a little worse for wear', chortled Ant. Jarred looked up at Ant with eyes that looked like two piss holes in the snow.

'Hey Ant, last night was a laugh but I'm paying for it now. Damn Bathtub made us drink till our heads caved in as punishment for picking on him', said Jarred.

'Yep, he's a big boy', confessed Ant. The two of them sat there chatting over a deliciously-satisfying breakfast that almost made them feel human again. When they finished, Ant asked Jarred if he wanted to go to the beach with him. Jarred thanked Ant for the offer but said he felt so crap that he planned to sit on his backside and do nothing except play Playstation 4 all day. Ant said fair enough and left Jarred to it.

Once home, Ant washed his face and slipped into a pair of budgie smugglers. Over the top, he put on a pair of jeans, accompanied with one of his favourite Isle of Man TT shirts that Lachie had sent him from the UK.

He grabbed his Brown Daniese motorcycle jacket and a backpack in which he placed a towel, shorts and a pair of thongs. He then wandered down to the ground floor of the house. Secured inside the house on the ground floor sat a gleaming, red, Ducati 999s. The bike was his pride and joy.

He loved the *Art Nouveau* look of the motorcycle, which was designed by Pierre Terblanche. In addition to the bike's visual appeal it could also propel Ant from 0 to 100 kph in around 3 seconds and that grunt put a smile on the old paratrooper's face.

Nimble, fast, beautiful and masculine summed the bike up. Its design was an ergonomic master stroke as it truly allowed the rider to feel as one with the bike, creating the illusion in the rider's mind that he was flying rather than being fixed to the road's surface. The engine roared as Ant threaded his way through the traffic heading south.

He opened his visor so he could feel the warm air buffeting his face. When he reached the open road south of Brisbane he cracked the throttle and he catapulted down the road. A smile crept across his face as a feeling of euphoria hit him.

He glanced down at the sleek, red race-bred machine as it sliced through the air. 'Yes, today is a good day to be alive', he thought to himself.

After thirty minutes Ant hit the Gold Coast. He decided to ride straight past the beaches as the tail-end of the tourist season was still underway and the beaches would be packed. Likewise, Tweed Heads looked like it was heaving, so he continued his journey to a beach just north of Byron Bay.

The southbound road had taken him inland a little and the curves provided him something to lay the bike over into before straightening up and blasting out of them again. The constant tipping into corners gave him the sensation of flying.

As he got closer to the beach his nostrils filled with the smell of the salt water. His excitement grew with the anticipation of hopefully a less-crowded beautiful Aussie beach to enjoy. Ant followed a small sign pointed to the South Golden Beach access that had a nearly-empty car park.

Apart from an old VW surf van, Ant had the car park to himself so he parked the bike and then sat himself under a nearby tree where he stripped off his motorcycle gear and placed it into a duffle bag that he had strapped to the back of his bike.

Now dressed in his board shorts and thongs he trotted down to the beach. When he got there he was beside himself with joy. The pristine beach stretched for miles and he was the only one on the beach except for what looked like two people huddled under a beach towel with four well-used surf boards strewn on the sand behind them.

Ant looked at the waves that looked like they had a bit of power behind them. 'Excellent!', he thought as he dumped his gear and kicked off his thongs. He then sprinted down to the water's edge and dived into a wave. The water was refreshing and energizing. It was so clear that he could see fish swimming through the waves. He splashed around for ten minutes, cooling down after his ride before swimming out to the deeper water for some body surfing. The waves weren't the biggest but they had plenty of power behind them. He bodysurfed for thirty minutes, having a blast, before he decided to walk back to his bag and grab a drink of water.

As he walked back to his gear he could see two young lads no longer towel-clad sitting in front of the surf boards. 'Wish I had my board with me', Ant thought.

The two lads looked up at Ant grinning. Their half-closed eyes suggested to Ant that the reason they were huddled under a towel before was because they were having a smoke.

'Hey man', the lad with the long blond hair said to Ant.

'Fellas, how's it hang'n?'

The two lads looked at each other and started to snigger, 'Loose and to the right bro.

You were carven them waves man', said one of the lads.

'Yeh, I wish I had my board with me, but can't bring it down on the bike so I am down to bodysurfing'.

The second lad with a shaved head said 'Yeah bro I went and checked out your ride in the car park. Ducati eh? Nice. Hey, use my board if you want bro, I'm too stoned to get out there at the moment'.

'Hey thanks for the offer man, my name's Ant by the way'.

'G'day Ant, I'm Spider and this here is Goldie. My board's the one with the orange on it'.

'Thanks Spider, be back in 30 minutes', Ant said, picking up the board. Spider grinned at him waving him away with a be my guest gesture.

'Hang on Ant I'll come with ya', called Goldie, grabbing his board. 'I'm not as stoned as Spider, he's a fucking dope gannet and barely shared his dabs with me.'

'Yeah fair enough', called Ant over his shoulder as he trotted off to the water. Spider's board was a short board and was easier to paddle out into the surf than Ant's 9'6" longboard, however that is where the easy bit ended.

The board was not designed to support someone of Ant's weight, so popping onto his feet was much harder than normal. Still he managed to ride a few waves. He was however totally shown up by Goldie, the little half-stoned beach bum who expertly carved the waves up.

Ant and Goldie sat out behind the breakers waiting for a good set just chatting away. It turned out Goldie was a top bloke. He and Spider were locals and had been mates since they were little grommets. Now they both worked for a local old age nursing home as carers.

Ant told Goldie he had just returned from overseas and was looking for work—probably a logistics job in supply and distribution. Ant then said after the next wave he would have to head back as he was expecting his mate Lachie to turn up.

The two men saw a big set approaching so they laid down on their boards and angled them towards the beach. Ant started paddling slowly as the wall of water approached. He felt a strong suck from the wave that made him smile as that meant this one would have some power in it. As the wave picked him up he popped onto his feet. The wave started to curl and he allowed himself to descend halfway down its face to pick up speed before leveling out so as not to get spat out of the wave.

He could see Goldie speeding off in front of him cutting up and down the face of the wave to milk every bit of excitement out of it he could. Both of them surfed the wave into the shore and trotted out laughing back to the now coherent Spider who was standing clapping and yelling, 'Not bad for a stoner and an old fella'.

Ant thanked Spider for the loan of the board and the company. Goldie swapped contact details with Ant and said next time give them a call in the morning he was coming down and they'd bring a spare board. Likewise, Ant said if they were up Brissy way to give him a call.

The men shook hands and Ant gathered up his gear and trotted back to the bike. He was buzzing with energy as he toweled off. He wrapped his wet gear in plastic bags and placed them back in his bike luggage before swinging his leg over the bike and fitting his carbon fibre AGV helmet. He fired up the brutish V-Twin motor and dropped the clutch as he did a semi-doughnut and sped out of the empty car park.

Before Ant hit the the highway a grumbling in his stomach gave him an idea. As he headed from South Golden Beach he took a small detour to New Brighton where he pulled into a parking spot at the Yum Yum Cafe Tree. As Ant walked into the cafe he observed the healthy and slim looking hippie patrons. 'Must be all yogis' Ant thought to himself as he took note of the ropey strong looking biceps of the smiling girl working behind the counter.

'What can I get you friend?' she asked.

'What's good here?' asked Ant with a cheeky grin.

'It's all good darling, but for you I would recommend the grilled fish, stone ground taco. It's a hearty, tasty and a healthy meal. I'm sure you won't be disappointed', said the girl.

Ant took her advice and ordered the taco. When it arrived he was glad that he did. It was delicious and filling, yet it didn't leave him feeling bloated, which was great given he had to ride back to BrisVegas.

When he finished, Ant waved goodbye to the friendly staff and jumped back on his Ducati to head for home. Ant roared through the quiet leafy suburb of Petrie Terrace to the garage gate at the rear of the house.

He pressed a button on the handle bars and the gate to his yard and the rear sliding-door of his house slid open. Ant gassed the Ducati and lurched into the downstairs room of his house that served as his man cave where his 999 took centre stage.

He hung his gear up and plodded up the stairs to take a shower and wash the salt water off. After his shower, he grabbed his small set of scissors and started trimming his moustache that was now starting to merge into his chin stubble as it continued to develop into a fully-blown beard. His once military-styled short, cropped hair was starting to grow out.

In the physical sense, he figured he no longer looked like a military man. This prospect excited him as he had spent his whole adult life looking like a soldier and now was developing his urban camouflage. He was starting to look just like another shabby member of society.

This notion was in a way therapeutic and made him feel like he was making progress in transitioning to a more stable lifestyle.

Dressed in his rugby shorts and his Same Same but Different T-shirt he walked to the kitchen where he fetched some almond milk, ice, banana, and strawberries to blitz in his Nutra Bullet blender.

He walked out onto the front deck with his frosty smoothie. Sipping it he felt completely refreshed and at peace. He glanced up and down the beautiful and quiet inner-city street. He sat there enjoying the Zen feeling he was experiencing after his morning surf and blast on his motorcycle.

He glanced up the street and noticed a big man dressed all in black, carrying an overnight bag walking down the street towards him. Odd outfit for this warm weather thought Ant. As the man got closer Ant tried to make out his facial features but the man had a black Irish-styled flat cap pulled down over his forehead. A thick black pair of Oakley sunglasses masked his eyes. The man's swagger exuded confidence and menace.

'Bloody Hell', thought Ant, 'This guy is huge'.

The man altered his direction and angled towards Ant's house. This could be trouble Ant thought as he got up out of his seat. Now five metres from Ant's front gate, he could see the man was sporting a bulbous broken nose and a priest's collar around his neck.

The big man stopped out the front of Ant's deck. The man slowly removed his dark sunglasses revealing two piercing blue eyes that seem to be able to bore into your sole.

A crooked grin spread across the man's face. 'Ant, how are you my son? Not starving I see by that long-range fuel tank you are sporting'.

Ant glanced down at his stomach then back at the man. 'What the fuck are you doing here Priest you prick?'

The man dressed in black looked at the ground and shook his head, 'Now Ant my son, is that anyway to address a man of God?'

'Are you serious Priest, he still employs you? He must have a need for a club-fisted moron'.

'Ant, are you still upset about that little incident at your party where I fell ill?'

Ant screwed up his face and parroted, 'Fell ill! Priest, you sprayed my downstairs toilet with vomit. It looked like a scene from the fucking exorcist! Took me two days to clean it up and there is still an unholy smell that lurks downstairs'.

'Ant I do apologise but I think your rum was off at that party. Anyway, don't you think it might be time to forgive and forget?' asked Priest.

Ant motioned towards the door, 'Come then Priest get inside and I shall fetch you a cool, non-alcoholic beverage'. Priest smiled and lurched towards the front door. Once inside, Ant's mood lightened and they spent the next hour catching up.

Despite Priest's somewhat unorthodox method of spreading the word of God there was no doubt he had been busy over the last couple of years. He had been somewhat semi-permanently assigned to East Timor where he supported several orphanages with some of the local sisters.

He maintained a small house in the Gold Coast hinterland, ten minutes from Nerang as you headed towards Canungra. Both men knew Canungra well as that area for some time has been used for land warfare training by the Army.

He still occasionally caught up with old Army mates although one of them he might have to distance himself from as he had turned to organized crime. Despite this Priest was pretty determined to serve God and do right by his fellow man where possible. This included trying one last time to save his old Special Forces corporal who now ran the Syndicate.

As the conversation developed, it became evident to Ant that Priest saw himself as more of a badass messenger of God who was prepared to do the dirty work and tackle evil head-on. The church had, as a result, assigned him the gig of being the one to visit the most hardened and terrifying criminals in need of religious counsel.

At the top of the list was an inmate named Michael O'Leary, who was doing life for murdering an English backpacker in the 90s. Prior to coming to Australia he had been a member of the IRA. Even though he had traveled to Australia to escape the 'struggle', he was unable to tame his radical views and his hatred for the people he saw as his oppressors.

Hence some poor English tourist and his girlfriend, enjoying the trip of a lifetime and hitchhiking to northern Australia, stumbled across O'Leary who offered them a lift from the Tennant Creek Roadhouse.

He took them 100km north before veering off onto a dirt road and taking a blade to the lad. He must have really been enjoying his work because the girl made a break for it without him noticing until 10 minutes after she had gone.

O'Leary set about trying to find her. After 20 minutes of searching he saw the girl climbing into a road train cattle truck.

Cursing his luck that the girl found help in the middle of nowhere he made the error of trying to stop the road train. The driver who was appalled by the brief story the hysterical girl had relayed decided not to stop when O'Leary swerved in front of the truck to try and halt him. Instead he plowed over the top of the van that was crumpled and spat out from under the rig down an embankment.

O'Leary laid there in the mangled van bleeding in the dust and heat for two hours before the police found him. To this day, he still remained unrepentant but called for Priest every now and again to bleat and to try and convince himself God would welcome him into heaven in due course.

Priest said it takes every ounce of his self-control not to reach across the table and strangle the evil little prick.

Ant had to admit Priest had been leading an interesting life in the service of God and his fellow man. He also confessed that Priest's dedication to the orphans of East Timor was inspiring.

The conversation was interrupted by a knock at the door, and a none too lady-like female voice asked, 'Hello is anyone fucken home?'

Ant got up and walked to the door to see an attractive redheaded girl in a very tight pair of denim shorts and a tight singlet that had crept up just enough to expose a perfectly toned stomach.

Ant's eyes slowly and subconsciously crept up from the woman's mid drift to her small, firm breasts, finally coming to rest on the familiar face. Ant smirked and said, 'Well hello gorgeous, what can ol uncle Ant do for you?'

The woman's response was swift and harsh, 'Oh fuck off Ant, get your fat fucken eyes off what you can't afford or I'll rip your fucken balls off and feed em to ya!'

Ant chuckled, 'Wonderful to see you too Baz, I take it Lachlan has invited you to my house as well for a quickening of the clan?'

As he opened the security door the redhead's demeanor changed as her eyes softened and a big grin spread across her face. She wrapped her arms around Ant and draped herself over him despite her being taller than him by some two inches. 'Great to see you Ant, my beautiful fat little wogboy', the girl crooned, rubbing her hand through his scrubby hair.

Ant allowed himself to cuddle his old friend for a moment just enjoying the moment of euphoria one gets when they see someone dear to them that has been absent for some time. 'Good to see you to Baz', said Ant.

His thick eyebrows knitted together as the tone of his voice changed, 'But what's with you and Priest insinuating I'm fat? I could probably still outrun you both'. 'Sure you could honey', responded Baz, patting his belly.

'Right, stuff it', said Ant. 'I start my health kick next week, I'm not copping this shit anymore.'

'Anyway Ant, enough about you. Through my powers of deduction, I take it this gentleman dressed in black in front of me is this Priest that you refer to?', said Baz.

Ant apologized as he had not realized they didn't know each other. The three sat there chatting for ten minutes before a familiar voice called from the front of the house, 'Well this must be the right place. If I am not mistaken that is the unmistakable ladylike voice of Baz', said a fit-looking bearded man with scrubby red hair.

Baz looked up at Ant and called, 'FOT, you little ripper'. Ant and Baz both raced to the door to let FOT in. As he walked in his infectious smile lightened the mood. The four of them were chatting enthusiastically about who might arrive next to be part of Lachie's dysfunctional crew. It seemed both FOT and Priest had found their calling in the civilian world and were doing well.

Baz was floating a little between running adventure training camps and trekking expeditions. She was enjoying the work but there wasn't much money in it so she desperately needed a payday.

FOT was the only one of them who was married with a family, so that, coupled with his steady employment as a GP, led the group to determine that he had the most successful transition to civilian life.

If FOT was in fact the most successful at making the transition, then the next to arrive was probably the one on the shakiest ground. Crazy Wayne's battered face appeared at the door. Sporting a split lip, a black eye and slight limp, Crazy looked like he had been in the wars.

'What friggin happened to you Wayne? Ant enquired. Crazy figured he might as well get it all out in the open and come clean. He told them about his encounter with the NZ girl that had left him battered, bruised, and covered in shit, to teach him a lesson for been a sexist pig. He told them in graphic detail about the incident. Ant was intrigued by the story, Priest was disgusted, FOT was gob-smacked and Baz was pissing herself laughing.

'Couldn't happen to a nicer guy!', she chortled.

Crazy went onto explain that incident got uglier as it turned out the house didn't belong to the Lisa girl he was with. Instead it was some innocent nurse living there that returned home from her busy shift to find Wayne chained to her bed with a painful erection and a big steamer on his chest.

That was it, all of them now joined Baz in a hearty laugh at Wayne's expense. Wayne went on to explain that the nurse hit him with her bag out of the shock of seeing a strange man in her bedroom and that's how he ended up with the black eye and split lip. 'God knows what she had in her bag, but I'm guessing by the damage it caused to my face it was a little more than lipstick and tampons', said Wayne.

Apparently after lashing out she calmed somewhat but still called the police. This kind of suited Wayne anyway as he felt as though he had been assaulted by the woman who tied him up, whipped him, tortured his old fella and shat on him.

The police informed Crazy Wayne that the woman he described was a repeat offender and took detailed statements. They let him off with a warning to be more careful with the people he went home with and slipped him a card for a rape guidance counselor that again sent Baz into hysterics.

Ant fixed some tea to calm everyone down after Wayne's story. Before long there was an unmistakable sound of a Porsche 911 engine being revved down the alleyway behind the house. Ant could hear the electric gates in the house next door activate.

Ant looked at the others, 'I take it His Majesty has returned from England'. There was another knock at the door. It was another large fella. The big man smiled at Ant and extended a massive mitt for Ant to shake. In a British accent, he boomed, 'Hi-yah Ant, I'm Si, an old acquaintance of Lachlan's. He and I just arrived back from the UK and he's just taking care of a few things next door before he pops in'.

Ant shook Si's massive hand and invited him in to take a seat. After introducing him to everyone he offered the Brit a cup of tea. The Brit responded with an extremely enthusiastic response akin to what you would expect from a teenage boy who had just been asked by little Mary rotten crotch if he would like to squeeze her boobs for the first time.

'Ha the British and their great love affair with tea', announced a posh voice from the balcony. 'Yes please Guv while you're up'.

Ant looked out onto the rear deck to see his old friend Lachlan. He could also see the step ladder spanning the gap between Lachlan's and his deck which had enabled the nimble man to appear at his rear door instead of the front.

The group all welcomed Lachie as he was the common thread for them all, other than Baz who had met Lachie through Ant. Once Lachie had said hello to everyone he walked over to Ant and gave him a hug. 'A long time no see Antonio', said Lachlan.

Ant smiled, 'Good to see you although I would have thought you'd be too jet-lagged to play trapeze artist across our back decks'. Lachie grinned at everyone and then looked back at Ant.

'Use it or lose it my good man', said Lachie as he patted Ant's slightly bulging stomach. 'Yes, use it or lose it!', he repeated for effect.

Ant snarled, 'Oh for fucks sake I'm starting back at the gym next week'. Lachie eyed everyone, 'That's good Ant, you will need to. In fact, you will all need to be in shape if you want in on this deal. This is it lady and men, the opportunity you have been waiting for. All the excitement of the military, except with more money. No one will be telling you what to do but, if you lack self-discipline or commitment, then you will be gone regardless of how much I love you.

Of course, I have picked a team of people who don't need to be told this. You are all extremely capable, tough and borderline psychotic, which will stand us all in good stead for when things don't go right, which invariably they won't', said Lachie.

'The plan never survives the first shot', mumbled Ant in an almost automated response whilst staring off into space.

'Exactly Ant', said Lachie, 'Although hopefully there won't be any shooting in this job mate. In fact, we won't even be armed. This is a privately funded international emergency response group, which will be called 'Global Angel'. We should expect to be called-out anywhere in the world at any time to respond to humanitarian response and disaster relief operations. You need to stay on 24-hours' notice-to-move whilst ever you are with Global Angel.

That means if you are off canyoning in the Blue Mountains you still need to be in contact so you can get your ass back to our base of operations within 24 hours from green-on go! For this inconvenience, you will all be placed on a retainer of $150k a year.

In the event of call-out you will receive a further 20k and then 10k a month until the operation is complete. Ant will be on a slightly different package as my deputy team leader. Is everyone cool with that?'.

The group exchanged glances amongst themselves and smirked their approval. For some of the group this was three times what they were used to earning. Wayne squinted at Lachie with a suspicious look, 'Hang on Lachie, you mean to tell me you are going to pay me 150k per annum for me to sit on my arse and wait for a storm that may never come?', asked Wayne.

Almost Wayne', said Lachie. 'You will have a lot of free time to yourself but there will be a requirement to train. You will follow the workout regime given to you by Baz given she is a qualified physical trainer and the fittest in this room. Ant, you need to shift some weight mate, there may be parachuting and roping work at some stage so you need to be able to easily lift your own bodyweight', said Lachie.

'Oh, for fuck's sake', protested Ant. 'I'm leaner than Si, why aren't you picking on him as well?', asked Ant.

'You're a sensitive little soul today aren't you Ant?', said Lachie. 'For your information, Si will be training hard as well, but remember you all have different roles. I have seen Si lift a car engine block with his bare hands, so he is never going to be light. Can you lift an engine block Ant?', responded Lachie.

Ant looked at the ground, a little red from embarrassment and mumbled an apology to Si. With the insubordinate outburst from Ant out of the way Lachie continued. Priest and FOT will of course continue their normal employment. After all, I don't want the orphans to starve and I don't want Doctor FOT to take a pay cut.

The rest of you will be required to do routine equipment servicing and any other random tasks Ant or I set for you. So yes, Wayne, other than the four odd days a month I require you to work, you are free to surf, sail, jump out of aircraft or in your case Wayne cruise the red-light district until I need you'. The group nodded their approval.

So, who's in?', asked Lachie. Priest got to his feet and grumbled, 'For the orphans', he toasted, raising his glass of water.

Baz screwed her face into a sneering smirk, 'Yeah why fucken not? I'm in Lachie, you fucken little ripper', she said.

Lachie looked at Crazy. 'Yeah alright Lachie I'm in, but I do currently live NZ and Fiji so the 24-hours will be to the wire', said Wayne.

Lachie responded, 'Yeah I know that Wayne but it's a good thing you are located in Fiji. There is a real chance that the natural disasters will occur within the South Pacific or South East Asia. Therefore, having you in Fiji and Priest in East Timor may serve us well in regards to setting up our forward operating base'.

FOT nodded his head, 'I'm in, this popping blisters and treating VD in otherwise healthy people is boring the shit out of me. I need some action before I give up on life and start driving a beige Camry whilst wearing a cardigan with elbow pads'.

Lachie turned his attention to Ant and said, 'Well Ant, I have already briefed Si in and he's on board, so that leaves you old China. Interested? Or are you too busy getting badly-drawn tattoos in Thailand?'

'You sure there won't be any shooting Lachie? I don't go for that caper anymore. I've had enough of war', said Ant.

'Oh Ant wash the sand out of your mangina. There won't be any shooting, we're there to help people, not dispatch them', said Lachie.

Baz started sniggering, 'Mangina, ha ha, let me know if you need to borrow a tampon Ant, sounds like it's that time of the month', she joked. The rest of the group cringed at Baz's crudeness.

Ant continued, 'Alright I'm in. But I know you lot well, except for Si, but you are all trouble. You're a bunch of nut-jobs with PTSD. If you guys start acting the goat and hurting people I'm out. But if there is a chance we can all earn some good coin, doing good and maybe save our souls in the process then I am in'.

'Couldn't have said it better myself', agreed Priest.

'I appreciate the support Priest, but you are one that I am most worried about', said Ant.

Priest shot Ant a menacing sneer.

The group sat there and chatted away until they decided it would be a good idea to bond over a few cold pints at the pub. Lachie even offered to pick up the tab as a business expense. The group strolled up the street to the Paddo Tavern to get their afternoon underway.

Ant offered to fetch the first round. Everybody fired their order at him. Ant eyed the group. 'You all realize that every one of you just ordered a different beer? Rather than me remembering seven different brands of low carb Nancy boy beer, you can all have a XXXX instead. You are in Queensland after all', said Ant.

He then looked at Wayne and sneered. 'Millers with lime, why don't you grow a pair Jessica?', Ant said as he stormed off towards the bar. Ant approached the young barmaid who was wearing the Paddo Tavern trademark cowboy hat and ordered three jugs of XXXX Bitter.

The barmaid offered to help Ant carry them to the table. Ant admired the frosty cold jug of liquid gold as he returned to the table. He was dying to tuck into the contents. When he returned the group greedily ripped into the jugs that only had a life expectancy of 15 minutes before the next round was ordered.

There were no protests about having to drink XXXX anymore. The beer was cold and delicious. It was the perfect accompaniment for long-lost friends catching up on a beautiful warm afternoon in Brisbane. The table they occupied gave them a view back over Brisbane as the sun started to set.

Lachie looked at Si and said, 'What did I tell you Si? Quite the view isn't it?'

'Stunning,' agreed Si. The big man sat there taking it all in. Si couldn't remember the last time he had been so happy. He had been a Staff Sergeant in the British Army before they made him redundant 9 months ago. He had been sitting in his little apartment looking out the window at the dreary London weather, thinking how lonely and bored he was since he had left the Army when Lachlan contacted him.

It didn't take much for Lachlan to convince Si he should pick up his life and move to Australia. Luckily Si had an Australian mother and company sponsorship that made the challenge of applying for a work visa post-30 years of age much easier.

Now here he was in Brisbane on a beautiful warm afternoon drinking beer with some of the most larrikin Aussies he had ever met. Whatever was around the corner on this new path he had chosen to tread was bound to be interesting.

As he sat there watching a Catholic priest chug a schooner of beer he thought to himself, 'Yes this could be the most interesting adventure I've had since Afghanistan'.

Down in Nerang on the Gold Coast another ex-military man was having a party of a different sort. The boss of the Syndicate criminal gang, an ex-mate of Priest's, was sitting in his office with a hot nude Russian hooker face down on his lap.

His nickname in the military had been Bossman when he had served as a corporal in an elite Army unit. Since getting kicked from the military he had turned to crime, steroids, coke, and hookers. Still it wasn't all bad, Bossman thought to himself looking down at Susan's perfectly-formed arse.

The beautiful Russian had moved to Australia a year ago, and started stripping. Unfortunately, she had developed a bit of a drug habit, which ate through her savings fairly quickly. She had turned to hooking to get some extra cash and that is when she met Bossman. She thought of him as some sort of a deranged tool but at the end of the day he gave her what she needed. Cash, an apartment, and a seemingly endless supply of high-quality drugs.

In fact, right now she had over a thousand dollars' worth of cocaine on her arse being neatly arranged in lines. Bossman took his rolled-up fifty dollar note and slammed one of the rails of coke off Susan's arse.

'Fuck yeah!', said Bossman with his watery eyes dancing around in his skull.

'When's my go?', protested Susan.

Bossman smiled, 'When you can reach it you can be my guest', he laughed.

'Bastard', said Susan getting angry at Bossman's mocking of her. She tensed her stomach muscles and farted. Bossman watched in horror as over a thousand dollars of coke was farted into his face.

'Cheeky bitch', he yelled, slapping Susan on the arse.

'Ow', said Susan laughing.

Just then Bossman's phone buzzed. Bossman tossed Susan off his lap onto the bed to answer the video call.

On the other end a well-dressed Japanese man named Takashi looked at the naked Australian crime boss. 'We have two boxes of the product you want. It will be available in three weeks and as discussed the price is 120k', said Takashi.

Good as gold, the job's on', said Bossman hanging up. 'Now', he said looking at the naked Susan snorting some more coke. 'It's time to celebrate', Bossman said, crawling down onto the bed next to her.

ANT LAY IN BED LOOKING AT THE CLOCK 6 am. 'Habit of a lifetime', he thought. After so many years of waking up at 6 am it wasn't possible for him to sleep much past it.

He heard some footsteps walking down the hallway towards his room. Must be Baz as he had offered for her to crash at his place for a few weeks while they pulled the Global Angel team together.

All he had to do today was shop for equipment and a Brisbane warehouse. Easy day he thought as he stretched out, grinning thinking of how great it would be to be earning money again.

His vision of utopia was interrupted by a bashing on his door, 'I'm coming in so drop your cock and put on your socks', said Baz before barging through the door.

Ant looked up to see a well-awake Baz standing in front of him in her lycra training gear.

'Piss off Baz', Ant said throwing a pillow at her.

She ducked the pillow and tossed a small box at him that he caught. 'What's this Baz? Did I forget our anniversary again?', Ant joked.

Baz looked at him grinning, 'Ant, you should be so lucky. Now in answer to your question my little pudding pie, inside that box is a fitness tracker.

We are going to use it to help us keep your heart rate over 120 beats per minute for as much of the day as possible. Now tubs, get changed and meet me downstairs in ten minutes with that tracker on your wrist.

Ten minutes later Ant slummocked down the stairs to the kitchen where Baz was sipping some water while waiting for him. She had one foot up on a stool while leaning forward on the bench reading her phone. In a box was half the contents of Ant's fridge and pantry.

'What's going on?', Ant protested pointing at the box full of food.

Baz looked up at him with a disappointed look on her face. She walked over to the box and started pulling things out of the box and slamming them on the bench, 'Coca Cola, chips, biscuits, pies, jam and muesli bars? Are you fucking kidding Ant? Are you hoping to die of diabetes or malnutrition?', she asked.

Ant stood there looking like little boy lost being berated by the principle. 'Yes, alright Baz, you've made your point, but what's wrong with the muesli bars?', he asked naively.

Baz picked up one of the packets and held it to his face pointing at the little panel on the back of the packet, 'Ant this muesli bar is a hidden fat bomb. It has more sugar in it than those biscuits. It is a clever ploy by the food companies to keep even those trying to do the right thing addicted to sugar. Now let's go outside and I'll demonstrate to you how long it takes to burn off the calories in that bar'.

Ant reluctantly followed Baz to the door. He had an impending feeling of doom and was regretting offering Baz a place to stay in Brisbane. He thought it would be fun to have a friend stay for a while, but it looked like it was going to be anything but fun.

Once outside Baz set up Ant's fitness tracker to monitor his workout and then said, 'Let's go', as she started jogging off. Three kilometers on Ant was beginning to wonder if she was lost. They descended the Story Bridge steps to the park below. Once in the park Baz stopped running and looked back at Ant who was still catching up, 'Come on Ant I thought you could out run me?'

Ant pulled up next to her, panting. He and Baz inspected the tracker that read 145 bpm. 'A bit high, for losing weight. We might stop for a minute and let your heart rate settle before heading back. Now drop and give me fifty pushups my little chip muncher', said Baz.

Ant was a getting a little annoyed at the taunts and having his day hijacked, 'Hey Baz how about we cut the fat jokes? I'm kinda getting pissed off with your shit'.

Baz's demeanor changed as she reverted back to the recruit trainer she had once been in the Services, 'Oh Ant, that is truly fucking pathetic. You know that I have largely found men to be a disappointment in my life. The only trait they have that I like is their ability to be resilient and not over-analyze things. Now here you go sooking. You have over-analyzed the situation and seem to have come to the misconception that you have a choice and that I am taking some perverse pleasure in spending my free time running your ample backside around Brisbane.

Now you have been kind enough to let me stay at your place and you have been a great friend to me over the years so this is me paying you back. We are going to get that 10 kg off you that you have stacked on since you left the Army. We are going to finish this exercise session and then we are going to restock your fridge with healthy food. I am going to teach you how to look after yourself. I am doing this all for you Ant, because you are like family to me and I love you.

Now I don't want any thanks. All I want is for you to stop fucking whingeing and to drop and give me seventy pushups', Baz demanded, pointing at the ground.

Ant gave a defeated look and got on the ground and started the exercise. 'I thought you said fifty', Ant said.

Baz smiled. 'Right you are Ant, better make it eighty. See how this works with us', said Baz in a caring yet condescending tone.

'Yeh I think I'm starting to get it', said Ant still cracking out the pushups. 'That's good to hear Ant, but there is one thing I should confess. I am taking a perverse pleasure in this, now keep going Mr Pushups', she said with a smirk on her face.

It was 11 am and Baz had decided they should shop to restock Ant's fridge. She stood with Ant at the door of the supermarket. 'Now Ant, this is a good place to stand. See how at one end of the shop you can see fruit and veg and at the other end we can see meat? That's good as that's all we need. There is absolutely no need to go into those middle aisles', Baz said.

'What about tomato sauce?' asked Ant. 'Packed full of sugar. I'll show you how to make your own. Now come on', she said, grabbing a trolley.

Once home Ant surveyed the bench full of greenery and lean meats as Baz stuffed them into his fridge. 'What the fuck is kale?', he asked eyeing the leafy vegetable with suspicion.

'Oh Ant, it will be everywhere in your diet over the next few weeks', said Baz gabbing it off him and stuffing it in the fridge.

Ant decided to get to work. He grabbed the Global Angel equipment list that he and Baz had drafted and began shopping online. Between his, Baz's, FOT's and Si's logistics experience they had been able to compose a comprehensive list of equipment and supplies to deal with any contingency.

Crazy was taking care of the communications gear through his contacts. Five hours later Ant was satisfied he could get his hands on most of what he needed. He assembled a quotation for the equipment and stores that he sent to Lachlan so he could organize the funds. Tomorrow's job would be to find somewhere to store it all.

He leaned back in his chair and yawned. He looked at his watch, 7 pm, and he was already buggered from the day's activity. Baz was right, he had let himself get out of shape he thought, as he heard footsteps coming down the stairs to his study. 'How are you going with it all?' she asked as she walked in the room. 'Good better than expected', said Ant.

'Good work. Now come on Mr Pushups, your dinner is ready', said Baz.

Ant sat down at the dining table and looked at the bowl of green stuff in front of him, 'What's this?'

'That Ant is everything a shrinking boy needs to be healthy and happy. It's lentils, your beloved kale, garlic, spices and some lean protein', said Baz.

Ant took a spoonful and was pleasantly surprised by the taste. He gulped the food down and then helped Baz clean up. He sat on the couch staring at the TV when Baz walked up with a beverage.

'Tea?', Ant enquired.

'Green tea to be exact, it's good for you', said Baz handing Ant the cup.

Ant might have enjoyed the lentils and kale but the same couldn't be said for the tea. At Baz's insistence, he gulped some of it down then announced he was going to bed.

'Good work Ant, get an early night. We are back into it 6 am tomorrow.'

True to her word Baz was waiting for Ant in the kitchen the next morning.

'Here drink this', Baz said thrusting a glass of water into Ant's hands. 'You need to hydrate before we get started. Ant, do you remember how you felt three kilometres into that run yesterday?', she asked.

Ant looked at her with a concerned look on his face, 'Yeah I remember', he said. 'That's how far you had to run to burn off the calories in that muesli bar," said Baz. She angled around her computer that had Ant's workout profile from yesterday displayed on the screen. She explained to Ant how to read the programme.

Ant was shocked at how bad for him the food was he had been eating. Then again, he wasn't sure how good Baz's food was for him either. He felt bloated and was farting like a brewery worker all morning.

At 6 am Ant and Baz were out the door jogging up towards Paddington. A kilometre up the street they arrived out the front of a gym. Ant looked at Baz, 'What now?', he asked.

'What now, I'll tell you what now. We head in there and get you signed up. Then we work you until you have burnt off three beer's worth of calories, so next time you go to stick one in your gob you'll think about how much effort it will take to burn one off', said Baz patting Ant's belly.

Once inside Ant had to admit the Fit 'n Fast gym was the nicest he had ever seen. It was stacked full of equipment and had views out over the city on one side and the Paddo Pub on the other.

'That's a bit cruel isn't Baz? I gotta sweat my arse off while I watch people drink beer?', protested Ant.

'Yeah I s'pose it is Ant, I tell you what, why don't you give fifty pushups to take your mind off it', said Baz watching for any further protest, but there wasn't any as Ant did what he was instructed.

The girl behind the counter smiled at Baz in amazement, 'Wish I could control my boyfriend like that', she said.

'Darling, training men is all about consistency and offering the option of a sugar cube or the rolled-up newspaper. Although in my case he just gets the rolled-up newspaper', chuckled Baz.

Baz put Ant through his paces. She made him do a thirty-minute weights session without rest breaks. She then had him doing sit-ups and squats. He then jumped rope and finished with a twenty-minute boxing session. By the end of it, Ant thought he was going to chuck. He stood hunched over gasping for air as Baz examined the fitness app on her phone.

'Okay Ant, well done. That was a tough session and that was three beers you just worked off. Now let's get you home for some kale, sweet potato and tuna', said Baz.

Once Ant had showered and regained his composure, he set about the task of finding Global Angel a home. Eagle Farm seemed like the obvious choice. Just outside of the CBD, the industrial precinct was within minutes of the airport and sea terminals. This would suit the internationally deployable nature of Global Angel.

Before long, Ant had short-listed a few warehouses and booked in with the estate agents to inspect them the next day. Baz called out dinner was ready so Ant headed upstairs. 'What are we having, not kale again I hope?', asked Ant.

'Relax, we are having grilled salmon and bok choy', said Baz.

'What in all that's holy is bok choy?', complained Ant.

'It's good for you Ant, that's what it is. Now would you like a beer with dinner? We'll just do a little extra exercise tomorrow to work it off', said Baz holding a beer up with a cheeky grin. Ant shook his head vigorously, signifying a definite no.

'Okay fair enough Ant, looks like that's two less kilometres you need to run tomorrow. But I think I shall have one given I have such tight buns and can get away with it', said Baz slapping herself on the arse to prove a point. She gulped down a third of the beer and looked at Ant with a strange look on her face. She then let rip with a burp that the Queensland State of Origin team at an after match piss up would have been hard pressed to beat.

Three weeks into the Global Angel preparation and the progress of the team had astounded Lachlan. He stood in their warehouse looking at the array of stocked shelves and light equipment. 'Ant, my man, you have done a fantastic job. How far are we off being operational?'.

Ant shrugged, 'We are now. The last things I'm waiting on are some parachutes and some beach matting', said Ant, staring at his electronic tablet.

Lachlan nodded with a satisfied look. 'How vital is the matting? And I thought we already had the parachutes?', enquired Lachie. Ant looked up at Lachie with a look that he was giving deep consideration to what he had just been asked.

'Well Lachlan, I hate to say it but it depends. If we have access to a sea and airport at our destination then it isn't needed at all, but if the existing infrastructure has been damaged then it is vital. In the event of no wharf being available then the beach matting allows us to easily drive our wheeled vehicles across the sand. Yes, we have our personnel parachutes but I have ordered some tandem gear and some cargo chutes. This will enable us to parachute in personnel not trained to jump and airdrop our stores and equipment.'

Lachie nodded, agreeing with Ant that such capability was important in case the airfield had been rendered inoperable from a disaster. Ant went on to say most of the team was qualified to parachute. Baz and Si had no qualification but had been booked in for training, starting in two weeks' time.

Ant still thought the tandem equipment might be a good idea anyway as you never knew what other specialists they might recruit in the future.

Lachlan patted Ant on the shoulder, 'Great work mate. I'll see you back at home for drinks at Kettle & Tin'.

Ant said he would see him then and started locking up the warehouse.

Ant opened the Ducati's throttle so he could listen to the exhaust note as he rode through the underpass. 'Drinks at Kettle & Tin', he thought as he rounded onto Heussler Terrace near Lang Park Stadium.

He hadn't had a beer in three weeks. I bet Baz won't let me have one tonight either. Well she will, but she would make me run it off tomorrow. What a ball-buster. Still my pants are getting loose and I can't deny I feel a lot fitter even after three weeks. I am even enjoying the fresh food she makes me eat. My guts have settled down and adjusted to digesting the fibre rich green vegetables that Baz had told him had something to do with his gut bacteria healing.

Ant smiled under his helmet, all in all things were going well. Without warning, there was a big flash which short-circuited Ant's brain. The dusts of Afghanistan swirled in front of his eyes as the flashes from the 107mm enemy rockets exploded in front of him. His Ducati mounted the gutter and the sand and rockets disappeared to reveal the reality that he was crashing his motorcycle.

He hit the brakes and jerked on the bars to steer around a tree. He succeeded in bring the bike to a stop but had lost his balance in the meantime. The beautiful bike toppled on the ground. Ant stood there shocked, looking at his bike on the ground wondering what had triggered the memory of explosions in his mind. Suddenly there was another dazzling flash and then another.

Ant spun around to see the cause of the distracting light. Behind him, parked on the footpath, was a speed camera happily snapping drivers for doing 55 km/h in a 50 zone. 'Fuckers!', thought Ant, 'They could have killed me.'

As Ant stood there glaring at the van, its window opened and a head poked out. 'Are you ok?', the head asked poking out of the blacked-out van.

Ant sneered, 'I'm not hurt but that flash shocked me and caused me to crash', he said.

The head responded with, 'Maybe you should pay more attention and get better at riding that piece of shit'. Ant was furious, it had nothing to do with his riding. The unexpected flash had somehow triggered a flash back to one of the many times he had been rocketed.

He picked up his beloved Ducati to see two big scratches in the glossy red paintwork. Ant started the bike, turned, and flipped off the head, who was now yelling something about having him charged for neg riding.

Ant arrived home to find Baz doing some yoga in the living room. Ant told Baz they were meeting up at the bar in an hour. She jumped up from the ground announcing that she had finished her yoga and was looking forward to going out.

Ant looked dejected, scuffing his foot on the floor bringing up what a shame it would be that he wouldn't be able to join in with a having a drink due to his strict training regime.

Baz smirked at Ant's obvious attempt at manipulation. 'Honestly Ant, you look so sad, how could I say no? I've been checking your workout stats today. Do you know you have a resting heart rate of 57 bpm and you have shed 3.5 kg in the last three weeks?

Do you know what this means? You are eight weeks away from being the Ant that all of us women lust after. I am so proud of your progress. So proud, I'm going to let you have one drink for free. Every one after that is a 2 kilometre run penalty tomorrow.'

Ant was so elated he let out a little woohoo.

An hour later he and Baz, Lachie and Si, were headed up to the bar cum café which reminded Lachie of the bars you found in places like Italy and France.

As they walked in, Ant commented on the crowd of young, trendy Brisbanites that frequented this place. Ant wasn't sure he belonged in there with the beautiful people.

Lachie gabbed Baz by the arm and announced that they did and strode in up to the bar. Before long, Crazy turned up at the bar, flashing his infectious smile.

The friendly bar staff suggested to Lachlan that on a hot evening the best drink to have was 'the Cyclone' which consisted of white rum, lemon juice and a slash of Bundaberg ginger beer.

Lachie agreed that sounded great and ordered a round. Once they had their drinks the group found a corner table and clinked their glasses in a ritual toast before they sipped the refreshing beverage.

Lachie eyed Ant, 'Baz, what have you done to our cuddly little Ant? He's starting to look lean and mean again'.

'Healthy living luvy, that's all it is. Give me three more weeks and he'll be ready for the parachute regiment again', she said with a grin.

'What? You aren't staying at my house for three more weeks', protested Ant. The group of friends laughed. They and Ant all agreed that regardless if he was enjoying it or not, Baz was good for him and probably should stay for a few more weeks to make sure the diet and exercise stuck.

The truth was that Ant enjoyed having all his mates back in Brisbane. Since they had been back his drinking had reduced and his dreams had also tapered off. He no longer felt lonely. Instead he felt useful, needed, and maybe even loved?

An hour passed and Crazy was on his fourth rum. Ant was still cradling his first so as to reduce the physical punishment he would go through tomorrow. Crazy had asked Ant how things were going and Ant let slip about the incident with the speed camera. 'Pricks!', announced Crazy. Then the look on Crazy's face changed to pure menace. 'I got an idea everyone. Tomorrow I need everyone, three radios and two screwdrivers. I got a plan to teach these pricks a lesson.

At 2:30 pm the four friends met Crazy at the top of Heussler Terrace. Crazy was crouched in front of his Nissan Skyline removing the number plate. He handed a radio to Si and one to Lachie. 'Si you stay here, and when I tell you, report to me every time you see a pedestrian, pushbike rider or vehicle go past you. Lachie, you take this radio and jog down to the roundabout and do the same for traffic going the other way. Ant, this screwdriver is for you. Baz, you bring along your beautiful sparkling personality.'

Ten minutes later Baz strutted up to the blacked-out van on the footpath. The little sign told of its purpose for being there. As she walked up to the van a big flash went off. Baz tapped on the blacked-out window and before long a chinless head popped out. 'Can I help you, young lady?'.

Baz smiled twirling her hair, 'Were you taking my photo?', she asked in a coy, playful tone.

The Head smiled, 'Oh I wish but no ma'am, I am photographing speeding offenders', he said. Baz leant forward, 'Wow that sounds like an important job stopping law breakers', she said, oozing femininity.

Crazy looked over at Ant as he crouched down in front of the vehicle. Ant was still shaking his head at Baz's overt act of seduction. As the first screwdriver was about to attack the van's plates Baz began to make sounds of arousal over Head's explanation that even someone doing 5 km over the limit was a potential killer.

Within minutes, Crazy and Ant were back in the Skyline. 'Are we clear?', Ant asked into the radio. 'All clear', said Lachie. 'No one on the road', barked Si. 'Hit it!', said Ant to Crazy. Crazy gassed the Skyline that shot up to 85 kph in the 50 zone.

As they got close to the van Ant dropped his pants and pressed his furry arse against the windscreen. The camera and flash initiated as the Skyline screamed past. 'Got another offender', said the Head to Baz in the deepest authoritarian voice he could muster.

Baz bounced up and down clapping, 'Yeah', she cried as her boobs bounced up and down in front of the hypnotized head. The Skyline lined itself up for another pass.

This time as it flashed passed the camera got a photo of Ant's ample junk. After ten minutes Baz saw Ant and Crazy crouched down at the front and rear of the van again.

Once they nodded to her and walked off back up the street Baz gave the Head a phone number and told him to call her sometime. She strutted off up the street with his eyes still firmly planted on her backside.

A week later the analyst would be reviewing their video files to see how a speed camera van could be photographed by itself doing six high-speed passes down Heussler Terrace. The photos would reveal that a Nissan Skyline with the speed van's number plates was the culprit.

When the photo was enlarged to try and get the offender's face they would see a driver wearing a Pauline Hanson mask and an unknown man chucking a brown eye.

The Head would later be called in to give a 'Please explain', but the best he would be able to give is a description of Baz's boobs and the fact that the number she gave him was actually the number for an erectile dysfunction clinic.

Eventually a department insider that didn't like the Head leaked the event to the media resulting in renewed debate on the usefulness of speed vans. Most laughed their arses off at the unknown pranksters but some were outraged at their disregard for public safety.

An investigation to try and track down the Skyline was launched but a coincidental hack into the department's database destroyed any evidence they had been able to pull together. Before long the police figured they had bigger fish to fry and the Head was sent back for refresher training after receiving a misconduct reprimand.

It was four weeks into Ant's workout regime. He and Baz were standing on the beach in the early morning still puffing from their run. 'Not bad Ant, I thought you had me there for a moment', said Baz still panting.

'Maybe next week Baz', replied Ant between gasping for air. Ant had now shed 4.5 kg, but had also increased his muscle mass in the process. He looked younger and felt much better. He only ate fresh, unprocessed food.

Baz promised Ant a trip to the Rosalie Gourmet Market as a reward for his hard work. 'Home-made pizzas tonight', she announced. Ant loved the market and was well known by the friendly staff there.

A visit there to peruse their extensive selection of cold cuts, olives and fresh fruit and veg was like a visit to Italy. 'Can't wait Baz, what about a swim first?' 'Race you', said Baz sprinting off into the surf.

Baz and Ant had just finished cooking two mouth-watering healthy pizzas when there was a knock at the door. Ant walked open to answer it when Lachlan and Si burst in.

Lachie placed his laptop on Ant's dining table. 'This is it Ant! Our first mission son', Lachie said excitedly. The four Global Angel team members gathered around the computer as the video link was established. A well-dressed man appeared on the screen.

'Prescott', acknowledged Lachie.

'Oh Lachlan, how good to see you. Please hold for Lord Erskin-Stamper.'

Before long Lord Erskin-Stamper sat down in front of the screen. 'Hello Lachlan. I see I have interrupted your tea time.' Lachlan turned around to see Baz stuffing pizza down her head.

Lachlan waved at her to get out of video shot. Baz snarled at Lachlan and moved away. 'Sorry sir, please go on', said Lachlan.

Lord Erskin-Stamper cleared his throat and continued, 'In my youth I visited a beautiful Island called Niue. I have fond memories of it and how charming the 2000 natives that lived on the island were. I have been using the island as an air and seaport since then for my other business interests. This has had the added benefit of injecting money into the community and providing them with a source of employment. Their only other source of income is a very modest tourist industry which revolves around fishing, scuba diving and a crazy local artist who has a world-wide cult following.

Twelve hours ago, a devastating cyclone hit the Island. Indications are that it will take a concerted engineering effort to clear the port. The Aussies are sending a Naval ship to fix the port and aid the Island's recovery but that is 12 days from arrival. The airfield is blocked so an airborne humanitarian assistance team from the Aussie and NZ Defence Force can't land until it's clear.

Now Lachlan, this is where you come in. We need a team to parachute in as no helicopter has the range to reach the island. They will need a dozer of some sort to clear the airfield. I'm not sure how you will get it there but that is why I am talking to you. I have hired an old SAFAIR C130 Hercules Aircraft, which arrives in Brisbane tomorrow.

Lachlan, I need your team to clear the airfield, treat the injured and prevent secondary effects such as disease outbreaks resulting from damaged sanitation infrastructure', said Lord Erskin-Stamper.

Lachlan was visibly excited, 'Don't worry boss, Global Angel is GO!' 'Yes, quite Lachlan, don't screw it up. Your actions reflect on me now', said Lord Erskin-Stamper as the screen went blank.

The Job Designated Day Zero

IT HAD BEEN A LONG FLIGHT in the commercially owned South African C130 but the Global Angel team inside of it was now coming to life as they had been given the thirty-minute call. They would soon be over the drop zone. The loadmaster was pouring coffee to make sure the team they had been contracted to deliver was awake.

There could be no delays. As it was the aircraft would be running on fumes by the time it got to Samoa to refuel upon completion of the airdrop. The loadmaster knew that if this disheveled-looking bunch of misfits faffed around then it would cost valuable minutes of fuel consumption. They needed to be alert and ready to go so they would be out the door as soon as the aircraft arrived over the closed Niue airfield.

He figured the group to be mercenaries of some sort, but then again, he would think that given the look of them and that they were about to parachute out of the aircraft at night. Sane people don't do that kind of shit. He didn't ask anything about their mission, as he and his crew didn't want to know. They took the job because they were paid big money into the aircrew's offshore business account and that's all he needed to know.

Ant took a big swig of the lukewarm coffee. It tasted like acid and prompted a look of utter distain to be returned to the loadmaster. 'An

Aussie of Italian decent can't drink this instant shit', he said tossing it into the aircraft's rubbish bag.

Ant took a deep breath and looked out the porthole shaped window. He could see nothing but black. Ant then turned and gazed around the C130. It was a fairly standard fit-out for this sort of 'military spec' aircraft. The C130 Hercules is the workhorse of many a military. The reliable medium lift aircraft can carry up to twenty tonnes of payload.

On this mission, it was only carrying half that, resulting in the aircraft being able to extend its range.

The interior of a C130 is anything but plush. It is a sparse, robust, and functional solution. The fittings include collapsible seats made of nylon webbing and anchors in the exposed aluminum floor to attach the hooks of the load straps.

No unnecessary aesthetically-pleasing cladding on the walls and roof was present. Instead, the inner workings of the fuselage are displayed, seemingly as a deliberate mess of cables, insulation, tubes, and pipes that spew cool white vapor into the cabin.

The aircraft's fumes and his nervous energy began to make him feel nauseous. It was a familiar feeling deep in the pit of his stomach that he felt every time he thought he might be about to die. He'd experienced it when undertaking activities such as parachuting, patrolling in warzones and racing his motorcycle. The early morning and the fumes added to the feeling so he decided to take his mind off it and get busy.

He inspected the cargo straps on the loads that had held them firmly in place for the last four hours. He removed some of the straps to prepare the load for quick exit and did a final check on its parachutes. Not a bad job rigging these loads he thought to himself as he climbed around the stores bundles, the medium-sized dozer and two John Deere Gator TUVs.

When he had finished his checks, he activated the Cyalume sticks attached to the loads so they would be able to see the loads on the ground in the dark and avoid them. Landing on these loads at 7 meters per second could shatter an ankle or worse. The Cyalume gave an eerie green glow in the dimly-lit aircraft.

The other members of the team had started to kit-up. Each had a blue Cyalume stick attached to them as well as a voice-activated earpiece that would allow them to communicate once on the ground. All except for Si and Baz were affixing their parachutes.

Baz and Si both stood there in a harness with a look of abject terror on their faces. Neither of them had served in an airborne unit, nor qualified on commercial parachuting courses, so they were to be strapped to someone that could.

Crazy had volunteered to parachute with Baz, an offer which she declined—she claimed she was disgusted by the thought that if they did plow in, the last thing to go through her would be Wayne!

Lachie told Baz she could jump with him. Crazy would pair up with Si instead.

The aircraft loadmaster peered out the window and tapped his intercom. A loud disconcerting noise of hydraulics started to whine followed by the sound of buffeting as the ramp door of the aircraft opened. The cold night air rushed in sending a menacing chill through every member of the team.

'Five minutes!', screamed the loadmaster over the cacophony of beastly sounds. Ant and FOT rushed around removing the last of the straps on the loads and then stood back with the rest of the group.

The aircraft slowed noticeably as the pilots flew low and slow over the drop zone that had been crudely marked by four sets of car headlights down below in the dark. At the western end of the DZ a battery-operated strobe marked the target for the pilots. They would try to drop the loads as close as possible to it.

The aircraft banked into a steep g-force pulling turn. It was at this point that Baz vomited, induced by a combination of sheer terror and motion sickness. Lachie was glad she was strapped to the front of him rather than the back.

Wayne who was standing directly in front of her was not so happy. Priest glanced at Ant with his usually piercing blue eyes softened with fear. Ant leaned across and yelled in his ears, 'Are you all right Priest?'

'I'm shitting myself Ant. It's been 10 years since I've done this'.

Ant screwed up his face as his natural leadership qualities kicked in to allow him to focus on others instead of wasting energy on his own fears.

'Priest, you never forget how to do this. It's just like falling off a bike except at 5000 feet. Plus, you are in good with the big fella should something go wrong. Most of the others are going to Hell if they mess up. So relax and enjoy the rush'.

Priest smiled in appreciation of Ant's efforts to calm him and responded, 'Thing is Ant if any of these lost sheep spud in, then I can perform their last rights which may just win their way into heaven. Who does that for me if I bounce?'

'You won't bounce Priest. There is just no way you would give me that satisfaction you big boof-headed prick', said Ant.

At that Priest started to laugh. Ant had succeeded in alleviating his fear-induced tension. God bless that rude little chubby bastard Priest thought to himself.

The aircraft straightened and the loadmaster nodded at the team moments before a green light came on followed by a loud clunk as the load platform couplings sprung free, allowing gravity and the drag chute to pull the loads from the inclined aircraft. Ant and the loadmaster moved to the large rear window to inspect the chutes blossoming open in the moonlight. 'Five minutes!', the loadmaster shouted as the aircraft banked into a steep climb to gain some more height before the human cargo could be dispatched. Lachlan shuffled to the front of the group with Baz.

'One minute', the loadmaster called.

'What the fuck?', Baz protested. 'Are we fucking going first? I'm not fucking ready!', she howled.

'You don't need to be', Lachie yelled back at her just prior to the load master calling, 'Green On go!'

At this call Lachie dived out of the aircraft with the somewhat limp Baz strapped to his front. A second later Wayne and Si were out the door. It was then a rush as FOT, Priest and Ant piled out together throwing themselves into a hard-arch body position to gain control of their fall.

FOT who was probably the most proficient of the lot flipped himself onto his back so he could watch the aircraft lights disappear in the night sky. Ant inspected the stabilization chutes of the two tandem jumpers as he screamed past them in a dive to find some clear air.

Ant was plummeting towards the dimly-lit airfield at terminal velocity. His altimeter flashed at the preset 2000 feet. Time to pull out the pilot chute that would fill with air and hopefully drag out the main canopy. He tossed the pilot chute and an almost immediate jolt shot through his body as his rate of descent slowed by 100kph.

He looked up and inspected the canopy to ensure all was as it should be. Satisfied that he was hanging from a functioning piece of nylon, he started to search around him for any other jumpers so he could avoid a collision. No one was in his immediate vicinity that he could see. He could just make out two blue Cyalumes in the distance.

How far away he couldn't exactly tell, but they were far enough that he felt safe for now. He looked at the DZ, which at 1300 feet was still well lit in the moonlight. He lined up on one of the TUVs that he was planning to spiral down onto.

As he got closer to the ground the moon illumination disappeared due to the reducing angle of light reflection from the ground giving the sensation that the DZ was getting darker the closer he got to it. It was now that he could spot the green Cyalumes of the loads that had already landed.

He could also clearly see the ground illuminated by the vehicles and that is what he aimed for. He was the first jumper to arrive at the ground. He flared his parachute, which washed off his forward speed, and hit the ground running.

Once his feet contacted the ground he kept his forward momentum going towards one of the vehicles to clear the DZ for the next parachutist.

Ant took a deep breath to slow his pulse rate down to a more normal pace. Night parachuting does tend to elevate your anxiety and adrenalin levels he thought to himself as he removed a scrunch bag from his leg pocket and begun stuffing the parachute into it.

Ant could now hear a female cry of exhilaration as Lachie skillfully glided himself and Baz in for a soft, almost elegant landing.

Ant had to admire the man's parachuting prowess as a landing like that took serious skill. Not so soft was the landing of Si and Crazy who arrived with a thud, followed by a booming British voice announcing his arrival with, 'Oh fooking hell bruv'.

Priest and FOT arrived next stacked beautifully as if they had been rehearsing the landing for some time. As they landed an excited cheer came from the darkness. It was only then that Ant and the others realised they weren't alone.

'Have you all landed?', an excited unfamiliar female voice asked in English.

'Yeah!', responded Lachie.

'Great', said the female voice, then breaking into a foreign language that triggered around two hundred flashlights being turned on. A lady in her early 50s with dark hair strutted over to Lachie and Ant with her hand extended.

'Well hello you mad bastards', she announced. 'That was one of the coolest things I have ever seen', the woman said.

A man of islander appearance standing next to her added, 'Yeah that was some real James Bond stuff'.

Lachlan stroked his hair back into place and then walked over to the man and the lady. He then extended his hand to the lady and introduced himself,

'Hello, my name is Lachlan, I guess you could say I'm the leader of this motley crew. We are all members of the Global Angel Group and our primary mission is to reopen your airport and prevent disease outbreak'.

The dark-haired woman stepped back and motioned to the man next to her who leant forward to shake Lachie's hand.

While Lachlan exchanged a hand shake with the islander the woman introduced the man to Lachie as the Premier of Niue. Lachlan smiled and stated what a pleasure it was to meet him.

The Premier thanked Lachlan for coming to help. At this the lady leant forward and introduced herself as the New Zealand Ambassador to Niue.

The Premier offered to meet with Lachie tomorrow in the Government Chambers so he could brief him on the situation. Lachlan accepted the offer and asked about the injured that he understood to number around twenty.

The Premier's tone tightened, 'Yes there are twenty-two people badly injured and two are dead. We are keeping the injured in the community centre just across the airfield since the hospital had been destroyed by the cyclone. They are being treated by Niue's nurse who has not slept since the disaster'.

'Right then', said Lachlan, 'How about we start there? I have a doctor and a priest with me who despite their rough-looking appearances are fantastic at healing and dealing with trauma.

Are you comfortable with them helping out your nurse?', asked Lachlan.

The Premier and Ambassador both agreed that would be fantastic.

With his permission to start Lachie begged his leave and proceeded to round-up his team. The other members of Global Angel were already attending to the loads, freeing them from their parachutes, cords, and platforms.

Lachlan tapped his earpiece, 'Team this is Lachlan, what is the situation?'

Ant was first to respond over the network, 'We're all ok. We have the Gators freed from the platform and are in the process of working on the dozer.

We will be all done in twenty-minutes and ready to establish camp', said Ant.

'Roger that Ant, good work team', responded Lachie before continuing. 'FOT, Priest, are you guys there?' FOT and Priest both responded their acknowledgement to the boss.

Lachlan continued his orders over the radio network, 'I need you two to jump in one of the Gators and head northeast for three hundred meters with the medical kits and some water.

There is a lone nurse over there out on her feet trying to look after twenty-two badly-injured locals. Let me know what the facilities are like. If they are not in good order let me know and we will set-up our field medical facility as a priority.

Did you copy my last?'

'Priest and I are on it boss', responded FOT enthusiastically at the thought of doing something more exciting than setting up camp.

Lachlan worked with Ant and the others to help set-up. Some of the crowd offered their help moving the stores to the side of the airfield where they would set up camp not far from the community centre. The additional assistance made light work of the task at hand and the camp was half set-up when FOT radioed in and said the facilities weren't too bad but they needed a scrub as mud and debris had entered the building during the cyclone.

With the multiple open wounds his patients had, he was worried about infection. Baz and Ant were busy setting up tents and stretchers, and Crazy was establishing their satellite communications, so that left him and Si.

'Sorry Si, it looks like you and I are on clean-up duty until the others are free', said Lachlan.

'Not a problem Sir, I am all over it like a seagull on a chip', responded the big Brit. As it turned out, two minutes into the cleaning job they were set upon by locals who insisted they should help.

With the extra helpers the place was scrubbed to within an inch of its life before the hour was up. Halfway through the clean-up Baz fired up a generator with some field lights that illuminated the community centre in lieu of the kerosene lamps the nurse had been working under.

The Niue nurse stopped working and looked around. She could see the building had been transformed in an hour from a ramshackle community centre into a hygienic health facility.

She now had a qualified Australian doctor with her to help her make treatment decisions. The pressure was now off her and her beleaguered, unqualified helpers.

She had done it, holding out on her own for some 40 hours since the event that killed and injured her people. The big redheaded doctor and his terrifying-looking priest were treating the injured in a calm professional manner and some of the injured were even laughing as the priest momentarily took a break from treating a woman to tease her son and daughter, who were trying to get the attention of the big scary looking white man by tugging on his shirt.

She beamed a tired smile at FOT and thanked him. As she did the pent-up emotion from being the strong one in the face of adversity caught up with her and she started to sob.

'It's okay darling', said FOT in a rare moment of compassion. 'You've done a great job. Why don't you get your head down for six hours and I'll see you in the morning.'

The nurse reluctantly agreed. She was a spent unit and she knew it. The problem with being over-tired is you tend to make mistakes. She once again thanked the doctor and then left for some well-earned rest.

By daybreak the camp was established and the patients had received a round of treatment, which included redressing wounds and meds to manage the pain and fight off any potential infection.

Lachlan called a meeting at 0700 hours to ensure everyone had a common understanding of the situation and to plan their duties and sleep rosters. By the looks of the situation they might be there for at least a week so he needed a rotation system to enable his team to continue for the full duration.

Any less than four hours' sleep in a 24-hour period and his team's performance would start to degrade by day three.

Sitting in a tent they had erected the night before that now served as their communications centre and meeting room, Lachie eyed his team carefully. They had worked like Trojans throughout the night without prompting. They had been on the go now for twenty-six hours and they still looked to be brimming with energy.

'Seasoned professionals', he thought to himself. 'They may struggle fitting into society's daily grind but they are absolutely perfect for this shit. Virtually none them can function happily in a routine-based environment. In fact, they almost all would have suffered from ADHD in their younger years but would not have been diagnosed back in the 1980s. They just would have been deemed underachievers or problem children. But in a chaotic environment with no structure, routine or guarantee of safety, their creative and adventurous nature comes to the fore. Their eyes were all buzzing from the stimulation of being on a mission again in foreign environment.'

'Okay lady and gents, let's quiet down and get this meeting underway so we can get back to work', said Ant in his acting role of meeting secretary. 'As per the agenda I have circulated, the first item is a situation update, followed by administration and logistics issues and concluding with Lachlan's guidance on what he requires from us in the next 24 hours.'

Lachlan thanked Ant for kicking off the meeting and providing the first situation brief. It appeared they were in good order overall. No one was injured from the night parachute insertion although Crazy was pissed that his clothes still smelt of Baz's vomit.

She had responded with, 'Oh come on, don't try to tell me that I was the first girl to vomit on you?' At this, Crazy immediately went quiet. In fact, she was the first girl to vomit on him, although one had done a more grotesque and depraved act to him recently.

He winced and put his head in his hands as he remembered the girl in NZ that had laid a steamer on his chest. He thought to himself, 'If these chicks keep grossing him out he might swear off them forever. Then they'd be sorry....'

Ant continued with his report; all the stores and equipment had been accounted for and were functioning except for a ruptured pallet of water which had lost half of its load resulting in a loss of 200 litres of drinking water.

FOT said the patients in the community centre were stable but there might be more injuries from people who were staying out in the villages. If so it's a race over the next day to track them down before infection can take hold.

Likewise, the island's drinking water would need to be checked as a priority to ensure it hasn't been contaminated during the storm. Lachlan agreed. Crazy reported on communications with AusAID, DFID and Lord Erskin-Stamper's assistant.

The assistant said Lord Erskin-Stamper wanted a video conference brief from Lachlan in six-hours' time when he awoke, to coincide with his morning tea. The group chuckled at Crazy's lame impersonation of a posh British accent. Lachie reminded Crazy who was bankrolling this operation and his pay for that matter.

Lachie then went on to outline what was to happen over the next 24-hours. Preventative health measures and working on opening the airfield remained the two priorities. He then issued the sleep rotation and thanked them for their efforts to date.

Ant confirmed who had what tasks and then closed the meeting. He and Lachie were to check the villages to assess the welfare of the people and bomb the water supply to reduce the chance of disease outbreak. Baz and Si were on airport clearance duty. Crazy was to meet with the airport manager to ensure the communications and lighting were re-established. FOT would continue on rotation with the nurse, looking after the injured at the airfield and prepared to travel to any untreated injured that Ant and Priest found in their travels. Lachlan would meet with the Premier, develop the mission plan and update the relevant authorities. Their next meeting would be that evening at 1800 hours to work out where to next.

Lachlan gazed out across the littered airfield. Baz and Si were now hard at work with the mini-dozer. He marveled at Si's strength as the gentle-looking Brit giant tossed a downed palm tree from the airfield with the same ease that an Australian political party tosses its Prime Minister.

'Who'd want to pick a fight with that bastard', Lachlan mused. Still they have their work cut out for them. He surveyed the wreckage and downed vegetation and figured that it was 4 to 5 days' work. Better get more hands onto that task as soon as possible.

We need to open this airfield in three days or risk being overwhelmed if there are any complications in the next week. Ships from Australia and NZ were on their way but they wouldn't arrive for another ten days. No, they needed the airfield open ASAP.

He dabbed his forehead with his sleeve. It was hot and sticky already and it was only 0930 hours. The sound of a car creeping along the gravel behind him prompted him to turn around in time to see an official-looking Landcruiser approaching.

It pulled up a few metres from him and two solid smiling islanders climbed out. A man dressed in a Queensland Reds shirt grinned and said, 'Hey bro. We are here to take a bloke named Lachlan to the Premier's chambers. Know where he is?'

'You found him', replied Lachlan.

'Great', replied the man. 'When you're ready we'll head off.'

Lachlan told them to give him a minute and jogged off to grab his ruggedized tablet.

Once in the vehicle the men introduced themselves. The man in the Reds' jersey was named Pio. Curiosity got the better of Lachlan who enquired what was with the Reds' jersey.

Pio smiled and replied that it had become his favourite rugby union side since they signed his cousin, Ramowhati. Pio then proudly showed Lachlan the slightly faded signature on the shoulder which said, 'Pio, WE ARE RED! Cheers your bro Ramo'.

Lachlan had to admit that the jersey was pretty cool and told Pio he planned on catching some games this season. Pio said to keep an eye out for Ramo who would be tearing it up at the inside centre.

He then started to point things out to Lachlan as they drove along the road that ran around the rugged coastline; Niue was the largest coral atoll in the world and tourism played a big part in the island's economy, which is what would make the damage from the cyclone even more devastating in the long-term.

He said they had checked on all the tourists currently staying on the island and that they were all safe and sound. The resort had somehow only suffered relatively minor damage. They had plenty of food and booze, but no generator power.

The 48 tourists were in good humour, but some were disappointed as they had come for the great fishing and scuba diving that unfortunately was temporarily average given the storm had churned up the sand.

He then pointed to a pile of rubble and explained that it was the clinic, which was the reason for the temporary setup in the community centre.

'Was anyone hurt?', enquired Lachlan.

Pio sighed and looked up at the sky, 'Unfortunately the nurse on duty was killed, that's why we only have one very tired junior nurse tending to the injured'.

Lachlan could hear a great deal of sadness in Pio's voice so he decided to leave that story be and moved on to the condition of the fourteen villages on the island. Pio explained that many of them had been badly damaged but that he would receive a thorough briefing at the Chambers.

They drove on for another five minutes and arrived in front of a modest yet, well presented, building. A sign at the front indicated it was the Premier's Chambers. The men climbed out of the vehicle and walked through the double glass doors. Lachlan was offered a cold Coca Cola or a tea. He declined both and asked for some water.

He was shown through to the main meeting room which was already three-quarters full with officials including the heads of each village through to government clerks and a padre. Men of the cloth tended to carry a fair amount of clout in places like this. Lachlan wasn't himself a religious man, but he understood the importance of such a man and he would hopefully win over his support and that of the community through him. That's one of several reasons why he enlisted Priest into Global Angel.

Lord Erskin-Stamper had thought he had made an odd choice but Lachlan knew this was one of the ways that you could win hearts and minds as well as rally support from the local community. Pio facilitated Lachlan's introduction to the room.

Several chiefs and the padre confirmed Lachlan's suspicions that there were injured still in the villages. Lachlan promised to get to them as soon as he could. He told the leadership group to expect a big orange boof-head doctor and an even bigger and more boof-headed priest.

'A real priest?', queried the padre in an excited voice. Lachie confirmed that as far as he could tell, Priest was in fact the real deal. He was however a bit rough around the edges, but had a passion for helping orphans and performing exorcisms.

The padre informed Lachlan that the Lord worked in mysterious ways and that some of those in his service needed to possess traits different to his other children.

Lachlan laughed and claimed that Priest certainly possessed many interesting traits and must be one of the Lord's most interesting but maybe not the most loveable of his servants.

The padre wasted no time in extending an invite to attend a church service on Sunday and suggested that Priest could participate in some way.

Pio told Lachlan he may as well as the island's population would all be there anyway, and that if Priest was a little different to what they might be used to, they might enjoy the experience.

Whilst Lachlan stood there, pondering what excuses he could come up with to avoid going to a church service, the Premier entered the room. Pio announced the Premier and the NZ Ambassador's arrival before encouraging everyone to take their seats.

The Premier wasted no time in welcoming the leadership group of Niue and thanking them for their efforts so far. The Premier then looked at Lachlan and said, 'Lachlan, thank you and Global Angel for their work so far, but to be honest I am not sure who to thank beyond that, as I don't know which country is funding your venture?'

Lachie took this as his cue to explain how they came to be here—after all this was free publicity for the organization to the NZ government. He explained that Lord Erskin-Stamper was the Chairman of the Board and key financier of Global Angel. In this case the organization had been contracted by AusAID to deliver this response. DFID had also kindly funded a flow-on building supplies delivery that should arrive in three weeks.

Lord Erskin-Stamper had negotiated the support in the order of some £1,800,000. There was a buzz of excitement and anticipation around the table over such funding being funneled to the small island with existing modest infrastructure.

Encouraged by the positive response and caught up in the moment, Lachlan went on to explain the enthusiasm and commitment that Lord Erskin-Stamper showed towards the island was nothing short of extraordinary for a man that resided on the other side of the planet.

Again, the Premier fixed Lachlan with a serious stare, 'Maybe not as extraordinary as you think young man. The good Lord Erskin-Stamper is no stranger to our island, but all the same we are very thankful for the support. Please convey my gratitude to him and let him know that those closest to him are safe and sound'.

Lachlan was a little confused by the Premier's comments but all in all they all seemed very happy with Global Angel so far.

As the meeting progressed it was announced that funerals for the dead would be conducted this afternoon. There would be a large church service this Sunday to further commemorate their loss. The village cleanups had commenced but there was smashed and broken asbestos scattered everywhere from the 1950s buildings.

Lachlan advised, that where possible, they should just leave the stuff for now. His team had brought with them protective suits and masks that he was happy to issue to the villages. He also advised his people could give some advice on how to handle the asbestos if areas needed to be cleared before the professionals arrived in the next fortnight.

Lachlan went on to explain that with the Premier's approval they were going to treat the water supply and commence vector control of rodents and insects to reduce the chance of any disease outbreak from disturbed creatures entering damaged infrastructure. This would include treatment of the village areas, the main town, the sewerage plant, and the rubbish tip. His medical team would get to the villages over the next twenty-four hours to ensure the injured were treated.

They would of course continue to clear the airfield as a priority so that further support could be flown in. Any local work teams that wished to assist would be greatly appreciated and, if they reported to him prior to commencing work, their efforts could be coordinated to ensure an efficient clearance effort. He asked if there was anything else he needed to know.

The head of the island police shuffled in his seat and explained there might be something he may want to check. He explained that all the islanders and tourists had been accounted for. The only people not accounted for were the people on the ship that was moored in the harbor, who had arrived three days before the cyclone.

To the best of his knowledge the crew weathered the storm on their vessel. Since the cyclone, they had been conducting repairs to the ship. When he had travelled out to the ship to check on their well-being he had been informed they were all OK and very busy. When he had asked to come aboard he had been told in no uncertain terms, no! He was informed the ship had been damaged and it was too dangerous for him to board.

The couple of crewmembers he had seen looked like trouble. The policeman emphasized to Lachlan that Niue was a long way from anywhere if things turned sour and right now they had bigger troubles than potential smugglers passing through their waters.

The NZ Ambassador added that she had already passed information on the suspicious behavior to the NZ Navy. If the ship passed close enough to them, they would intercept the vessel and have a little poke around. Lachie explained the ship and its crew were not really their concern but he might get his doc to check on them after the village visits. Satisfied, the Premier closed the meeting and wished them all good luck in their endeavors.

Now that the meeting was over, before rushing back to the airfield, Lachie decided to take a few minutes to inspect some paintings that had caught his eye when entering the chambers. There were two large, colourful canvasses hanging on the wall. Both featured a beautiful island girl frolicking in crystal-clear water near a waterfall. The bright colours, coupled with the stunning scenery and such a striking copper-skinned young lady created a captivating sight.

As he stood there staring at the paintings he felt as though the young woman was dragging him into the canvas with her. He could feel the coolness of the water at his feet that offset the warm air, which had been causing him to perspire. She smiled at him before slowly forming an expression of shyness. Entranced by her emerald eyes he reached towards her and gently stroked her hair. The shyness disappeared as she sensed the man was enticed by her beauty. She tilted her head and purred as Lachlan run his hand through her hair, over her shoulder and down the side of her perfect partially-exposed breasts. He looked at the beads of water from the waterfall form on her skin. He wasn't so much aroused as he was captivated by her beauty.

'Ah yes, everyone loves Rose', said Pio.

The intrusion shattered the illusion as Lachlan was torn from his blissful waterfall frolic and cruelly flung back to the entrance foyer of the government chambers.

Lachlan composed himself and faced Pio, 'This woman and this place, is it real?'

Pio smiled, 'Ah yes, she is real and so is this place. This was the work of a local artist'. Pio agreed to show Lachlan the waterfall and introduce him to the beautiful Rose in due course, but in the meantime, they should get going.

Lachlan followed Pio back to the car. Pio said he would take Lachlan for a tour of the island on the way back so he could gain his bearings.

As they drove along, Lachlan replayed the meeting through his mind. 'Hey Pio, what did the Premier mean saying Lord Erskin-Stamper was no stranger to the island?'

Pio shrugged, 'No idea my friend. The Premier has been around for a while and travelled a bit, maybe they bumped into each other somewhere. He travels all around the world. Being Premier is a good gig. That's what I'm working towards. I don't want to leave Niue like Ramo has, but I do one day hope to see more of the world than just this island'.

'Yeah, well Pio, don't be in too much of a rush. The world is a strange place sometimes and if you have places like that waterfall and women that look like Rose you might find you have already hit the jackpot', said Lachlan.

On the way back to the airfield Lachlan marked all the infrastructure and settlement locations that didn't appear on his map. He also took note of their condition and formed a priority task list for his team. Accurate reconnaissance, prioritization, and correct allocation of resources would create efficiency. Efficiency provides timely responses, and timely responses would save lives and result in mission success. This is what Lachlan understood. He was a planner and a leader.

He was not burdened with compassion or empathy therefore he could remove emotion from the equation to enable him to plan accurately. Some might describe Lachlan as somewhat of a sociopath. He thought of himself as professional and strong. No sad-looking injured child could sway his priority list as it was all a simple case of mathematics, 20% of the effort to achieve 80% of the result.

He would achieve his mission priorities. Priority one: prevent disease outbreak, priority two: repair key infrastructure to allow follow up support to reach Niue, Priority three: if possible save lives of individuals. Underpinning all of these priorities was the enhancement of Global Angel's reputation. Because of his priorities, when he did see the wretched-looking ship mentioned in the meeting floating in the harbor, he made no note to check on it. No, better to treat the locals and the tourists as a priority as they fell squarely within his mission parameters.

The Job Designated Day +1

PRIEST AND SI STOOD AT THE RUBBISH TIP. It was putrid and baking in the hot sun. A seething mass of insects, deprived of their natural food sources since the storm, were swarming on any vegetable or protein matter they could find.

'That is bloody disgusting', said SI.

'It's an apocalyptic plague!' announced Priest. Si looked down at the fogging machine in his hands that was shaped something like a massive leaf blower. 'Yeah, well either way it's time for this plague to gulp down an unhealthy dose of pyrethrum. Light me up Priest', said Si while pulling a mask down over his face.

Priest flicked a switch and the savage-looking device in Si's hands sprung into life. Si slumped his backside on the tray of the Gator facing the fogger to the rear of the vehicle. Priest pulled his mask over his face and started up the Gator. He drove the vehicle upwind of the rubbish tip. Once in location, he signaled to Si who then flicked a lever on the fogger that spewed a pyrethrum fog into the air. Insects started dying instantly. Several hundred thousand took to the skies only to go into spasms and plummet to the ground. When the fog cleared, the tip looked like an insect warzone. An unfathomable number of dying insects writhed on the ground.

Si smiled under his mask, 'Insects of the apocalypse, meet Armageddon!', he said shaking the fogger above his head.

While Si and Priest were waging war against the island's vermin and insects Ant and Lachlan were busy chlorinating the Island's communal water tanks to ensure the drinking water was safe. They were at the last tank when Lachlan stopped and muttered something indiscernible.

'What was that mate?', Ant called out to him as he finished reading the scanner that confirmed the water was fit for drinking. But no response came.

He peered around the side of the water tank to see Lachlan walking off down a little ravine. 'Hey!', called out Ant, but Lachlan continued to ignore him. In a trancelike-state he foppishly walked down the hill.

'What now?', thought Ant, 'I'd better go see what His Majesty is up to'. Ant trotted towards the edge of the ravine to be met by an awe-inspiring sight. There in front of him was one of the most perfect waterfalls he had ever seen. The waterfall itself was only around three stories high but had a perfectly formed plume of water splashing down onto well-worn boulders below. The boulders sat in a pond of crystal-clear water that fed a small stream that flowed out to sea. The rim of the pond was lightly vegetated, but protected from direct sun by a high tree canopy that had somehow survived the storm.

Lachlan was now standing up to his ankles in the pond. 'This is the place, she was here', he muttered.

'Who was here you goose?' called Ant.

'Rose was. One of the most beautiful girls I've ever seen', replied Lachlan. Lachlan looked across the pond and could just make out a trail snaking its way up the other side of the ravine. On the ridgeway above was a partially concealed house. It looked much larger than any other dwellings he had seen on the island.

Lachlan pondered the possibility that occupants of the house might know about Rose and the painting, given they virtually lived next to the pond that was the subject of the artwork. Maybe the house belonged to the Premier or the NZ Ambassador. If it did it wouldn't hurt to touch base with them again anyway.

Lachlan convinced Ant that they should check to see the occupants were okay as, given their relative seclusion, they might not have been checked on by the village.

Ant agreed they should, so the two men trudged up the steep trail. The trail was lined by rich green vine-clad vegetation that someone had taken care to hold at bay. Within five minutes they reached the garden perimeter of the large house. There were no fences except for a large chicken run. The house was a Mediterranean-style, which looked like it belonged in Spain rather than in Niue.

Surrounding the house were orchards containing various fruit trees. There was definitely some damage to the orchard. Some of the trees lay on the ground completely uprooted. Several trees were now on an angle with snapped off branches. Damaged fruit lay on the ground baking in the sun. The sweet smell of the decaying fruit was a little overpowering as they approached the front door of the house.

Lachlan straightened his clothing and pushed his disheveled hair back into place. Ant didn't really pay that much attention to Lachlan's preening as the man was as vain as they come and they were clearly about to meet a big cheese on the island.

Ant knocked on the door. After almost a minute they heard someone approach the door. The door slowly opened to reveal a well-presented island woman who Ant guessed to be in her sixties. In addition to being well-presented, Ant could tell straight away that the woman would have been beautiful in her day. Actually, to be fair, she was still somewhat attractive. She had a shapely body, well-groomed silver hair, an enticing smile and emerald eyes that had just started to go cloudy with age.

'Can I help you boys?', asked the woman. Lachlan just stood there silently staring at the woman so Ant thought he'd better do the introductions and enquire if the woman was okay.

The woman said she knew who they were. She was in the crowd on the night they parachuted in at the airfield. She told Ant how impressed she was by the spectacle. It was the best entertainment they had witnessed on Niue in some time. She assured Ant that they were okay and were clearing up the mess around the homestead. Nothing that couldn't be fixed but they did lose a lot of fruit, which was a shame for the island as they tended to trade the fruit for labor assistance from the villages.

Ant and the woman chatted for a moment before Lachlan interjected, 'You said, we are okay. Who else lives here? Do you know Rose? Is she your daughter or granddaughter by chance?', asked Lachlan.

'Wow, you're a little socially awkward aren't you, young man?', replied the woman. She looked at Ant and said, 'Why don't you boys come in for an iced tea. It sounds like the heat is getting to your friend', said the woman.

Ant thanked her and said that would be great. She told them to follow her as she disappeared into the house. Ant turned around and slapped his embarrassed-looking friend 'What the hell is wrong with you Lachie? Snap out of it and who the hell is Rose?', whispered Ant.

Lachie seemed to return to reality and mumbled, It's nothing', as he followed the woman into the house. Ant shook his head and walked into the house closing the door behind him. He was thinking how nice an iced drink would be as he followed the woman into the house's reception area, where an unexpected sight met him.

Several large, colourful canvases depicting a beautiful woman at the beach, in the forest and at the waterfall that they had just seen, hung on the wall.

The two men stood drinking iced tea and admiring the extraordinary artwork. 'That's Rose', muttered Lachlan.

'No that was Rose', said the woman.

'This is Rose now', the woman said pointing to herself.

'That painting was done 50 years ago darling', said Rose. Lachlan stood there gawking as he came to terms with his falling for a woman who could well be in her 70s.

Ant started laughing, 'Is this why you have been a vacant lot for the last two days? First time I have seen you emotionally investing in someone in my life.

Well there she is Lachie, ask her out on a date. Who knows she might say yes even though you're probably a little inexperienced for her', laughed Ant with tears welling in his eyes.

The woman giggled, the thought of a young man falling in love or lust with an image of her 18-year-old self certainly appealed to her sense of humour as well. So did the fact that the young man was now as red as a Scottish backpacker sunbathing on Bondi Beach.

She fixed her eyes on Ant and said, 'I can tell you now chuckles, you wouldn't have said no to me back in the day either'.

Ant agreed that in her day he would have been chuffed to have had the opportunity to take her out, but since his parents weren't even born at the time he might pass the baton to Lachie. 'Cheeky', remarked Rose with a smirk on her face.

With that the backdoor slammed shut 'Is someone here mum?', called a voice. Rose replied that two of the parachutists from the other night were here to check on their well-being.

Heavy footsteps made their way towards the reception room and a forty-something-year-old islander and a teenage girl entered the room. Rose introduced her son Loto and granddaughter Tina to Lachie and Ant. She invited everyone into the living room.

As they made their way there, Lachie couldn't help think how familiar the son looked. Also quite interesting was that he suspected the son and granddaughter were mixed race.

As they entered the dining room the two men noticed the array of photos hanging on the wall. Most were of the son at various ages, his wife, daughter, and his son. They were largely unremarkable to Ant and Lachie but what was of interest were the black and white photos of a young Rose in Europe. There were photos of her in front of the prominent landmarks in Paris and on the French Riviera.

Lachlan enquired if they travelled to Europe much to which Rose responded just that one time in her twenties after her husband had died. Her husband had been the artist who had painted the canvasses of her. When he had died, she had gone into mourning for seven-years before a rich Englishman arrived in Niue for business. He, like Lachlan, was captivated by the canvasses hanging in the Premier's chambers. He had sought her out to buy one of her paintings.

Rose didn't want to sell any of the paintings but the man offered her more money than she could have fathomed at the time. She sold him one of the paintings despite the guilt of letting-go one of her late husband's works of art.

The man felt remorse so offered to take her on a week-long cruise on his yacht to visit some of the other South Pacific Islands. Rose had never left Niue, she had no family and had been grieving for so long that she couldn't remember the last time she had any fun so she said yes.

During the cruise she and the Englishman fell for each other. He whisked her off to Europe where they stayed in expensive resorts and ate expensive food. Her favourite place was Monaco as it had a fabulous view of the sea from their hotel room.

Rose turned to her grand-daughter and told her to cover her ears. She continued that she thought that was where her son was conceived. When the Englishman found out she was pregnant he returned with her to Niue where he had the house constructed for her and planted the orchards. He erected the farm pens so she would always have enough to get by.

He admitted to her that he was due to marry another girl in what was essentially an arranged marriage between two English families. Rose paused for a moment and stared off into space as Lachie and Ant sat there eagerly awaiting the story's conclusion.

She turned back to face them with a tear in her eye. 'He then told me he would always take care of me and his son and sure enough every now and again large sums of money turn up in my account.

I never married again as I never met anyone that I loved as much as my husband. Although fond of the Englishman, I probably didn't really love him, although I am thankful to him for my family that he gave me through our son and the fact that he financially supports us. He often assists the Premier by funding infrastructure projects for the island, which is very generous. He always asks to remain anonymous so as not to embarrass me', said Rose, placing her hand on her son's giant forearm.

Lachlan and Ant sat there stunned. 'That's quite a story Rose, where is the Englishman now?', asked Lachlan.

'Oh, I never saw him again', said Rose but there is a picture of him over there on the mantle'. Curiosity got the better of Lachie and Ant who both leapt up from their seats to have a look.

Ant looked at the young Rose and the neatly-dressed Englishman in the photo. 'Yep, he looks English', conceded Ant.

Lachlan turned to face Ant, 'that man is our boss, Lord Erskin-Stamper!'

'So he's still looking after us then?', said Rose in more of a statement than a question. 'Tell him we are all ok and that I said hello'.

They had a conversation about Global Angel and its role in the clean-up. Rose worked the orchard full-time with Loto's help when heavy lifting needed to be done. Loto's other job was to manage the dock in the harbour.

Apparently, the good Lord Erskin-Stamper still had a warehouse near the dock that he also looked after as part of the family support deal. Lachie thought it weird that his boss hadn't told him anything about the warehouse. Lachlan enquired if there was anything in it.

Loto replied nothing except for some shelving and trolley jacks. No one had been near it for two years or so until recently. He had gone down to check on it after the storm and was pissed-off to find the lock on the door cut. Inside were about ten men who he had never seen before. They were the crew from the *Merdeka* sheltering from the storm.

'The *Merdeka*?', enquired Lachlan. 'Yeah, the *Merdeka*, the foreign ship in the harbour that no one is allowed near', said Loto. He explained that anyone that went near the ship had been politely but firmly sent packing.

The crew in the warehouse were a mix of Irish, Asians and Middle Eastern men. One of the Irishmen paid Loto $NZ 500 for the damage and the inconvenience caused by their occupancy. Loto told them no problem and that they could stay as long as they needed to. The Irishman said they would be gone sometime in the next week when their repairs were finished.

Ant looked at his watch and announced that Rose and her family's hospitality had been fantastic but that he needed to get Lachlan back to base before he tried it on with Lord Erskin-Stamper's old girlfriend.

Rose laughed and replied, 'Ant, you truly are a delightfully cheeky little chubba'.

'What do you mean I'm chubby?', protested Ant, lifting his shirt to reveal some partially-formed abs. 'I've lost four kilos in the last four weeks', he continued.

Rose looked Ant in the eye and said, 'Tell you what Ant, you stop picking on me for my age and Lachie for his fine taste in women and I'll let that little layer of middle-aged flab covering your abs slide'.

At this, everyone in the room started to laugh. Even the red-faced Ant had a chuckle and had to concede he deserved it.

The two men thanked Rose again for her hospitality and started towards their vehicle. Once far enough away from the house the two old friends looked at each other and burst out laughing.

'Our boss is a dirty little fucker', announced Lachlan.

'Oh, you're just jealous he got to bang Rose and you didn't cause you're younger than her son', retorted Ant.

'Shut up Chubba', Lachlan teased.

Ant stopped laughing, 'Honestly I thought I had lost some weight and was starting to look good'.

'Don't worry Ant, you have and you are looking better. I worded Rose up when you went to the toilet that you are sensitive about your weight and it was the best way to shut you up if you kept gobbing-off, which I knew you would, you chubby little smart arse. I was genuinely in love Ant, albeit in love with a painting of an 18-year-old girl that turned out to be the 70-year-old mistress of our boss'.

The two men looked at each other and again burst into a fit of hysterics.

As they looped back around the Island to the airfield the harbour appeared on their right, as did a large warehouse. In the harbour was a small ship.

'The *Merdeka*', commented Ant. 'A bit sus isn't it?', he continued. 'I don't care Ant, it is none of our business'.

'Well that may be true Lachie, but that warehouse would be handy for any follow-on disaster relief stores that the ships are going to offload here. I think Lord Erskin-Stamper would expect us to seize this facility and use it to achieve mission success'.

Lachlan pondered Ant's suggestion for a moment before he replied, 'Yeah you are right. We'll come back tomorrow evening and check it out. I imagine the crew are no longer hanging out in there now that the weather has improved'.

The two men, comfortable with their decision, drove through the town back towards the airfield camp. When they got back they saw the impressive progress the team had made.

A reasonable amount of the airfield had been cleared but there was still a good day or more work to do before it could be deemed operational and re-opened to commercial traffic.

Despite this positive progress what was of concern was to see Si poking around the dozer with a wrench and an oily rag whilst Baz looked on with her hands on her hips and what could only be described as a pissed-off look on her face.

The two men climbed out of the vehicle and walked over to the dozer. 'What's up?', enquired Lachie.

Baz looked up and snarled, 'The fucken thing is fucken fucked up, that's what's fucken up!' Lachlan flinched at Baz's foul language.

'Wow Baz, do you kiss your mother with that mouth?', asked Lachlan.

'No but I've fucken kissed your mum with it!', she retorted angrily before turning on her heel and storming off.

Lachlan watched Baz disappear into the kitchen tent. Lachlan turned to Si and asked if he could give a more insightful explanation as to what was going on. Si sat up and smiled at Lachie. 'Well, Mr Lachlan, a hydraulic hose has blown. It's a messy time-consuming job but I can fix it. I just need two more hours and I should have it going again.

What I can't fix is that Aussie vixen's temper. She may be easy to look at but she has anger issues. She went off the rails when she was sprayed with some of the hydraulic fluid', said Si.

'Okay Si I'll leave you to it and I'll go calm Baz down', said Lachie, rolling his eyes.

When Lachie walked into the tent Baz was leant up against the counter, downing a cool bottle of water.

'Baz, how are you?', asked Lachie with a sympathetic look on his face.

Baz smirked at his best disarming little boy lost look. 'Oh Lachie, I'm fine I'm just a bit tired and emotional. When the dozer jizzed all over me I just lost my shit', said Baz.

Lachie started laughing at her crass joke. 'Baz, you are just too much. But seriously how much sleep have you had?'

She sighed and looked at the ground 'Oh I don't know, maybe three hours since we landed', she said.

Bloody hell Baz', said Lachie. 'You should have had at least three times that. You are lucky you haven't passed out behind the wheel of that dozer.

Now listen to me Baz, it's going to take Si at least two hours to fix that dozer, but I don't want to see you go near it for the next six hours. Go get a shower and five-hour's sleep', demanded Lachlan.

Baz shot a lecherous look at him, 'Aye, aye boss, are you going to tuck me in?', she said. 'Sleep Baz, I mean it', said Lachie, pointing sternly at her whilst exiting the tent. 'Oh, and one more thing. Si is a good guy, you might want to smooth things over after you yelled at him, you terrifying woman', and with that he was gone leaving Baz to ponder her apology.

THE JOB DESIGNATED DAY +2

HER EYES SLOWLY BLINKED OPEN but there was nothing to see in the blackened tent. The gentle hum of the generators comforted her. It was a familiar sound that she had been exposed to for her entire adult life whilst she served in the Army and the later in the Air Force.

The generators were always used to power field camps on military exercises and operations. It also acted as a white noise that washed away the tinnitus she had suffered during a heavy rocket attack in Afghanistan. In the dead quiet of night, the constant high pitch ringing in her ears would drive her mad and keep her awake.

The only way she had found to deaden the ringing was to replace the quiet with white noise like a generator, an air-conditioner or her night-time music file of ocean noises that she would play every night. Her insistence on using white noise at night sent her last boyfriend mad. It was one of the reasons he left her, that, and she was always away with the military.

She left the Air Force for him in an attempt to keep her relationship alive. But the damage was already done. She later realized that while she had been away he had been bonking anything that moved. In fact, it wasn't until she was home with him for three months straight that he realized just how much she irritated him.

One night with a few beers under the belt he told her that he had been screwing around. In true Baz fashion, she had let rip at him. Her usually beautiful face was ugly and contorted with rage as she spat insults at him. She kept going on and on until he couldn't take it anymore. He wanted her to stop but she wouldn't. He threatened to hurt her but she still didn't stop. Instead she got right up in his face and taunted him. 'What are you going to do big man?

Hit me and then go and screw some whore with that weeny little dick of yours?' At this he cocked his right hand and backhanded her across the face. She stumbled backwards clutching her face. It hurt, she hadn't been hit that hard since her step-father used to beat into her when she was 17-years-old.

It was the situation with her step-father that caused her to leave home and join the Army. Now this bastard also thought he could lay into her. Well she wasn't that little girl anymore. The military and war had toughened her. She could feel the anger welling inside of her but she didn't let it out.

She remembered her unarmed combat training and went into a fighting stance. She scanned the room for a weapon. There, in the corner of the room behind the bastard was a broom.

'What the fuck are you doing you silly little bitch? Are you shaping up to me? You'd better pull your head in or I'll bitch slap you again', he yelled at Baz.

Instead of seeing fear in her eyes he only saw defiance. In a fast and fluid movement, she threw a jab punch that struck him in the nose. It wasn't hard, it barely hurt but it was perfectly-timed and struck him square in the nose causing his eyes to water.

'You bitch!', he howled moments before he was struck in the face with a rapid six-punch combination. Some of the hits had hurt him, but not enough to stop him.

He wiped the water from his eyes so he could see. Time to finish this mole, he thought, as his eyesight started to return, but before he could do anything there was a searing pain in his groin that dropped him to his knees. Baz removed the broomstick from his groin as she scanned his crippled body for her next strike point. The throat she thought, jamming the broomstick end into it.

The man gasped in pain now completely incapacitated. Fear set-in as he looked up at the woman he had wronged. There was no emotion in her eyes. She was like a machine scanning for another strike point. Baz pulled the broom handle back like a spear and that was the last thing he remembered. The court later found that Baz was just defending herself against a man who was 40 kg heavier than her.

It was unfortunate that the final blow to the man's temple had left him with minor brain damage. But given the fracture she had suffered to her face, it was understandable that she felt herself in significant danger and had used an appropriate amount of force to extricate herself from the danger of further physical harm.

As Baz awoke she subconsciously rubbed her now-repaired cheekbone. For a while after the incident she had sworn off men more out of disappointment for their kind than anything else. For a long time, they just didn't seem to offer anything that she needed. However, she had now been alone for over a year. She had no real companionship since leaving the military and nearly killing her ex-boyfriend. She had little in common with women other than her mother.

Most men were too soft for her. She needed someone more masculine than she was at the very least. They needed to be entertaining and they needed a dick. Yes, she thought to herself, it had been 14-months since she had had sex. Indeed, they must have a nice dick.

She felt sorry for the first man she was going to sleep with. She smirked as she thought of herself writhing, screaming, and clawing. The poor bastard whoever he was. She sat and pondered what was right under her nose. A group of masculine men who were on this mission with her.

Obviously, Priest is out as he is either really a priest or a delusional nut job that thinks he is a priest. FOT was handsome and masculine but unfortunately very happily married, so he needed to be ruled out. Si was too old for her and had a fair-sized beer gut. Crazy was a fully blown man-whore and she just couldn't deal with someone cheating on her again.

Ant was perfect and she had deep affection for him. Problem was he was firmly in the friend zone. He was like a brother to her and she just couldn't get her head around being romantically involved with him. She had tried on several occasions to develop a sexual attraction to him as she knew he would be perfect.

Once she even got herself drunk and threw herself at him hoping he would take advantage of her. Instead he acted the complete gentleman and put her to bed on her own to sleep it off. This act gained her respect and admiration but landed him permanently in the friend zone.

'Damn it!', she thought, such a shame. 'It looks like he is packing some serious weaponry in those pants she thought to herself. That leaves one, the most unobtainable Lachlan. He is handsome, rich, educated and very masculine in a men's health magazine kind of way.

Yes, maybe Lachlan'. She certainly felt attracted to him and she hadn't entirely been joking when she asked him to tuck her in. Problem is would he be attracted to her? She had caught him perving on her a couple of times. But, then again, most men do as she has a stunning athletic physique.

Except for the chubby chasers, she wouldn't appeal to them at all as there wasn't an ounce of fat on her that shouldn't be there. The smirk on her face started to disappear as her fully-awaken presence of mind returned.

Shit', she thought, 'I was a bitch to Si yesterday. Beer gut or not the man is a darling and didn't deserve the shit I lumped on him. I think I'll go apologise to him'.

Baz walked out of the tent whilst pinning her matted hair back into a pony-tail. 'Great', she thought, 'Four days without shampoo and my hair is starting to form dreadlocks'.

Si must have gotten the vehicle going again as she could hear the dozer humming away in the darkness. As she walked towards the dozer she could make out the silhouette of Si and Ant in the light of the generator-powered beach lighting sets they had set up. When the two men saw her they both stopped work and looked up at her refreshed smiling face.

Ant switched off the motor of the dozer and climbed down, out of the seat. 'Well, well if it isn't sleeping beauty', he said.

Baz walked up to the dozer, putting her hand gently on it, 'You did it Si, you got her going again'. Si nodded at her. 'Ant, I wonder if you could give Si and me a moment, I need to talk to him in private?', she said.

Ant smiled as he knew it was apology time as Si had told him how she had gone off. 'Sure Baz, it's time for me to get a bit of sleep anyway', said Ant.

Ant walked over to the quiet side of the airfield sipping on his bottle of water to check out the dark early morning sky prior to going to bed. He stood there watching a shooting star cross the sky thinking how good it was to be in the bush again. He was enjoying the peace and quiet when a shiver went through him.

It felt like his senses had become hyper-alert. A shot of adrenaline entered his veins and the hair on the back of his neck stood on end. 'Great', he thought, 'My nerves are still shot. Goddamn PTSD', he thought to himself. 'I am completely alone trying to enjoy nature and my nerves play up'.

Ant commenced the breathing exercises he had been taught in an attempt to calm his pulse rate. Little did he know that he should have trusted his sixth-sense. Just 30 metres away a slender figure all clad in black lay in the bushes watching Ant through a night-vision riflescope.

Behind the crosshairs, Ant's beaming face was looking up at the stars oblivious to the lethal weapon pointed in his direction. Ant suddenly stopped smiling and with a new uneasy look on his face scanned his immediate environment.

At one stage, he looked directly back down the scope. The shadowy figure tensed at the thought of somehow being discovered. 'He can't have seen me', the figure pondered while caressing the weapon's safety switch.

Suddenly Ant's face showed a look of discomfort. Through the scope the figure saw Ant's hands fumbling at something. 'Was he reaching for a weapon? Shit, I have been discovered', the figure thought, moving the scope from Ant's head to his hands to see what he was holding.

It was no gun Ant was holding but it was definitely a weapon the figure thought as their crosshairs were now placed directly on Ant's huge dong. No missing that, the figure thought, as the noise of Ant letting rip with a massive fart while he had himself a hard-earned pee. 'Disgusting', the figure thought, wiggling back down an embankment to slink away in the shadows.

The Job Designated Day +3

ANT AWOKE EARLY and started fumbling in his kitbag to look for his watch. 'Five-thirty in the morning, time for coffee', he thought to himself.

He walked out of the accommodation tent into the kitchen tent. There lying on the ground in front of the hot water urn was the biggest centipede Ant had ever seen.

'Bloody hell!', he thought as the 20cm long black and red centipede became suddenly active as the sunlight Ant let in the tent left the creature feeling exposed.

Out of survival instinct it made for the nearest cover it could find which happened to be Ant's foot. Shocked by the sudden movement Ant leapt back letting out what could be best described as a none to masculine squeal. The centipede shot past Ant and crawled under some water jerrycans.

'Right', thought Ant, 'It can just stay under there. I'm not messing with that monster'. It was then that Ant heard a noise behind him. He spun around to see Lachlan standing there with a grin on his face.

'A little jumpy aren't we Ant?', asked Lachie.

'Oh shit', Ant thought to himself, 'One moment of weakness and of course his Royal Highness had to be there to see it'.

'Massive centipede nearly bit me', mumbled Ant in a way of explanation.

'Stung Ant, not bitten', replied Lachlan.

'What?', sneered Ant. 'I said stung Ant, technically the centipede stings its prey, it doesn't bite them. Painful as hell too. There is only one true defence against an attacking centipede. The prey should leap back into the air and squeal like a five-year-old girl. Apparently this humiliating act causes the centipede to feel sorrow for its intended victim which will cause it to lose its will to attack', joked Lachlan, standing in the tent doorway looking smug at his attempt at early morning humour.

'Oh piss off', retorted Ant. 'I tell you what Ant, you make me a coffee and I won't tell everyone what a little sugar britches squeal you let out', offered Lachlan.

'Alright you gotta deal', mumbled Ant as he headed towards the brew urn to make two coffees. A couple of minutes later Ant walked out with two cups of coffee to Lachie who was sitting there in conversation with Priest and Crazy. Lachie looked up at Ant with a mischievous grin, 'Why thank you Ant, my good man you didn't need to go to any trouble'.

Ant looked at Priest and Crazy who were also both smirking at him. 'Prick', Ant thought, 'He's gone and told everyone anyway'.

'Hey Florence, is there any chance you could fetch Priest and I one as well? That is unless there is some godless creature lurking in the shadows of the kitchen tent that would see you too terrified to risk it', sniggered Crazy.

Ant's thick eyebrows knitted together as they tended to do when he was getting pissed off. 'Certainly Wayne, I'll get you and Priest a coffee and I'll rim them just like I did Lachie's', said Ant.

'You'll what?', said Crazy.

'You know, rim it. You see I got Lachie's cup before I put the coffee in it and I rubbed my knob around the rim cause I knew that prick would say something', said Ant, with a sinister look on his face.

At this Lachie spat out his coffee, which caused the three other men to burst into laughter. Baz walked out of the tent looking at the three men laughing and Lachlan retching.

Baffled by the scene she enquired, 'What are you bunch of cocksuckers laughing' about?'

'Exactly!', cried Wayne.

Sometime later Lachlan regained his composure after Ant assured him he didn't rim his cup. The team met over a feast of bacon, eggs, and coffee to take stock of where they were at.

In the daylight, the airfield now looked fairly clear. The airfield manager would be there at seven o'clock to assess if the runway was operational or not.

'Great work guys', said Lachlan, 'If all goes well I will give you today off'.

'As long as you are right for church tomorrow', said Priest.

'What?', protested Crazy. Priest fixed the group with a purposeful stare.

'I said, you can have your day off and hit the piss as long as you are fit to attend the local's church service tomorrow. They have been kind enough to invite us all and we are going to foster good relations by all being in attendance.

Besides I've heard their services are something to behold and let's face it some of us need forgiveness for our sinful lives', said Priest leaning forward towards Crazy's face, stopping an inch away from him and glaring menacingly into his eyes.

'Alright, alright, I'll go Priest, just stop freaking me out with that psycho stare', said Crazy pulling away from Priest.

The airfield manager appeared at the camp on time. Unexpectedly, he had the Premier and his entourage in tow. Both men beamed as they declared the airfield operational. There were handshakes and backslaps all round as they all acknowledged a job well-done.

Lachlan and the team were invited to the Matavai Resort to celebrate that evening. The Premier informed Lachlan the a medical aircarft would arrive late afternoon from NZ, so Global Angel's doctor could be stood-down to join the team at the Resort after his handover with the incoming medical team.

'Great work Global Angel, now what do you have planned for today?', asked the Premier. Lachlan pondered for a moment, 'Well, we thought we might try some of your famous scuba-diving sites and then off to the Resort for drinks this evening.'

'Sounds like a great plan. Apparently, other than the water visibility dropping a little, the reefs and aquatic life are still in good shape. Anyway, I must get going, we have a lot of aircraft due in in the next 24-hours to prepare for with the NZ Ambassador. See you tonight at the Resort', he said to the team before leaving with his entourage.

Lachlan, Ant and Crazy disappeared into the meeting tent to set up a briefing with Lord Erskin-Stamper to update him on their mission success. It took five minutes and Crazy had established a video link back to the UK.

A prim and proper-looking woman appeared on the screen. She introduced herself as Lord Erskin-Stamper's personal assistant and proceeded to tie in some administration with Ant, including invoice verification and an extraction date.

Once the admin was complete Ant moved away from the video link camera to allow Lachlan to take up his briefing position. Moments later Lord Erskin-Stamper's image appeared on the screen. He was dressed in a navy blue woolen lounge suit, accompanied by a yellow silk cravat.

Although his formal attire did not surprise Lachlan it certainly seemed odd to Ant and Crazy that someone would dress so formally at 10:30 pm in their own home. What they didn't know was that Lord Erskin-Stamper's outfit had only ever been worn in his own home.

It was a bespoke Savile Row-tailored suit that cost in the order of £7,500. If they had known this information they would have thought him completely delusional. To Britain's elite this is simply how one dresses. To Lord Erskin-Stamper, Ant and Crazy looked like filthy simpletons who he paid handsomely to advance his reputation and international standing.

He made a mental note to himself to design a uniform of sorts for Global Angel. Can't have these antipodean proletarians representing his company while dressed in soiled rags and marsupial skins.

The briefing continued for five minutes and Lord Erskin-Stamper seemed very pleased with their success. He then started asking odd questions about the areas worst hit and even went as far as to ask for the names of the dead and badly injured.

Lachlan turned to face Ant and Ant nodded his approval. Lachlan turned back to the screen and said in a sympathetic voice, 'Boss is there a family here that you specifically want to know about?'

Lord Erskin-Stamper shifted uneasily in his seat.

Ant motioned to Crazy to follow him out of the tent to leave Lachlan to his delicate task. When they had left, Lachlan continued, 'Boss, we know about your friendship with Rose and her family. It's ok, they are all perfectly ok, we checked on them personally. She spoke fondly of you and asked us to pass on her thanks to you for your continued support'.

A look of relief spread across the normally impervious face of Erskin-Stamper. After a moment, he regained his composure and started to stammer, 'Oh, oh yes, I remember Rose. We were once friends who shared an interest in her late husband's artwork. Just friends of course– I felt sorry for her–single mother on an island with no means of support–so I decided to support her family.

You understand Lachlan? It's the type of thing one does from time to time in an attempt to buy one's way into heaven'.

Lachlan fought back the smirk desperately attempting to break out on his face, 'Oh yes boss, of course, that's just how Rose described your relationship. May I say sir that your generosity and kindness in supporting Rose's family touched Antonio and myself greatly. All the same Antonio took a photo of Rose and her family in case you were interested to see how an old friend is faring?'

Lord Erskin-Stamper told Lachlan that it would be nice to see the photo, but he could just send it with the other photos from the mission. He then thanked Lachie for his report and bid him goodnight.

Once the conference ended Lachlan allowed himself to chuckle at how uncomfortable the normally stoic English gentleman looked. Then he thought to himself, 'Oh bugger, I forgot to ask about using the warehouse.

Oh well, not to worry'. He reflected, 'As if the boss would mind us using his empty warehouse. I think I've put him through enough tonight and I might just let him drift off to sleep having pleasant dreams about the beautiful Rose'.

The Global Angel team, minus FOT who was caring for patients and Priest who was preparing for tomorrow's sermon, met at the dive shop to get kitted-out with some gear. The team sorted through the collection of rental scuba gear looking for a good fit.

Baz, Crazy and Lachie were easily fitted but for big Si he was out of luck when it came to a wetsuit. The man was just too big for the standard wetsuit sizing. It wasn't that Si was fat, he was just a big unit.

The shop owner said to leave it with him and he would see if he could tee something up. Ant, on the other hand, was able to be sorted out. It wasn't beyond their ability to fit him into a wetsuit, it was just for the 95th percentile he was too solid for his height. The solution was that he simply wore a wetsuit designed for a taller man.

This brought much delight to Lachie who enthusiastically pointed out that Ant's legs were too short for the suit.

Ant's bushy eyebrows started to furl as he observed that Lachie's suit looked like it had been tailored to him. Ant was annoyed partly because Lachie always looked immaculate and partly because he always took such delight in pointing-out everyone else's shortcomings.

Lachlan wasn't the only one who looked like their suit was tailored. Walking in from the back of the shop was Baz, rocking an incredibly tight wetsuit. Simultaneously the four men lost the power of speech as Baz slinked past them to her kitbag where she promptly bent over to rifle through it. Ant immediately felt bad staring at his friend's perfect peach-shaped backside and looked away out of respect, but Lachie, Crazy and Si all stood there gawking.

Baz looked over her shoulder, and out of defensive reflex, let loose, 'What the fuck is wrong with you three perverted window lickers? Can't you be gentlemen like Ant?'

'And there it is', said Crazy, 'The illusion that Baz is in fact a lady is yet again shattered, sorry for staring mate, it's just you don't look like the other blokes!'.

Baz screwed up her face, 'You won't look like the other blokes either after I tear your balls off', she said.

'Wow that escalated quick', said Lachie. At this they all burst out laughing. Underneath the laughter, Baz was kicking herself. Why did she go off like that?

She had squeezed into a wetsuit two sizes too small and strutted in her entrance to get Lachlan's attention. She didn't mind them looking. She was glad they looked. Why did she go off? Maybe it was they were enjoying looking a little too much that annoyed her? Great way to confirm you're a Tom Boy, she berated herself.

Before long there was a shadow cast in the doorway as massive islander lurched into the shop holding a wetsuit in his massive right hand. 'Where is this big white guy?', the man announced.

'Miaga!', called the shop owner, 'Thanks for bringing the suit out cuz. This is Si, the guy that needs to borrow it'.

Miaga looked Si up and down and with a big friendly smile on his face said, 'Hello Si, you don't look that big. You're welcome to borrow my suit cuz. Think of it as my way of saying thanks for your help on beautiful Niue. No peeing in it though', he said, stabbing a finger the size of a cucumber into Si's chest.

'Yeah, yeah thanks for the loan Miaga, I will look after it and clean it before I give it back', said Si feeling awkward, due to the rare occurrence of being in the presence of a man significantly bigger than himself.

Miaga chuckled and told them of an underwater swim that went through the middle of a rock and coral formation.

Si thanked Miaga for the local dive tip and again for the loan of the suit. The big islander told him to think nothing of it and waved a goodbye as he lumbered out the door.

Half an hour later, the five Global Angle team members were down by the water. It looked remarkably clear given the recent cyclone. It didn't take long for them to wade out into the warm water in the calm conditions.

Ant was first to signal his intent to submerge as he let some air out of his buoyancy control device or BCD as they are commonly known. He slowly submerged and scanned his new underwater environment. Four metres down the water was teaming with wildlife. The coral was stunning.

He neutralized his buoyancy, giving him the sensation of flying above the ocean floor. Ant just stayed there floating for a moment which allowed the sea life to get used to his intrusion into their world. Before long the creatures were back to going about their normal business of eating, fornicating and swimming.

A big beautiful-looking crayfish crawled around the coral and appeared right in front of Ant. After several days of tinned food Ant could think of nothing better than a nice big juicy crayfish. He made a grab for it but the cray shot off at lightning speed. 'Damn!', thought Ant, I didn't know they could move that fast'.

Ant linked up with the rest of the team who were now also submerged. They began swimming as a group and looking around their environment. Before long they found the spot that Miaga had told them about. It was only three metres in length but it was very pretty.

Baz looked up at the rock formation as she swam through, to see her air bubbles trapped against the rock as they attempted to make their way to the surface as physics would dictate.

What a spectacular site she thought to herself as she exited the formation.

They continued deeper into the water until they found a bommie.

Circling above it was a large Manta Ray. The group floated above the coral bommie, just metres below the Manta Ray.

The creature seemed as fascinated by the humans as they did it. It swam over towards their direction and started circling their air bubbles streaming towards the surface. The creature looked totally majestic gliding through the water while it circled above their position. They sat there mesmerized for five minutes, taking in every detail of the experience before they decided to move on although they were thoroughly convinced they had just witnessed the highlight of the dive.

After a fantastic 30-minute dive, the team exited the water. Their excited chatter about their shared experience continued all the way back to the shop. They cleaned their gear and handed it back to the shop owner. He was keen to know how they enjoyed it as from an islander perspective it wasn't worth diving yet due to the muck in the water from the cyclone.

From the team's perspective, they thought it was fantastic and couldn't imagine anything better than what they saw on their dive.

They piled into the dive shop vehicle and were dropped off at the camp where they got cleaned up.

FOT came over to greet them and tell them that the first aircraft would be landing in the next two hours. When Ant told FOT of their underwater adventures FOT shook his head in disappointment at having to remain on duty and miss the dive.

Still, in two hours a medical team would arrive and his hand-over of his responsibilities would be complete, freeing him up for a night of drinking. If there was one vice FOT had it was beer. It seemed odd that an extremely fit man would have such a love for beer. He pretty much stayed away from it day-to-day, but when the call for drinks went up he was the first in line.

Sometime during the night he would be seen cuddling and caressing his beverage, announcing over and over, 'I love beer!'. The team prepared the briefing tent for the NZ authorities and the Niue Premier to whom they would be handing over responsibility.

At 2:30 pm Niue time the first aircraft arrived. It was Royal NZ Air Force C130 aircraft. It landed majestically on the clean and fully operational airfield. Seeing the aircraft land safely filled the Global Angel team with pride. Their first mission to date was a complete success.

The aircraft taxied towards them before shutting down 50 metres from their position. The Global Angel crew joined the locals in cheering the arrival of the NZ Defence Force relief team who soon disembarked from the aircraft. Before long two Royal Australian Air Force C130s also landed bringing with them some heavy engineering equipment.

The mixed Aussie and Kiwi team formed up and set about their tasks in an impressively professional manner. The Kiwi commander and her second in command, Aussie counterpart, introduced themselves to the Premier and the Global Angel team.

The Kiwi Commander introduced herself as Lieutenant Colonel Millar but insisted they all call her Michele. The Aussie major who accompanied her introduced himself as Brian. The team set about to brief Michelle and Brian on the situation.

FOT was relieved to learn that Brian was actually an Australian Army Reserve doctor with a great deal of experience in humanitarian and disaster relief operations. In his normal life, he was a cosmetic surgeon from the Gold Coast. FOT admired people like Brian that would be taking a massive pay drop to do their duty for humanity.

After a 30-minute briefing and a two-hour trip around the island, during which the team explained their work that they undertook, Michelle looked at the team and said, 'Well you boys and girl have done a cracking job.

I will make sure I include in my report to my and the Aussie's headquarters what a fantastic start Global Angel made to this operation. I imagine we will see more of you guys in the future. We will take over from here. We are not going to hang around the airfield—we are going to push out to the villages and start helping them with their reconstruction effort.

A contracted civilian medical team will be arriving in approximately 20 minutes and they will set up next to your camp, to continue to assist the injured in the Community Centre until we can finish constructing their new medical facility, which should be complete within two weeks. So, when is you team going to leave?'

Lachlan advised that they would fly out Monday morning. Michelle thrust out her hand and said, 'Well, given this is Saturday afternoon and we are about to push out to the villages and get into the reconstruction effort, we probably won't get a chance to see you guys again before you go, so farewell it is then.'

The Team shook hands with the Aussie and Kiwi leadership group before they mounted-up and disappeared off into the island's interior. Only Brian and a driver remained to relieve FOT until the civilian medical contract team arrived.

A weight had been lifted off the Global Angel team's shoulders. They were now officially relieved of their duty. Now all they needed to do was pack up and redeploy back to Brisbane. Oh yeah, but in there somewhere they needed to get drunk, then sober up and attend a church service.

The Global Angel group piled onto their two Gators and headed off to the Resort. Fifteen minutes later they were flooding through the front door of the resort. 'Please tell me there is beer here!', said FOT, clutching the bar with his big orange paws.

The girl at the bar giggled at FOTs desperation. 'We sure do, and it's cold again since your man Si stopped by yesterday and repaired our generator.'

FOT turned around to see a grinning Si as the barmaid placed a carton of cold beer on the counter. 'There you go Si, as promised for your help yesterday', she said.

'It was an absolute pleasure to help my lady', replied Si with a grin like a split watermelon.

'Could I tempt you with one?', Si said, handing one of the ice-cold beers to FOT.

FOT snatched the beer and ripped the cap off in what looked like one movement. He gulped down half the beer in one swig and then sat there for a moment in a sheer state of bliss. He looked up at Si and said sincerely, 'Thank you Si, you are a true gentleman and a scholar'.

Si laughed, 'Well I'm neither of those but I will settle for how do you Antipodeans say it? A good bloke?'

'That you are Si, you are a good bloke', FOT said, while not taking his eyes off his beer. The rest of the group piled in and commented on Si's genius and vital importance to the group on future operations.

The Premier stopped by to shout the team a beer, before disappearing to greet the next aid aircraft due to arrive. They sat there on the rear deck of the Resort as the sun started to lower and the day cooled. Ant had seen his fair share of sunsets in exotic places in his time, but he had to give Niue accolades for the one looking out over the ocean—it was a cracker.

The group sat there enjoying the beers and swapping stories about the mission whilst taking in the natural beauty that surrounded them. Before long, some of the stranded tourists staying at the Resort started flowing into the bar.

Two men of average height in their forties walked in, scoping out the bar. One had a shaved head with squinty eyes. He had a solid build and looked like he sported a constant smile on his face. The other had wavy black hair and a laconic look on his face.

Mate the bloody powers back on. Do you know what that may mean Mick?', said shaved head.

'I sure do Frosty my old China', answered the wavy-haired man.

Frosty leant forward over the bar looking the barmaid square in the eyes with a huge grin on his face, 'Does a man dare to dream?' he asked.

'He sure can', replied the barmaid, slapping two cold beers on the counter.

Mick and Frosty picked up their beers and toasted by clanking their beers hard enough together to shoot beer all over themselves.

'Cold Piss!', Frosty and Mick toasted in an enthusiastic gesture.

'Blimey FOT, those two blokes look like they enjoy their beer as much as you do', said Si. 'Kindred spirits', admitted FOT as they watched Frosty and Mick vaporize their beers.

Before long Global Angel's beers were running low. Just as they were about to order some more, a new carton was slapped down on their table.

Frosty stood there in front of them sporting a contagious smile. 'I hear you boys and girls fixed the gene?', he asked.

'Well yeah, well actually Si did', said Ant.

'Great work', said Mick appearing from behind Frosty, 'We tried to fix it but couldn't get it going. Thought I knew what I was doing as I have a couple on my farm. We've been stuck here drinking warm beer for a week, so we'd like to share these cold ones with you as a way of saying thanks'.

Lachlan thanked the two men and invited them to join them. Frosty and Mick introduced themselves. Mick was a Queensland farmer from near Rockhampton and Frosty was an Aussie Government contractor living in Fiji.

Each year the two old friends would meet up and go on a fishing trip. This year they had chosen Niue. The fishing had been great until the cyclone hit. Since then they had been stranded in a resort with no power and only warm beer. Still these two hardy men had made the most of their time helping the locals with the clean-up. But today was a step forward. They had cold beer and tomorrow morning a commercial flight was landing to take all the tourists back to Auckland where they could make arrangements to head home.

During the ensuing conversation, it turned out that Mick actually knew Lachlan's father. Mick's farm was only 150 km from Lachlan's family farm, so they were practically next-door neighbours. Given the size of farms in that region it wasn't far from the truth, probably only 75 km from being real neighbours.

Si asked Frosty what the attraction was to living in Fiji given he was an Aussie who had spent seven years living there. Frosty explained it was mainly about the people and the way of life. The pace of life was much more relaxed than Australia. People took the time to catch up with family and socialize with the community.

He explained that people living in cities of Australia and the other western countries had no idea how lonely and stressful their lives were. In the evening in Fiji people got together and socialized. If you needed help with something there was a whole community behind you ready to assist. If you acted the goat and did something wrong by your family or community, then they cut you off. No government handouts to reinforce your anti-social behavior. It made for a more tight-knit and rewarding social fabric.

The group was fascinated by Frosty's islander insight. It certainly left Ant pondering if that could ever work in Australia.

Eventually the bar closed so the Global Angel crew decided it was time to go. They bid Frosty and Mick farewell and wished them a safe journey for tomorrow morning. Frosty and Lachlan exchanged cards, given he was an Aussie Government representative in a country that was prone to natural disasters.

Priest, who had remained sober during the evening to ensure he was in good shape for tomorrow's church service, by default became the designated driver. He had to make two trips in the Gator to get his wayward flock back to their camp. One of the Gators would just have to remain at the Resort until they could pick it up tomorrow.

THE JOB DESIGNATED DAY +4

A BEAM OF BRIGHT LIGHT STRUCK Ant's closed eyes. He slowly blinked them open to see the sun had penetrated through the crack of the tent flaps. He sat up on his stretcher fumbling for his watch, which indicated it was 6 am.

'Shit', he thought, rubbing his head. That beer caught up on him as he hadn't had one for a few weeks. He looked around the tent to see everyone else was still passed out snoring and farting.

'Coffee!', he thought as he stumbled out of the tent towards the field kitchen. There, sitting there at the table, was Baz happily reading a book in the shade while having some breakfast.

'Morning Baz', said Ant.

She looked up from her book and smirked, 'Ant, is there any girl on this planet who hasn't been subject to seeing you stumble around butt-naked after you have had a night on the wallop?'

Ant looked down, 'Oh shit not again, sorry Baz', he said as his hands shot down to cover his bowl of fruit while he retreated into the tent.

Baz sat there chuckling, shaking her head. What a moron, but as I suspected that boy is packing some serious heat, she mused.

By 7 am everyone was up having breakfast. Priest walked out of the tent dressed in his white vestment. 'Ready to be saved my children?', he growled.

Ant looked up, 'Wow you actually look legit for once, rather than an extra from an exorcist movie,' he said.

Priest looked at Ant menacingly, 'Well Ant, I guess you are referring to how I usually look when dressed in my black cassock, which is the standard dress of day for a Catholic priest such as myself.

Now in regards to exorcisms you shouldn't make jokes about things you don't understand. They are real Ant and so am I. I am a servant to God and a warrior that fights evil. Be careful which side of the fence you fall on Ant or you might meet my bad side. I'm not all sugar and biscuits. One more thing Ant, stop flashing that weeny little peenie at everyone,' said Priest in a tone that pretty much terrified everyone present.

Ant scuffed his feet on the ground looking like a chastised school child. 'Yeah well I'm sorry Priest and I apologized to Baz. It was an accident I was still half-asleep.

But where do you get off calling my dick weenie, it's friggin' nine inches long,' Ant boasted. Priest sneered and leant over Ant, who suddenly felt very small and vulnerable in Priest's monstrous presence. 'Like I said Ant, weeny peenie,' said Priest confidently.

Everyone burst out laughing. 'I knew you fags were all into measuring each other's penises but this is the first time I have seen a priest involved in such a competition,' chortled Baz.

The group continued to laugh and carry on until Priest pointed out that they should get cleaned up as he wanted to be at the service early so as to greet the locals when they turned up to the church.

Thirty minutes before the service the locals started turning up in some of the most colourful church attire Ant had ever seen. The women were all wearing colourful hats and were, in themselves, somewhat of a spectacle.

They eventually moved into the church and took some seats at the rear. Ant looked at Crazy as they sat down. 'That's odd Wayne', Ant said. 'What is?', asked Crazy while taking his seat.

'Well Wayne, it's just that I was expecting you to burst into flame when we walked in', said Ant.

Crazy looked at his smart-arse mate and replied, 'No, I didn't burst into flame, but it really burns when I pee, do you think praying might clear that up for me?'.

Ant pointed out Crazy might be better to put that issue to FOT rather than the good Lord.

The Niuean Padre introduced the Global Angel team to the congregation who promptly showed their appreciation with enthusiastic applause. Priest then said a few words of condolence for those lost in the cyclone. He also told them that the thoughts of thousands of people overseas were with them in their time of need.

Before long the Niuean Padre took over the service again which all seemed fairly standard stuff to Ant, except that some of it was in Niuean. Then suddenly the congregation burst into beautiful song.

It shocked Ant that the singing was so exotic and uplifting. He felt as though he was an intrepid explorer who had just discovered some wonderful island and was now basking in their music in their native tongue.

He looked at the others who also looked like they were getting into it. Their tired cynicism had been washed away as they all seemed to be having some unexpected fun.

After the service, they all stood around talking and saying goodbye to some of the Niueans they knew such as Rose, Pio and Miaga who were all at the service.

After all the locals had left, Priest wandered back over to his team, 'Well, what did you think', he asked. Ant replied, 'Well Priest, I have to admit that I'm glad you made us all come along. The singing and indeed the whole service was kind of, well how can I put it? Uplifting?'.

Priest shook his head, 'It's called a spiritual awakening bonehead'. At hearing the agitation in Priest's voice, Crazy smirked at the opportunity to needle the man of God further, 'Spiritual awakening? Hey Priest, will that do anything useful like stop it hurting when I pee?', he enquired.

FOT put his big hand on Crazy's shoulder, 'Don't worry Wayne, I have a big needle and a tiny little umbrella scraper that will take care of that for you', FOT said with a sinister smile. Crazy gulped at the thought of FOT let loose on his genitals.

The team returned to the camp. Lachlan directed them to start preparing all non-essential equipment for redeployment to Australia. He then asked Ant and Priest to join him in commandeering Lord Erskin-Stamper's warehouse so the ships that would be arriving later in the week could use it.

The two men agreed to come with him.

Priest got changed into his standard work khakis that once again transformed him into looking more like a run of the mill thug, rather than a holy man. Thirty minutes later the Gator with the three men pulled up near the warehouse.

There were no signs of any occupants but when they went to enter the warehouse they were surprised to see a cypher lock fitted to the door. 'That's odd, Loto said he wasn't going to put a new lock on it so we could access it', said Lachlan.

'Stand aside Lachlan, I have certain skills I picked up before the Lord showed me the errors of my ways', said Priest. He walked over and took the lock in his left hand. He turned the small dial-shaped handle to the left on full lock. He held the handle in place with his left thumb and index finger and then began caressing the numbered cypher buttons.

'What are you doing?', asked Ant.

'Well', said Priest, 'When you turn the handle to its opening position, it is trying to find the gates on the programmed numbers to open the lock. Until those numbers are pressed there will be a small degree of pressure on those buttons making them slightly firmer to the touch. Here is one, number 1', said Priest, pressing the button.

He then released the handle and turned it again to the left repeating the process except this time pressing 3, followed by 5 and 7. Suddenly the lock sprung open. 'There you go, whoever put that lock on likes their odd numbers,' said Priest.

Lachlan and Ant looked at each other in amazement and then shook their heads at the ridiculous notion of a priest picking a lock.

Lachlan opened the door of the warehouse and the three men entered the building. Instead of seeing an empty warehouse, stacked in the far corner were thirty timber boxes. As they got closer to the green boxes they could see yellow serial numbers and a UK Ministry of Defence stamped on them.

'What the fuck!?' said Ant. 'They're weapon boxes'. 'UK MOD weapon boxes at that', added Lachlan.

'Guys, this isn't right, we need to report this to the Premier', he said with a worried look on his face. Ant and Priest both agreed. The men decided to take one of the boxes with them as proof.

Ant grabbed the box's rope handles. He hoisted the box onto his left shoulder and headed for the door with Priest and Lachlan in hot pursuit.

Ant loaded the box on the Gator and began quickly strapping it down. Priest stopped and suggested he should go back and lock the door so no one would be the wiser. He headed the fifteen metres back to the front door and had just locked it again when he heard someone call out, 'Hey what are you doing?'

Priest spun around to see three men of Asian ethnicity dressed in T-shirts and camouflaged trousers that were tucked into their heavy boots. Priest maintained eye contact with the men as he stepped backwards towards Ant and Lachlan who were not yet aware of Priest's predicament.

'Stop!', said the leading Asian man, lifting his T-shirt to reveal a 9mm Browning automatic pistol.

'Oh shit!', thought Priest as his senses focused. His piercing blue eyes fixed the eyes of the man with the pistol 'Look, I don't want any trouble', said Priest holding his hands up.

Suddenly the man with the gun froze. 'You!', he said, staring into Priest's eyes. 'You are one of the green ghosts, I remember your evil blue eyes', the man went on.

Suddenly Priest's memory placed the man, East Timor 1998, war criminal.

One of the other men reached behind his back brandishing a Berretta pistol. 'Screw this, I'm out of here', the big man thought, ducking around the corner of the warehouse with surprising speed.

The three men didn't give chase–he could just hear the war criminal calling out, 'What are you doing here ghost?'

Priest legged it towards the vehicle as Lachlan and Ant finished-up loading the box. 'They're here, let's get going!' yelled Priest as he ran the final five metres to the Gator.

'Shit' said Ant, starting the vehicle.

Once Lachie and Priest boarded the vehicle, Ant floored it in an attempt to flee as he rounded the first bend. The three men appeared on the road in front of the vehicle. The war criminal was face to face with Ant a mere ten metres from each other. Unlike with Priest, the recognition between Ant and the war criminal was instant.

'You!', the man shouted at Ant. 'Your ninja bitch cut my finger off', he protested, while pointing his pistol at Ant.

Ant didn't hesitate. He slammed the vehicle into reverse and started back the way they had come as fast as the vehicle would travel. Twenty metres up the road, Ant yelled out to Priest and Lachlan to hold on as he pivot-turned the vehicle so he could travel in the forward gears.

It was then that the three Global Angel men heard the unmistakable sound of gunfire as several subsonic pistol rounds whizzed past their heads less than a metre away. Now facing forward, the moving vehicle sped away out of sight of the attackers.

'Who the bloody hell was that?' yelled Lachlan. Priest was first to pipe up, 'A war criminal, that's who that was'.

'What? I'm pulling over now that we're out of range', said Ant.

Now with a good 4 km between them and their attackers, Ant drove the vehicle off the road and stood looking at the box. 'Priest, I don't suppose your super powers extend to picking padlocks?' he asked.

'They sure do', said Priest picking up a rock and bashing the hinge that the padlock was attached to. The box sprung open to reveal six neatly-packed assault rifles.

'They're SA80-A1s', said Lachlan while examining one of the distinctive British-designed bullpup weapons. The bullpup design is unmistakable as unlike a more conventional weapon this 5.56mm rifle's magazine is fitted to the stock of the weapon behind the trigger mechanism.

He explained the weapon was taken out of service in the UK military, around mid-2006. 'Oh shit, what's the bet these have been stolen—the Brits certainly don't sell this type of hardware to just anyone', said Ant.

'Agreed Ant', said Lachlan.

'Now you two, who the fuck was that shooting at us? You guys all seem to be having some kind of a fucked-up reunion', he asked Priest and Ant.

Ant was first to pipe up, 'Well, I don't know how Priest knows him, but the bloke yelling and shooting at us was one of the blokes that attacked Tatsu and me in Phuket. We fought him and several others who attacked us for no reason. Two of them died in the scuffle and that bloke got his finger chopped off by his own knife.

It was dark and confusing but Tatsu told me she saw the crowd join in the fight and that they killed the two men. Anyway, we were lucky to get away with it. Tatsu had to use her Japanese Government contacts to smooth it all over and convince the authorities we were innocent victims that had nothing to do with the deaths of two assailants and a severed finger of a third', explained a slightly flustered Ant.

Lachlan rubbed his chin while deep in thought. 'Alright Ant, fair enough. I must say that is quite the coincidence. Priest how do you know this nut job?', asked Lachlan.

Priest stared at the trees concentrating to remember as much detail as possible. 'Well my meeting this man goes back a lot further. In 1998, I was a young trooper in Special Forces. We were on a mission which, to be honest, I shouldn't even be talking about even now all these years later.

It was reported that the Indonesian military were losing control of the local Timorese militia who were committing criminal acts including mass killings of civilians. My team was sent into Timor to get eyes on the ground and to report back if the situation was deteriorating. We went covertly, we were not to be seen nor interfere with what was going on.

We were there for two months, living in the jungle conducting our surveillance mission. The situation was bad for the Timorese and the Indonesians. There was a three-way slugfest between the Indonesian TNI, the Indonesian-sponsored Timorese militia, and the Portuguese-trained FALINTIL that roughly stands for the Armed Forces for National Liberation.

We had remained largely undiscovered for months other than for a few civilians who supplied us with occasional food and information. It all came to a head one day when we were investigating a site where some FALINTIL had ambushed a group of TNI soldiers while they were bathing in a natural spring in the jungle.

Generally speaking, the FALINTIL came out on top of the TNI in the jungle, so the Indonesians formed a specialist unit which they used to hunt the FALINTIL. This unit was well-trained and equipped, and operated largely independently.

One of the key personnel in this unit was a guy called Sergeant Pramana. The man who just shot at you. One day we came across him in a rage after a gunfight with the FALINTIL in which some of his unit were killed. He was happily in the process of murdering civilians when my team leader snapped and decided to interfere.

It was a good decision for the village but a bad one for us. For breaching our orders and interfering we were all kicked out of Special Forces. My team leader became a drug-fucked gangster on the Gold Coast and I took steps to follow my calling and become a priest.

When the TNI found out what Sergeant Pramana and his unit had been up to, the Indonesian Government handed their details to a UN War Crimes tribunal. They got all of them except for that evil little shit who just shot at us. He went underground and become known as Tiger or the Lone Tiger as he refers to himself. Various government organisations have been hunting him as he is a notorious gun for hire', concluded Priest.

Lachlan maintained his look of concentration trying to piece it all together. Lachie looked at his two colleagues, 'He was passing through Niuean waters on the *Merdeka*, smuggling some stolen weapons when he got hit by the storm. Now that he's trapped with an ever-increasing group of foreigners arriving, he is at risk of getting caught and will be getting more desperate.

We need to tell the authorities quickly before it turns to shit. How far away are we from town?', asked Lachlan. Ant looked at his digital map. 'Well- we need to go the long way or we risk running into Tiger and his crew. Twenty-minutes, twenty-five if we swing by the airfield and brief our people first', said Ant.

'We swing via the airfield, our team's security takes priority over trapping an international fugitive', said Lachlan

It was going on to 1700 hours when the boys pulled up in their Gator at the airfield. Ant piled out of the vehicle and called out for everyone to drop what they were doing and get into the briefing tent.

Lachlan and Priest drove off at speed to the Premier's Chambers. Ant explained the serious nature of the situation to the others. 'These guys are dangerous and armed. We, on the other hand, have no weapons', said Ant.

'What about the SA80s? We could use them', said Si.

Ant shook his head in response, 'No ammo mate, just the rifles'.

'Bugger', replied Si.

'Exactly', said Ant, 'No, our best chance is to notify the authorities and adopt a passive defence. We will keep a low profile, so stay out of sight and away from the equipment until this all blows over', said Ant.

'Aye, aye, boss', the group responded.

While Ant's team gathered up their essentials, Lachie and Priest had arrived at the Premier's Chambers to find Colonel Michelle and a team of Kiwi and Aussie diggers already there. None of them knew what the situation was, they had merely heard some distant gunfire and thought they should report it.

On arrival, Lachlan was able to fill in the gaps that caused a great deal of concern amongst the group. Colonel Michelle radioed her teams still in the villages to remain vigilant. She then turned to Lachlan, the Premier and the police, which were now in attendance.

'Right, who here has weapons? We sure as shit don't as we are a disaster response team and not geared for security operations', she said looking annoyed at having to expose her team's impotence.

The law enforcement officer looked at her and said, 'We only have two old service revolvers. Not much use against military spec automatic rifles'.

The Premier looked at the group, 'I don't expect you to risk yourselves unnecessarily. Let them go. Just keep our people away from them until they leave. We will notify the NZ Navy and they can deal with them'.

'Agreed', said Colonel Michelle, 'We will help you cordon off the harbour'. Lachlan also agreed that the Premier's plan was a good one and that he would return to his men and keep a low profile.

Their discussion was suddenly interrupted by one of the island's law enforcement officers.

'It's gone, the *Merdeka* has gone', the officer said. There was a general look of relief around the room.

A short while later and Lachlan was back at the airfield briefing everyone that the bad guys had left the island and the *Merdeka* was nowhere to be seen. Ant asked about the warehouse. Lachlan explained that he, Michelle, and the cops had checked it but it was empty again. Even the cypher lock had gone. If it hadn't been for the SA80s they had in their possession, there would be no evidence at all of them ever having being there.

You could feel the tension in the briefing tent as everyone reflected on the day's close-call.

Crazy puffed himself up, 'Well, lucky they pissed off or I would have had to have made them my bitches', he said.

Baz screwed up her face, 'Make them your bitches, what does that mean? You were going to take them out for a cheap meal, then bore them to death with your inane chatter prior to taking them back to your room and trying to hump their legs?', she said.

The group all started to laugh. 'Don't know what you are all laughing about, that sounds like the perfect date', Crazy chuckled.

The mood in the tent relaxed and Lachie took the opportunity to focus the group's attention on the final phase of their mission, the pack-up and redeployment. 'I want everything except the accommodation and kitchen tent packed-up. Let's get to it', he said clapping his hands together to signify his intent for them to get cracking.

No Escape

PADDY MONITORED THE RADAR as he steered the *Merdeka* for open waters. He smiled to himself at the thought of their ship being intercepted. If they were to be picked up by the Kiwis, there would be no dramas.

He and his Irish mate were cleanskins as far as the authorities were concerned. They had only done a short stint in the IRA just prior to peace being declared. They were trained soldiers looking for action and adventure with no war left to fight.

That's when he and his mates had been recruited by a rich benefactor to fight for him. They had never met him or her and probably never would. They didn't give a shit so long as the money kept coming and keep coming it did. He himself was well on his way to being very well-off.

He would already be there if it wasn't for a fairly unhealthy coke and prostitute habit. But that aside, life was good for him and his mate. Especially now that they had gone their separate ways from Tiger and his psychopath killers.

They had thought Tiger was a bit of a joke when they first met him. For starters, what kind of a twat introduces himself as the 'Lone Tiger', honestly what a douche.

Over the coming weeks of working with the man and his team, which consisted of another Indonesian, a Malaysian and two uptight Middle Eastern guys, they realized just what a maniac he was.

They had picked up their weapons shipment from Thailand and were headed for Fiji where they were to be delivered to the commander of the next military coup. Everything was going well until they had been forced to travel further north to avoid some nasty storm cells.

They realized after two weeks at sea that they had picked up a tail. A smaller ocean-going ship would intermittently appear on their radar and then disappear again like some sort of ghost or stealth ship. They weren't sure it was following them until they deviated and headed for Niue.

The vessel followed them right into the cyclone. They knew then it was tracking them and they needed to get the weapons off the ship. They were compromised and needed to enact Plan B. While Paddy and his Irish and Filipino crew navigated the storm, and tried to ditch their tail, Tiger and his team remained below completely unfazed.

It all came to a head when Shamus, who was Paddy's second-in-charge, did a crew head count and noticed one of the Filipino crew members had gone missing during the storm. They assumed he had been washed overboard and continued focusing on battling the storm.

Once in clear water Paddy did an inspection of the ship to assess the damage. When he got to the lower deck where Tiger and his crew were staying he couldn't believe his eyes. Tied-up, naked, beaten and with his throat cut was the missing crewmember.

Paddy stood there staring in shock. Someone had crudely put makeup on the deceased man's face and there was clear evidence he had been sexually assaulted. Paddy drew his pistol on them and demanded to know what had happened.

'Bored', said a contemptuous, smirking Tiger.

A stand-off between the two groups occurred until Tiger agreed his team would remain confined to quarters until they got to the nearest landmass where he, his team and the cargo would be offloaded.

'Sick fuck!', thought Paddy, even more relieved at the thought of getting rid of that nut job. What's more it was a smart move. Their Fijian contact had charted an aircraft to make the short flight to Niue to collect Tiger and the weapons, which meant pay day for all involved.

Paddy's crew had cleaned up the murder scene and with no contraband left on board they were as pure as driven snow in the event the authorities intercepted them. The only illegal thing on the ship was a packet of white powder in Paddy's pocket that he would get rid of at the first sign of a vessel attempting to board them.

The *Merdeka* was steaming along at a comfortable ten knots. Niue was now back beyond the horizon and the sun had gone down. Shamus walked into the wheelhouse and offered Paddy a cup of Earl Grey tea. Paddy eagerly took the cup, slightly scalding his lip in his eagerness to drink the hot beverage.

He stood there for a moment savoring the taste. A degree of calmness washed over him for the first time since they began this mission four weeks ago.

Paddy grinned, 'What are you going to do with your cut Shamus?'

Shamus chuckled, 'Well I'm going to have some fun that involves a fast car, a girl, a donkey, a ton of smack and some fireworks.'

Paddy also chuckled and was about to ask Shamus to go on, when a huge clanging sound outside the wheelhouse interrupted them. Paddy quickly glanced at the radar but saw nothing to indicate any other vessels. Paddy looked squarely at Shamus and directed him to check it out.

Shamus nodded and drew his gun before exiting out the door. Once outside, Shamus slowly walked along the gangway to give his eyes a chance to adjust to the dark. On the lower deck, he thought he could make out something hanging off the railing.

He descended the ladder and walked towards the object. As he got closer he could make out two black metallic hooks attached to the ship. He looked over the railing to see the hooks supported a ladder. A few metres away in the dark waters was a black vessel of some sort. It was quiet and extremely low profile.

Shamus watched as the vessel suddenly pulled away at speed. He estimated it must have been traveling at thirty plus knots. 'What the?', he thought to himself, 'I need to get back and let Paddy know about this'. As he turned to make his way back to the wheelhouse two people dressed from head to toe in black blocked his path.

Shamus lifted his pistol and muttered 'You can go to he...'. Several heavy and lightning fast blows to his body incapacitated him before he could fire a shot.

Paddy kept steering the boat while regularly glancing down at the radar to check for approaching vessels. There was nothing. Suddenly a blip appeared 500 meters from the *Merdeka* and then vanished almost immediately.

'That's unusual', thought Paddy, 'So is it that Shamus has been gone for so long'. Paddy put his tea down and drew his pistol. He looked down at the crew alert button. I don't want to appear jumpy if nothing is going on he thought.

He decided against alerting the crew and instead locked the wheel in place so he could quickly stick his head out the door. Just as he turned the handle the door burst open, knocking him backwards. He regained his footing to see the blade of what looked to him like a samurai sword.

Holding the sword was someone dressed in black from head to toe. The person's face was covered so all he could make out was a pair of eyes which looked Japanese.

'Drop the weapon or lose your head', demanded the person holding the sword in a thickly-accented voice. Paddy looked at the little figure holding the sword and instead of complying swung his weapon towards his assailant. 'Fuck you Shintaro!', he yelled, moments before his head separated from his neck.

Shamus was now conscious again and was bustled into the wheelhouse along with the crew. Their upper limbs were tied and they were shoved along by some identically-dressed, darkly-clad people wielding swords.

The man whose sword was still stained with Paddy's blood walked over to Shamus. In his thickly-accented but very clear voice he demanded, 'I will ask only once. Where is Tiger?'

Looking at his dead skipper on the ground, Shamus panicked. 'He is on the Island, we dropped him off with the weapons shipment.'

'Lock them up and set the *Merdeka* on a course for Papua New Guinea', said the lead man in black.

It was completely dark at the airfield except for some lights powered by generator at the terminal. The military estimated they would have the main power supply back on in the next two days. They were in the process of ensuring all the power lines and junction boxes were deemed safe before the engineer flicked the switch to restore power to the island.

'Yep, the military loves being thorough', thought Ant as he stared out into the darkness. Suddenly another shiver went thorough him as again he felt like he was being watched. Well on the off chance there are still bad guys out there, I'm not going to dick around out here too long on my own, he thought to himself as he finished labeling some pallets that had been prepped for flight.

Unbeknown to Ant, his sixth-sense was right again. Lying flat on the ground not more than 15 metres away was a woman dressed in black remaining perfectly still. Again, the figure was cradling a high-powered rifle. This time the rifle was not pointed at Ant.

The figure slowly scanned the perimeter of the airfield in search of movement. Another figure identically dressed was perched up high in a blacked-out area on the air terminal's roof. Again, the figure on the roof scanned the airfield's perimeter.

He placed his cross-hairs on the stocky bearded Aussie near the pallets than scanned across to his colleague. 'She's too close to him', he thought as he activated his throat radio. In Japanese, he instructed his colleague to hold her position until the man left. He would let her know when she was clear and she could head to higher ground.

After ten minutes, Ant had finished his labeling and headed back the short walk to the camp. Lachlan had just finished delivering a report to DFID and AusAID when Ant walked into the tent. 'How are you, mate?', enquired Ant.

Lachie looked up at Ant and smiled, 'Yeah good mate. We're all set to go tomorrow. All the agencies and our boss are all happy. The only thing is, I still just can't get over the chances of running into that Tiger bloke and his crew'.

Ant conceded it was hard to accept the coincidence. He had been running it over in his own head regarding their chance altercation in Phuket. In a way, it was understandable Priest knew him. There are only so many professional soldiers on the planet, so it makes sense that you will occasionally encounter each other given the similar circles in which you all move, regardless of which country you originate from.

'I guess the guy was just doing some casual gun-running when he got waylaid by the storm', said Ant.

Lachie rubbed his smoothly-shaven chin as he sat there thinking. Unlike the others, he hadn't allowed stubble to appear on his face. In contrast, Ant stood there looking like a castaway who had been stranded out at sea for a month.

I get that Ant. But how did you just happen to run into him on your holiday?', asked Lachie, not really expecting an answer.

Ant chuckled, Well actually it was Tatsu who ran into him. She was the one in the knife fight with Tiger and his four mates when I arrived. In fact, I think she may have been the one who cut his finger off. No doubt about it, that girl could look after herself', said Ant going all dreamy-eyed as he remembered his time with the beautiful Tatsu.

Lachie cleared his throat to bring Ant back to reality, 'Ant, what was it you said Tatsu did for work?'.

Ant sat there contemplating their discussions during their time together. 'Not one hundred per cent sure mate. I mean she was clearly rich, but she reckoned that she worked for the Japanese Government. That's right, she was over in Phuket having meetings with the Thai Government to secure some trade agreement.

That's why she had sweet little Yumi there with her. She is Tatsu's assistant', said Ant.

Lachie shook his head, 'Really Ant, it didn't seem weird to you that Tatsu, a supposed public servant could fight off five men with knives, in fact didn't it seem strange to you that she was even in a fight to begin with?'.

Ant sat there a little embarrassed as a result of Lachie's mocking tone and his raising of what now seemed like a fairly obvious conclusion that Tatsu was not your average public servant.

Ant suddenly felt defensive. 'Well women can fight. Look at Baz nearly killing her boyfriend', said Ant, trying to regain some dignity.

Lachie shook his head again, 'Oh piss off Ant. Baz was fighting for her life against one man and used her military unarmed combat training knowledge to get the better of him.

She didn't square off against five armed men, making short work of three of them, at least one of which was ex-Indonesian Special Forces and a god-damned war criminal mercenary. I'm thinking he might be just a little more capable than the bozo Baz decked.

What do you reckon Ant?', said an annoyed Lachie.

'You were pussy-whipped Ant. Because you were, you failed to see what was going on in front of you.

This is all linked Ant. You'd better start engaging the big head instead of the little one and help me work out how before we all end up dead', said Lachie.

Ant wished he could crawl into a hole. Ant was a confident and strong guy, but somehow Lachie had this hold over him.

He had a knack of making Ant feel inadequate. Truth was, Lachie was like that with everyone. It was one of his less-endearing features and indicated that he truly didn't care to foster relationships.

In Ant's case however, Lachie did. He looked at his mate sitting there, dejected and wracking his brain for clues. Lachie felt bad. 'Damn, it's not Ant's fault', Lachie thought to himself, 'The guy just naturally thinks the best of everybody, he's untainted in his views despite the shit he has seen'.

Lachie was about to apologize to his long-term friend when the sound of a small aircraft interrupted what would have been a very rare and welcome occurrence. 'That's weird', said Ant, flicking through a ring binder folder, 'There is no flight listed here.' 'Let's check it out', said Lachlan, heading for the door.

Priest was just leaving the Community Centre having just checked on the welfare of the patients. The commercial medical team seemed to be doing a good job. He walked out of the light of the Centre into the darkness that led to Global Angel's camp.

Not long after he entered the darkness he heard the noise of a weapon being cocked. He stopped and slowly turned to where the noise had come from. By the time he had completed a quarter-turn he was staring straight at a pistol that was pointed at his temple. Standing back from the person holding the gun was a sinister-looking Tiger, accompanied by four of his men.

'Well, well, one of the green ghosts', said Tiger, 'Where are my fucking weapons you stole?'.

Priest smiled, 'Well Tiger, I'm not walking funny, so I guess they're are not shoved up my arse'.

This impertinence resulted in Priest been rapped across the head with the butt of Tiger's weapon. It was a hard blow, sending Priest back several steps. Priest regained his footing and stood up straight smiling, 'I keep my eyes always on the Lord. With him at my right hand, I will not be shaken'.

Angered by Priest's complete lack of fear, Tiger hit him again. This time the heavy blow concussed Priest, rendering him unconscious.

'Fuck, tie him up', said Tiger. Tiger could now hear his aircraft approaching. His chances of getting the missing box of weapons were getting low. Damn it, he thought. That's $60,000 I just lost.

He turned to his men who had finished zip-tying Priest and instructed them to get the weapons ready to take out to the airstrip.

Si stood straining his ears. He had been draining some of the fuel out of the vehicles to prep them for flight when he thought he heard an angry voice off in the darkness. An approaching aircraft was now making it impossible for him to hear anything so he decided to walk towards where he thought he heard the voice.

He walked forty metres before he heard a vehicle start up in the darkness. As he got closer he could see several men. Two of them were dragging a man into the bushes. Si started to run towards them. As he got closer he could see the man on the ground was Priest, 'What in the fook are you twats doin' with Priest?', an outraged Si demanded.

The Middle Eastern man who had just dragged Priest over to the bushes looked up to see the big charging Brit headed their way. The man pulled out his pistol and started depressing the trigger, 'Crack, crack, crack, crack', as the pistol bucked in his hand releasing its lethal load.

Two rounds struck Si. His momentum carried him two more steps before his legs buckled underneath him and he collapsed to the ground. He couldn't feel any pain, but he was well-aware of what had happened to him. He had been shot and he was badly injured. He was out of breath, which suggested to him that he had been hit in the torso.

He felt jelly-like and helpless. 'Lie here quiet in the dark for a moment and assess the situation', he thought.

There was another shot. A distant high-velocity shot that Si expected to hit him, but it didn't. Instead there was thud in the direction of where his attacker had fired on him.

Some panicked yelling followed the thud. The voices were not familiar to him, nor was the language being used.

The aircraft came in for a landing as Tiger's vehicle, stacked with weapons, moved at speed towards the southern end of the runway.

Four hundred metres from Tiger's position, on top of a water tower, was a woman with blue/hazel eyes clad in black. She tracked the vehicle with the cross-hairs of her rifle.

Her partner was now out of range for this fight. He had just dropped the guy who shot the Brit. Her partner was now retreating to the rendezvous site as his position had been compromised.

Some airfield workers with torches were still looking at the air terminal roof to try and find where the shot had come from. No, she would need to handle this herself. These weapons and Tiger couldn't be allowed to leave the island. Not in one piece anyway.

She took a series of deep breaths to settle her nerves. She had killed before and these guys were bad through and through. She knew the world would be a better place without them. It still didn't change the fact that she was starting to regret her career choice.

Three months ago, she would have relished the opportunity to be on a mission, perched above her prey waiting to pounce. But now all she felt was nerves and emptiness. Someone had changed her life priorities. She was thinking of settling down and maybe even having horrid, little demanding half-Japanese and half-Caucasian babies.

She continued her deep breathing. 'Snap out of it' she demanded of herself. She needed to enter her emotionless trance-like state; a technique that has been used by soldiers for centuries, enabling them to control fear and operate in an almost automated manner when executing their duties. 'Calm, breath, prioritize your targets. Tiger first, then the others', she told herself.

'I don't frigging care Lachlan, I'm going to stop this Tiger prick', said Ant, holding the pistol that had shot Si which he found on the ground. He checked the magazine. Four rounds, enough to stop Tiger.

Ant looked back down at Priest with his head bashed in and Si who was being treated by FOT. Si was starting to cough blood. He looked pale and in pain. To his credit, he still had a healthy dose of English pluck, telling everyone he was fine and not to worry. But FOT's overly calm demeanor and sense of urgency suggested otherwise.

'Alright Ant, if you're going then I'm coming with you. Best to give me the pistol though Ant, I'm a better shot than you, you fat pogue', said Lachlan, holding his hand out.

Ant frowned but handed Lachlan the pistol. Lachlan looked at the rest of the team. 'Stay together guys and stay safe, this is likely to go to shit.' Crazy looked up and nodded before going back to helping FOT treat Si.

Baz sat there nursing Priest who had started to regain consciousness. She sat there with his head in her lap and a single, perfectly formed, tear rolled down her cheek. Lachlan was shocked, he had never seen Baz display any emotion other than unadulterated happiness or anger, never sadness.

He turned to walk away but Baz called out, 'Boys push those bastards' shit in!' Lachlan smiled to himself, 'My mistake, it was anger, not sadness', he thought.

The aircraft taxied towards the parked vehicle before shutting down. A fuel truck also made its way across the airfield to the aircraft. The truck driver jumped out, started up the truck's pump to begin filling the aircraft with fuel. The other men started loading the crates onto the aircraft.

Up in the water tower the assassin tried to pick a target but the aircraft obscured her view. At this range and at night, she needed time to line up a clear shot. Her position on the tower was useless due to the pilot's choice of parking spots.

Time to move, she thought to herself, folding her bipod back into the weapon's foregrip. She silently slid down the ladder and started a crouched run towards her prey. She was in position no more than fifty metres away, concealed in a drainage ditch when she decided to set her rifle.

The water in the ditch left over from the storm was putrid, but it didn't distract her from her task. Mosquitos attacked her as soon as she lay down, but this didn't distract her either. She was in her trance, methodically setting her night vision scope for the new and much-reduced range. Such was her fitness that 20 seconds after her run to her new position her heart rate had returned to normal. She needed this to happen to aid in her accuracy.

She scanned the targets looking for Tiger. It was difficult to pick him at night, but she had narrowed down to two possibilities. She was getting ready to execute a shot when she saw two men running across the airfield towards the rear of the aircraft. One of them was carrying a pistol and the other one was..., no it couldn't be. She recognized the run and the barrel-chested physique.

Suddenly she snapped out of her trance into the here and now. A wave of panic shot through her. She was uncertain what to do. She didn't want to be here anymore, she wanted to be somewhere safe with him. For that to be so she would need to act. 'Screw the mission', she thought. 'I'm going to protect Ant' Tatsu murmured to herself.

Ant and a man she assumed was Lachlan burst out of the darkness in front of Tiger and his men. She could hear Ant's voice yell at the men to put their weapons down. What Ant and Lachlan didn't see was one of the men was in the darkness on sentry duty while the aircraft was being loaded. He was circling behind Lachlan and Ant.

The man ducked down on the other side of the fuel truck out of Tatsu's sight. She muttered, 'Kuso!', while slinging her rifle back over her shoulder. Shooting near a fuel truck should be avoided. Instead of the rifle, she needed a close-quarter weapon that couldn't ignite the truck's fuel load. She reached behind her right shoulder and drew a short sword. She held the sword low by her side as she ran so as not to allow the blade to reflect any light from the truck.

The sentry made his way around the truck. He assumed both men were armed so he decided to shoot the curly-haired man giving the orders first. He raised the butt of the SA80 into his shoulder.

Suddenly the man felt an impact to his back. His core strength gave way as if he had no stomach muscles to hold himself up. He looked down to see the blade of a sword protruding from his belly. As he watched, the sword was withdrawn, to be replaced with dark blood bubbling from the wound. An intense pain like nothing he had ever felt shot through his body. A wave of mixed emotion hit him. He was angry someone had gotten the jump on him, but most of all he was scared as he knew a wound this grievous was fatal.

He only had time to let out the beginning of a scream before it turned into more of a sickening gurgle as his throat was slashed. Tiger and his men heard the sounds of their colleague dying.

Tiger yelled 'Shoot them!', as he leapt to the ground, drawing his pistol.

'Oh shit!', said Ant hitting the ground and trying to hug the earth as rounds whizzed above his head.

Lachlan too, was eating a mouthful of dirt, when he managed to spit out some direction to his mate, 'Get back to the darkness mate'.

Both men leopard-crawled back to the darkness. It seemed to take them no time at all. Ant was at that moment glad for all the fitness training he had been doing which allowed him to execute this task at speed. All those push-ups and sit-ups probably just saved his life.

Tiger ordered his remaining men to continue loading the aircraft. He took off alone after Ant and Lachie. Despite their concerted effort to escape, they now had Tiger hot on their heels chasing them through the darkness.

Tiger fired at the direction in which he thought they had escaped. Lachlan took aim at the flash from Tiger's weapon and squeezed off one of his remaining rounds. Given the darkness it was a good shot, missing Tiger's head by mere millimeters.

Tiger crouched as he realised he wasn't dealing with an amateur. He quickly assessed his chances of being able to get the jump on the two men in the dark. He assessed the risk was too great. He was getting ready to return to the aircraft and cut losses when he heard an almost undetectable sound of footsteps moving at speed across the grass towards him.

He instinctively spun around towards the noise while dropping to one knee to take aim at his would-be attacker. Before he could squeeze off a shot at the black-clad figure, a blade flashed in the moonlight as it drew down across his face causing a deep laceration. Tiger cupped his left eye which had been sliced by the sword blade and rendered useless.

Unlike the prior victim, Tiger felt no emotion at all. This was just business and the way the world was. This was survival of the fittest and there was no way this Jap bitch was going to get the better of him. He squeezed off several rounds, one of which grazed Tatsu's upper right arm as she dive-rolled away from the shooter.

Despite the pain, Tiger smiled as he had the bitch in his sights and was about to fire again when a commotion 100 metres away caught his attention. In the light of the airfield, he saw Lachie and Ant running towards thirty Aussie and Kiwi soldiers who were sprinting towards the aircraft.

'You lucky moll!', Tiger screamed as he turned and ran towards the aircraft.

Unaware of Tatsu's presence, Ant and Lachlan joined Colonel Michelle and her troops sprinting across the airfield towards the aircraft. They were unarmed, but this didn't deter Colonel Michelle, or her soldiers inspired by her bravery, who charged with her across the airfield yelling threats which they planned to see through if they got their hands on Tiger and his men.

Tiger and his men now assembled at the aircraft, looked back at the approaching soldiers. Tiger wasn't convinced they were armed, so he squeezed off two shots at the soldiers. The soldiers didn't falter, they continued tearing across the airfield like a horde of blood-crazed berserkers. 'Get on board!',

Tiger yelled reluctantly. He knew the weapons hadn't finished being loaded but the soldiers would be upon them in 30 seconds and then it would be a blood bath. The aircraft was already revving its two engines ready for take-off. Tiger climbed on board last looking back at Colonel Michelle and her soldiers with his one remaining eye.

They were twenty metres from the aircraft when it started pulling away faster than they could run. Tiger glared at Michelle and flipped her off.

Colonel Michelle stopped and returned the gesture.

Her thirty soldiers and Ant thought this was a great laugh and all joined Colonel Michelle in flipping off Tiger's escaping aircraft. Tiger snarled as he watched Colonel Michelle and her soldiers disrespect him. He consoled himself with the thought that they didn't know what he was capable of but maybe one day they would find out.

While Ant and the soldiers had their fun at Tiger's expense, Lachlan looked in the back of the vehicle to see six boxes of weapons still in the back of the truck. He smiled to himself as he thought that there were now in total seven boxes of SA80s that weren't going to fall into the wrong hands. Not bad for a small disaster relief team.

As Michelle and her soldiers gathered around their bounty, Tiger's aircraft climbed into the sky with the remaining twenty-three weapons crates. On the ground in the darkness, an unseen wounded woman dressed in black made her way to the rendezvous point. She stopped briefly to look at Ant, the man whose life she had just put in front of her mission.

Tiger had slipped through her fingers twice and she had saved Ant's life twice as a result. 'It's worth it', she smiled to herself while clutching her wounded arm. Ant was mid-high fiving with Lachie and the soldiers when he suddenly felt the same uneasy feeling that someone was watching him.

He withdrew from the celebration and walked to the edge of the darkness on the airfield. As his eyes readjusted to the darkness, he thought he could just make out a dark figure looking back at him.

He called out to it, 'Who are you?'.

The figure didn't respond. Instead it turned and fled into the darkness.

THE HOME COMING

ANT WALKED IN THROUGH THE FRONT DOOR of his Petrie Terrace house. It was as he had left it except that it smelt a bit musty. He walked around the house opening the sash windows to air the house out. He opened some windows on the rear deck and noticed his herbs had died during his absence.

Well, Mad Max the possum will be pissed off now that he doesn't have my carefully-cultivated herb garden to decimate.

A warm breeze wafted through the house. The musty smell dissipated and was replaced by a lovely beer smell from the Milton XXXX Brewery.

'Good idea', thought Ant opening the fridge door and removing an icy cold beer. He sat on the front deck daybed and watched the sun slowly disappear over Mount Coot-tha.

Ant sat there in the quiet, contemplating what had happened on his time away. He logged into his bank account to see an extra $30,000 had been deposited into his bank account. He would normally consider this a good earn for a few weeks' work, but given the government was about to take almost half of it, he had been working fifteen hours a day and he was nearly killed in the process, it just didn't seem like an easy way to earn his money.

Maybe on Monday I'll jump on line and apply for a commercial logistics job in the city. It might pay a little less, but it's predictable safe work. Besides what am I going to do with the extra money I already have everything I need. But the thing that working with Global Angel had going for it was the people.

He grinned as he remembered his time with them. It was like been back in the warm embrace of the military. Then he thought of Si laying on the ground coughing up blood. 'Yes, a little too much like the military', he thought, subconsciously rubbing the Afghanistan remembrance tattoo on his forearm.

A sudden feeling of loneliness washed over Ant as he took another sip from his beer. Lachie wasn't home next door as he had flown direct to Sydney getting ready to fly out to the UK to brief DFID and Lord Erskin-Stamper.

The Global Angel team members all had interviews with the Federal Police over the next few days to give statements about Tiger and the like. Ant figured he would just talk about the Niue encounter as there is no way the cops would consider the two run-ins in a matter of months a coincidence. Even Ant couldn't get his head around it. No best to leave that bit out.

Ant opened his second beer when his watch pinged a message. He opened and saw it was from Tatsu. A feeling of excitement shot through him as he read the message as he had barely heard from her in months.

Then a feeling of dread forced its way into his head as he considered the possibility that Tatsu might be contacting him to say she would never see him again. Ant tentatively opened the message to read:

Dear Antonio, I hope this finds you well? I have given the distance between us a chance so I could clearly consider how I feel about you and the early stages of our impossible relationship.

Truth is I thought I would get over you when I returned to Japan.

I know I have been a bitch not responding to your messages and for that I ask for your understanding. Truth is no matter what I do I think of you constantly. I hope you feel the same about me.

I will be at the Japanese Embassy in Canberra next week and thought maybe you would like to meet up? If you don't I completely understand, but if you do you will make a girl very happy.

I am falling hard for you Ant and I don't understand why. Maybe I'm a chubby chaser;) Tatsu

Ant sat there staring at the message. He read it three times before he let out a cheer that could be heard halfway up the street.' You better believe I'll be there', he said typing a reply. Besides he needed to go to Canberra anyway, there was something else he had to take care of there.

Lachlan sat in the Sydney Airport Lounge having a fairly-disappointing cheap scotch. He had booked a room in the airport hotel so he could head to London the next day.

Baz was sitting there with him as she had flown to Sydney to visit a friend before continuing on to Canberra to stay with her mother for a week. Lachlan was grateful for her company as he always found airport hotels particularly depressing places.

Baz sat there looking at the beautiful Lachlan while she sipped champagne instead of a beer in an attempt to look lady-like. She had gone to some effort to make certain she looked feminine and sexy without looking like she had tried too hard.

The conversation flowed effortlessly between the two of them. An outsider would have picked them to be a good-looking couple in the early stages of their relationship, given the amount of casual leg touching and the regular hair twirling. Baz had engaged Lachlan in lighthearted discussion for an hour and a half.

The drinks left her with a champagne glow. If she had too many more she would get drowsy and her witty banter would disappear and be replaced by a less-charming, possibly even crass subject matter. No, she had to make her move now. She was certain that Lachlan was interested as he couldn't get his eyes off her perfectly-formed boobs.

She knew she looked fantastic tonight. She had done everything right, she had told him what a great leader he was and laughed at his crappy jokes. 'Lachlan I don't have to go to my friend's place tonight', Baz said.

Lachlan looked down at his drink as if contemplating what she had just suggested. 'I mean, haven't you ever wondered what it would be like? I have', she went on. Lachlan pursed his lips as he prepared to deliver a response.

'Baz, you are an attractive, sexy and intelligent woman, but I honestly don't think it would be a good idea given we work together and it would never last'.

Baz was a little shocked at his assumption they wouldn't last and responded out of reflex, 'Hell I wasn't suggesting we form a long-lasting loving relationship, just that we have a bonk. But I'm curious Lachlan, why wouldn't we last', she asked.

Lachlan didn't overly appreciate her tone, nor her putting him on the spot. She didn't look hurt, just a little angry, typical Baz, happy or angry, nothing in between. 'Baz, let's face it, you and I are from different worlds. I enjoy art, classical music and socializing with society's elite. You hate every sip of that champagne and would rather be chugging a beer, while scoffing a pie at a rugby league match.

You would despise my family and friends, thinking them a collection of abhorrent snobs. You are much more comfortable with the proletarian masses. Indeed, happier with the very people in society that bore me', Lachlan mirthlessly responded.

Baz looked at Lachlan for a moment and then her trademark sneer crept onto her face. 'Well Lachlan, this proletarian won't bore you any longer', she said standing up from the table preparing to storm off.

'One last thing Lachlan, just so you know what you're missing. I am a top fuck and can suck start a tractor engine', said Baz and then she was gone, leaving Lachlan shaking his head while ordering another drink.

Once outside the hotel Baz allowed herself to reflect upon what had happened. She stood out the front of the hotel waiting for the car she had ordered to arrive and take her to her friend's place. She caught her reflection in the window.

Ten minutes ago, she looked glamorous, now with her shoulders slumped forward and robbed of her confidence she looked unremarkable at best. A tear started to roll down her cheek, followed by another and then another. Lachlan had been wrong, Baz wasn't angry. She was upset and embarrassed.

She stared at her own reflection with a degree of self-loathing while she continued to sob. A car pulled up and she whipped her eyes smearing her mascara in the process. She assumed this made her look even less attractive.

The young Welsh driver pulled up and saw a beautiful woman standing waiting for his pickup. He could tell she had been crying and was still rather distressed by the look of her body language. 'Poor pet', he mumbled to himself as he pulled up alongside her.

'Hello, Barbara?', he asked.

'Yeah that's me, kind of. Tom, is it?', Baz asked.

'Yeah that's me, definitely. Can I help you with your bags lovely lady?', the driver asked.

Baz gave a coy smile and responded, 'If you did, you would be the only gentleman I have met today.'

In a large country mansion in Oxfordshire, England, Lord Erskin-Stamper reclined in his armchair facing a large video screen. On the other end of the link sat an equally well-dressed Japanese man.

Despite his well-groomed appearance the Japanese man was anything but a gentleman. He was a killer, a gangster, and a business partner of Lord Erskin-Stamper.

'*Konbanwa* Takashi, how much do we stand to lose?', asked Lord Erskin-Stamper.

Takashi shifted in his seat, 'We estimate in the order of £1,250,000 worth of cargo and equipment has been seized in the form of weapons and the *Merdeka*. Two members of "Tiger Team" and two members of "Team Irish" are dead. The remainder of Team Tiger escaped with what was left of the cargo.

Team Tiger's Zero Alpha has sustained a severe injury to his left eye, but he will be operational the week after he comes out of surgery.

The remainder of Team Irish is in the Japanese Police Agency's custody. But it isn't the police who have them, it is more likely the intelligence agency known as the Naicho.

My organization will arrange to silence the Team Irish members. They don't have that much information but as the old Japanese proverb states, '*kuchi wa wazawai no moto*', the mouth is the origin of disaster', said Takeshi.

Lord Erskin-Stamper frowned, 'What blessedly bad luck that my Global Angel Crew just happened across the warehouse. I just needed them to open the airfield so I could get our cargo out', he said.

'Lord Erskin-Stamper, I think it was more the Naicho that were responsible for our misfortune. Global Angel, the Australian and Kiwi Army just got in the way and added to the confusion. If anything, it appears they may have even hampered Naicho's operation', said Takashi.

'Yes, maybe you are right. Do we still have enough cargo to meet our client's requirements?', asked Lord Erskin-Stamper.

'Yes, we do. Two boxes are headed to the Syndicate in Australia and the remaining twenty-one to Fiji', replied Takashi.

'Good, good. *Konbanwa*', said Lord Erskin-Stamper. '*Konbanwa*', repeated Takashi as the two men bowed to each other and the screen went blank.

Si lay in a hospital bed in Auckland with a big grin on his face. What an absolutely bizarre turn of events he thought to himself. Years in the British Army, an Afghanistan veteran and not so much as a scratch. First tour with Global Angel and he cops two in the shoulder for his troubles.

Bloody Aussies, he chuckled. Still what a top bunch. They had all spent several days by his bedside before he told them all to piss off home. After all he was completely stable now.

Apart from some fairly impressive-looking scars and an expected thirty-per cent reduction in his left shoulder movement, he should be fine.

He had stopped coughing up blood resulting from a minor hemorrhage which the surgeon in Auckland managed to repair. Lucky FOT and that Army doctor were there to stabilize him in Niue or else it might have been a different story.

Priest and Crazy were still lurking around Auckland and would pop in to check on him once a day. The biggest surprise was that Lord Erskin-Stamper had paid $500,000 into his bank account as compensation for his injury.

'Blooming hell', he muttered to himself, 'That will pay off his apartment and leave him with enough to get a new Land Rover. Not bad for a month's work', he thought as he shifted in his bed grimacing in pain.

He heard a voice down the hallway and the smile returned to his face. The money wasn't the only cause of his happiness. 'How is my big brave soldier today?', asked a buxom Maori nurse with one of the most infectious smiles Si had ever seen.

'All the better for seeing you Katy. Are we still on for a visit to the Canary Islands when I am better?', asked Si with a little boy lost look on his face.

The smile on Katy's face disappeared and was replaced by a mischievous look. 'A free trip to the Canary Islands, I'm there, in fact I have already submitted my leave. That way I can keep nursing you while we sip cocktails on the beach', she said leaning forward over his face to fluff his pillows.

She deliberately pressed her ample bosoms against his face as she executed her task. Si made sure he looked up and managed to catch a glimpse of the edge of a big, beautiful, brown areola through the partly-unbuttoned blouse. 'I am ready to go now!', said Si.

'No darling, you will stay here for the next seven days recovering. Then I'll administer my own treatment to you when we get to the resort', said Katy turning to leave the room, slapping her own backside as she exited into the corridor.

Lachlan sat in the piano bar of the hotel. He was slightly toasted having increased his normal drinking rate, post the run in with Baz. He sat there kicking himself, not because he cared about her feelings but mainly because it was one root he would never get. The way he felt right now he could do with one. There has to be something here he mused as he scanned the bar.

He spotted an attractive brunette sitting on her own at the bar. She was staring into a half-finished glass of the house sparkling wine. Lachie called the waiter over and ordered a bottle of Dom Pérignon with two glasses.

When the waiter returned, he slipped the waiter a rock lobster and asked him to invite the lovely lady over at the bar to join him for a drink as he returned to his phone to casually review some emails.

The waiter accepted the tip despite his suspicions that Lachie was a wanker of the tallest order. Still twenty bucks was twenty bucks so he walked over to the young lady and delivered Lachie's proposal.

The woman looked over at the elegant man who was now casually looking at his phone rather than making eye contact with the very woman he had invited over to join him.

The woman smirked, what an arrogant arse, he will be perfect she thought to herself. She stood up from her chair revealing a stunning slender figure clothed by a tightly-fitting red dress. Half the bar's punters were captivated by the woman's assertively sexy display as she strutted towards Lachlan's table

It was only when she arrived at Lachlan's table that he looked up from his phone. 'My goodness!', he said in a sophisticated tone, 'What a privilege to be in the presence of such beauty.

Please do me the pleasure of joining me for some fine champagne. Although I can't guarantee the quality of my company, I can guarantee the quality of this champagne will far exceed the pleasure delivered by the house sparkling wine', said Lachie with an oily smile.

'Thank you', said the beautiful woman taking a seat. Lachlan leant forward thrusting his hand towards her, 'Marvelous, I am Lachlan and it is a pleasure to meet you.'

'Hello Lachlan, I'm Lisa', responded the woman, shaking Lachlan's hand.

Lachlan began pouring two glasses of champagne. The woman was stunning but lacked the air of sophistication that her elegant looks promised. Still, she gave off a sexy vibe so she would be perfect for what Lachlan wanted her for.

To start some small talk Lachie asked, while handing her a glass, 'So Lisa, is that a New Zealand accent I detect?'.

'Why yes, it is Lachlan. A fascinating place New Zealand, do you know it was the first place to give women the vote?'.

Lachlan smiled, 'Great, a feminist', he thought, 'Still, all the more fun to bag', he thought, raising his glass,

'Well Lisa, let's toast to the plucky little country prepared to break the mould'.

'I'd prefer to toast the country prepared to fight for equality', she said raising her glass with a lecherous smile.

THE END ;)

.

.

www.ingramcontent.com/pod-product-compliance
Lightning Source LLC
Chambersburg PA
CBHW070221030726
47505CB00006B/1762